2014 ELIT AWARD WINNER
BRONZE BEST MULTICULTURAL FICTION

CWWA's BEST FIRST CRIME NOVEL
FINALIST*

*Crime Writer's Association of Australia 2007

LAURENT BOULANGER is a novelist and scriptwriter. He has a Ph.D. In Writing and teaches in creative writing at Swinburne University, Australia. He is the writer-director of the feature film *Six Lovers*. His novel *Better Dead Than Never* was shortlisted for the CWAA's Best First Crime Novel and won a Bronze Medal at the 2014 eLit Awards for Best Multicultural Fiction.

BETTER DEAD
THAN NEVER

BETTER DEAD
THAN NEVER

Laurent Boulanger

SNIPER BOOKS

FOR
CAROLYN

CHAPTER ONE

"**M**s. Patricia Lunn, I'm John Bain, you were on a murder case ten years ago—"

"Yes, I know the case," I interrupted, "and I remember who you are."

In my mind's eye, I saw his jet black hair and his captivating green eyes. I also saw the young man with the severe strangulation mark around his neck and the blue, cotton shirt torn from his pale body. Blood rushed through my brain. My right hand tightly gripped the telephone receiver.

He said, "Well, something has come up, and I'd like to meet with you."

"Do you still work for the State?"

"I'm a solicitor for Smith & Gordon."

"I'm no longer a cop, so I'm not sure how I can be of assistance."

"I'd like you to come see me at the office in one hour, if it's all right with you." I didn't reply, so he added, "We'll pay you generously for your time."

I looked out of the kitchen window. Monday morning. The sky was pencil grey all the way to the horizon where the heavens and the ocean became one. It was not raining, but it had been, and the forecast was more showers throughout the day. City-bound traffic was congested as always so early in the morning. The window was wide open and the scent of saltwater roamed throughout the apartment. I was wearing my blue shorts and white tee from an early workout at Terry Bennett's on High Street. Percolated coffee was brewing, and I had nothing on the agenda for the next twenty-four hours.

"Money is not a problem," I said. "I'm just wondering what it is you need from me. I no longer have access to the case file, and I wasn't deeply involved in the investigation. I was only present on the last day because I happened to be on shift. Honestly, I'm really familiar with the case. I'm sure the Crime Investigation Unit will be more than happy to help you." I had the dreary suspicion whatever Bain wanted wouldn't include a fourteen-day paid vacation on a tropical island with two first-class return tickets.

"I'll explain everything when you get here. If you can be here in one hour, it would be great. I've got a court appointment at eleven."

"Look—"

"This is really important. I wouldn't have bothered tracking you down if it was just a routine matter. You come highly commended for the job."

I rolled the telephone cord around my left middle finger. It would just be a meeting after all, wouldn't it? Free breakfast, and then I'll turn him down flat. "All right, I'll see you in one hour."

I hung up.

Judging from the assertiveness in his voice, Bain had become used to making requests that turned into orders. He had been a hot catch back when I was still in a cop's uniform, and the horny little devil at the back of my mind suggested he might be worth checking out—even if I had been promised to another man for the last ten years.

CHAPTER TWO

"It's so good to see you." John Bain stood up from his high-back, leather-bound executive chair. "I'm so glad you could make it. You're going to save me a lot of trouble."

We shook hands firmly like old friends who'd survived The Gulf War and were forever changed. He smiled and locked his green eyes with mine. I knew that very second I was dealing with a professional who could make you feel at home, even if you were someone who kept chopped body parts in the freezer compartment of the fridge next to the ice-cream and the baby peas.

He checked me from head to toe as if I were a Christmas tree he was thinking of taking home with him. My black skirt was too short and my white blouse too tight, but I liked it that way. I wasn't one of these women who suffered from a frigid sense of post-feminist existence. Nature had given me a body for men to sin over, and who was I to argue with Mother Nature? All in all, I convinced myself I could pass for a slut-turned-lawyer if real lawyers walked past me at one hundred miles per hour while blinking.

"You look great," he said.

"Thanks."

"You work out or something?"

"I work out *and* something. You're not bad yourself."

"Well, thank you. Please, take a seat."

I took my place on the visitor's chair facing his desk.

The south wall of his Collins Street office was panelled tinted glass overlooking the Yarra river, the Casino complex and the recently built battalions of apartments in Southbank. Filtered sunlight bathed the room in a coffee colour, and his expensive citrus aftershave travelled through time and space. His desk was large and made of solid oak, and the only decorations on the walls were his university degrees and several postgraduate qualifications he must have earned since I had last seen him. An impressive array of leather-bound, legal volumes stood to his left in a bookshelf, which probably cost more than the total price of all the assemble-it-yourself furniture at my place. In those days of interactive multimedia resources, the legal volumes were probably just for show when consulting with prospective clients. People wanted the reassurance they were getting value for money, and an empty office didn't inspire confidence.

I said, "You love it around here, don't you?"

"I worked hard for it." He smiled like someone in a toothpaste advertisement.

Ten years ago John Bain looked more like a young model than a recent graduate from The University of Highton with a double degree in psychology and criminal law. He was still handsome but more assertive in a power suit that made me look like a Salvation Army Shop regular. He wore a gold pin set with three diamonds over a red silk tie. His face reminded me of one of those singers in a boy band who always looked ten years younger than he was—eternal youth without the expensive plastic surgery. He was disgustingly attractive and he knew it.

He added, "It beats working in a cage in Queen Street."

"I bet it does."

"And the pay is not bad either."

I nodded.

"You're still with—"

"Gérald."

"That's right, Gérald." He glanced at the window and back at me. "Wow, amazing. Ten years with the same person. I've got everything, but I can't find the right woman. I mean it's not like there's something seriously flawed with me. I work long hours, but who doesn't these days? Women are just as power hungry as we are, so you'd think by now my Cinderella would have turned up."

"Ever been in a serious relationship?"

"Once."

"Anyone I know?"

"A complete bitch, a gold-digging whore who used me as a floor matt to climb the corporate ladder."

"Uh-huh. Good partners are hard to find."

"You mean they exist?"

"All the good ones are already taken, and in your line of work, it's unlikely you come across many."

"Yeah, it's what I heard too. I don't know who are the worst arseholes—lawyers or crooks!"

We both laughed wholeheartedly. He still had something , which turned me into jelly when I was young, horny and had no self-control. But now I was older and wiser—and still horny—and knew the devil has the power to assume a pleasant appearance. Still, sometimes the only dance you want to dance is the forbidden one. A brush with the devil can be more exciting than a brush with an angel.

I said, "I gather this is not a social meeting, and I am not your last hope at throwing the anchor?"

"Very funny, Patricia."

I swallowed hard. "Well, I was only joking, of course."

"Of course." He shuffled some paper on his desk and pulled one white sheet filled with ticked boxes and word-processed paragraphs.

He said, "How much do you remember of the State verses Bah Sheh Mohammed trial?"

I shifted uncomfortably on my seat. The leather screeched like someone letting off gas. "Last case when I was still in uniform. Mohammed got thirty with no parole for the rape and killing of Steven Donnelly. The victim came from an affluent family, and Mohammed had three priors for sexual assaults and one for aggravated burglary, not exactly a saint and kind of a good deed we got him off the streets."

"Can't disagree with you on the last point, but see, I've got

5

a little problem. Do you remember who took his defence?"

I shook my head. I had only been present at the trial when it had been my turn to testify on the arrest, and in those days I had far too many other errands to run. I did remember the story of the murder had been covered in every major newspaper, and any front-page mention of this unusual case guaranteed an extra 30,000 print sales for the dailies. Compassion for homosexuals and foreigners was at an all-time low that year, and civil libertarians argued the media's portrait of the aggressor was accountable for the escalating number of gay bashings around the state.

Bain passed me the court paper cover sheet. "Some redneck straight out of law school got appointed pro bono for the defendant because he couldn't afford his own lawyer. One lawyer to defend him, and there was a bunch of us on the other side. Mohammed didn't stand a chance and neither did his cheap-as-chips lawyer. And the fact it was a homosexual rape sealed the case for us."

He pulled a cigarette from a silver case and lit it up.

"You're allowed to smoke in here?' I asked.

"No, but I won't tell if you don't." He smiled his gorgeous smile and inhaled. "Anyway, my problem is not whether I think Mohammed is a good guy, but whether he hasn't had a fair trial."

"What do you care? He's scum. He killed a man and he got convicted."

"Yeah, well, I agree with you, but Mr. Redneck came to visit me last Friday, and he was almost crying, telling me we framed the wrong guy."

"Ten years later?"

"It's how long it takes for some people's conscience to work around things."

I looked through the tinted windows and across the street. Some suits were having morning coffee in an outdoor terrace and billing some unsuspecting client two hundred and fifty bucks per hour, per person.

I said, "Why the sudden interest?"

"Peter Murray grew up in Moe. He is the first person since his ancestors arrived here from Tasmania who managed to get out of the mining industry and into university. He is clever, no doubt, but the Mohammed case was his first criminal case, and he had no idea what he was doing. Mohammed would have done a better job defending himself, even with his pigeon English."

"What's your point?"

"I believe Murray. He thinks Mohammed got done for racial and political reasons, and he was head-hunted to work for Legal Aid because the State knew he was going to screw up the case. It didn't help his resume when he decided to move on."

"You want to polish up Murray's resume?"

"As far as I'm concerned, it's water under the bridge. Fresh-faced attorneys always get done in the first year. Shit shuffling is part of the in-house training of every legal firm even government outfits such as Legal Aid. You know it's not much different from being the new cop on the block."

"So you want Mohammed out of jail?"

"Not particularly. We both know he's a dangerous man whether he killed Steven Donnelly or not. My concern is not with Mohammed but with what Murray told me." He looked straight into my eyes.

"You think if Mohammed didn't kill the young student, someone else did?"

"Exactly."

"And he got away with it?"

He poured me a glass of water from a bar fridge without my asking and passed it over the desk.

I took the glass. "Thanks." Then: "You know how I feel about injustice."

"Same here."

"But you're a lawyer now, and lawyers want to get rich and screw up people's lives. They don't care about the truth. You don't strike me as the type of person who needs to right the wrongs of this world. Well, maybe you did once when you were an undergraduate law student…"

"What's in your heart doesn't change, Patricia. It never does. I might have made the big time, but I still believe in the truth, even if most lawyers don't know the meaning of the word. There's more to this case than meets the eye, and I was part of the team that convicted the sonofabitch. Let's just say my vested interest is to get a full night's sleep."

I drank my water and placed the glass on the table. "I'll help you. Just tell me what it is you want me to do."

"I'd like you to meet with Murray."

"When?"

"Tomorrow morning."

"You don't give much notice, do you?"

"I wish I could, but Murray has to return to Sydney the day after tomorrow."

"Okay, but if I don't like what I'm hearing from him, I walk away."

"No problem."

So much for turning him down flat.

CHAPTER THREE

"**M**urray is not hiring you," Bain said, "Smith & Gordon is."

"And how is the firm responding to this?"

"I'm a senior partner, so let's just call it my pet project for the time being. And I'm not paying you to get Mohammed out of jail, just to find out who the hell killed the young student." He frowned. "So, what does a P.I. charge these days?"

I told him my hourly rate.

"Why did I bother going to law school? I could have just got a P.I. licence instead."

"My work is not as regular as yours, and believe me it's not at all what it's cracked up to be. A lot of the time you just sit in a car in the middle of the night and chew on cold pizza until dawn. You can't even get out for a pee. Do you know how many empty plastic bottles I have to bring with me during a stakeout?"

"Okay, Patricia, spare me the details, I was just commenting on the income you're generating."

I smiled.

He smiled back.

I was on to my second glass of water when Bain and I agreed on how to approach the whole situation. To begin, we were both aware with the current political situation in Iraq, sniffing around and trying to get an Iraqi convicted rapist and murderer proved innocent after he had been found guilty more than a decade ago wasn't going to sit too well with a lot of people, including the Federal Government. The recent armed raid by the Federal Police on some Islamic homes reflected clearly the state of mind of the nation. And the fact the victim was of the same gender as the predator would once again cause a lot of eyebrows to knit. A decade had passed but people's sense of justice was still stuck somewhere in the middle ages. If public bludgeoning had been legal, I wouldn't be sitting in Bain's office discussing the possibilities of a re-trial.

Bain squashed his cigarette butt into a black marble ashtray with the company's logo engraved in gold lettering and pulled another one straight out of his silver case. "After you've seen Murray, I'd like you to have a chat with Mohammed and see how much you can extract from him."

"And you think he's going to cooperate with me? We're the ones who put him away in the first place."

"You've got a valid point." He lit his cigarette, the third one since we began this conversation.

I said, "Maybe I can bring Tyron with me."

"You're still hanging out with your friend from New Zealand?"

"He could pass as an Iraqi if he stopped shaving for a couple of days."

"Does he speak the lingo?"

"No, but visuals do tend to have a strong effect on people. You told me so when you insisted on blowing up pictures of the dead man for the jury to see ten years ago. Show them a victim who looks like he's gone through a meat grinder and you'll be hard-pressed to find someone coming forth with a not-guilty verdict. That's justice for you."

"You've still got a sharp tongue, you know. I hope your detective skills are as good as your reputation."

"I guess it's for you to find out."

He took a long drag from his cigarette and blew the smoke like a kid making bubbles with soapy water and a straw. "This is coming out of my account, so I just want to make sure I'm on the right track."

"John, if you thought you were on the wrong track, you wouldn't have called me. I can't make any promises, but I'm going to seek the truth from Murray on this one, and we'll see where it leads."

"Sure, and don't forgot to keep me updated with what you find."

"Don't worry, soon enough you'll be fed up with the sound of my voice."

He smiled. "I doubt it very much, Patricia, it's been too long."

We said goodbye, and I left the building, my heart pounding like a kettledrum.

Another five minutes, and I would have forced him into the office storeroom and made him undress at gun point.

CHAPTER FOUR

Tuesday morning I jumped in the shower and stayed under the hot water for a whole ten minutes. My biceps were round and warm like bread rolls from the workout. At the age of thirty-five, even though I looked mid-twenties, it was crucial to look after oneself. Past your mid-thirties, every bodily part has a tendency to sag, and if you don't pump some iron now and then, you end up looking like a farm girl who feeds on nothing but white corn, fresh cream and maple syrup.

I was back at the gym after a three-month break. In a previous investigation, I had lived in hell after some over-zealous cop took me for a burglar and nearly fractured my spine. I spent a whole month with a wheel chair as my best friend. Instead of suing the Victoria Police, we patched things up under the table. The Deputy Commissioner agreed to provide me with unrestricted assistance in the course of my duties. This was not on paper, but I had his word for it, and according to undisclosed sources, this was as good a deal as I was going to get.

My skin softened under the hot water. I lathered my brown locks in jasmine shampoo and massaged my scalp as if it were dough. The morning light coming through the glazed window bathed the whole room in glowing amber. Hot morning showers and going to bed at night were my two favourite events of the day. The only moments when I didn't have to be accountable for anything.

Work had come nice and easy over the past few months, and I had been in no hurry to take on a new client when Bain's phone call came through the previous day. In fact, I had been winding down some of my activities and for months planned a vacation in Broome with Gérald. My daily routine would consist of sipping ice-cold, light beer and simmering in the scorching sun. Tons of books were sitting on my desk, begging to be taken for a holiday and read cover-to-cover. The voracious reader I once was would soon become illiterate if I didn't take these books on the trip with me.

Someone outside my apartment was calling someone else a bastard, and the clacking of a tram coming around Fitzroy Street grew louder.

I lived in St Kilda, in a secluded warehouse apartment above Impression Plus, a desktop publishing firm that designed and printed for free my business cards and letterheads. In return I did the odd debt collecting on customers who extended their credit beyond what was deemed reasonable in normal business practice.

I stepped out of the shower and dried my face with a clean, white hand towel. I spread a generous amount of moisturiser with the tip of my fingers all over my forehead, my nose, cheeks and the back of my neck. I put on a light foundation and brushed my teeth until the gums bled, not a good habit to get into, my dentist told me, but neither was tooth decay.

When I was done with the daily scrub, I snuggled into Gérald's oversized, blue bathrobe and headed for the kitchen. I poured freshly brewed coffee in a mug and stared through the open window at waves crashing into the shore. The metallic smell of a recent downpour filled the room like someone's cooking. More rain had been forecast for the rest of the day, and the air was chilled.

I had been working as a private investigator for almost a decade, and the last time I saw John Bain, I wore a uniform and carried a gun. The average lifespan of a cop on the job is eight years, even less for a woman, and I was no exception. I tossed the promising vocation to the side and hung my shingle on the wall. I was good at my job. Word got around quickly, and most of my assignments were derived from referrals. Other than the annual block advertisement in the Yellow Pages, my marketing budget was non-existent.

I washed down a multivitamin and a vitamin E with the black coffee, no milk, no sugar. The caffeine wasn't all that good for my body, but combined with my daily nutritional supplement of pills, it was as effective as a kick in the pants so early in the morning.

At 9.15 a.m. I was inappropriately dressed in a mini and tank-top, ready to cast my charm on the unsuspecting world of male chauvinist pigs.

I checked on Gérald before leaving the apartment. He was still sound asleep after a double-shift at St Vincent's hospital. His blond hair was messed up like someone's toilet brush.

I stepped outside the apartment and headed for the city to meet Murray, the defence lawyer who guaranteed his clients a life sentence, even if all they'd done was to run through a red light.

CHAPTER FIVE

"You know," Murray said, "I fucked up, and I am not scared to say I fucked up."

I said, "We all fuck up now and then, but it really doesn't matter. What matters is what you do after you've fucked-up."

"Exactly my point. So when they gave me this case ten years ago, of course I was eager, I had never been offered a criminal case before. Straight out of law school, how the hell was I supposed to say no?"

We were sheltered from the cold and the rain that blanketed the city since the early hours of the morning. People were coming in and out of the Little Lonsdale Street eatery for a quick snack or a coffee to keep up the pace for the rest of the day. The aroma of Brazilian roasted beans and toasted croissants filled the room like at a Parisian café. If you half closed your eyes and stopped listening to other people's conversations, it was easy to make believe you were having breakfast somewhere on the other side of the world. Every street in Melbourne had a story to tell, and it was the reason I never felt the need to move to another state. With murder, mayhem and corruption right at my doorstep, business had never been so good.

Peter Murray was a tall guy who looked more at home

driving a 4WD somewhere between Ayers Rock and a cattle station than sitting at a club sandwich bar and sipping tap beer from a highball glass. His face was square and ruddy and he carried beefy shoulders and forearms. His tone was assured, but he spoke like a country bumpkin, not a lawyer.

He took a gulp of his tap beer.

I was drinking chilled light ale from a bottle, breakfast on the run.

I said, "So what happened exactly?"

He placed his glass down on a paper coaster. "How well do you know the case?"

"John Bain gave me the transcript to go over."

"Have you read it?"

"Most of it."

"And what's the verdict?"

"I thought you were going to shed some light on that."

"Okay, fine, I'll start then." He called a young waiter over and asked for another beer. He asked me if I wanted another light beer, and I said I was fine for the time being. Instead, I ordered a club sandwich with avocado and thinly sliced red capsicum, topped with tasty cheddar.

After the waiter left with our order, Murray turned back to me. "He didn't do it, and I know he didn't do it because I have a hunch about these things."

"A hunch?"

"Yeah, you know what I'm talking about, you're an investigator. You know when people tell the truth. This guy wasn't a smart arse about anything. He admitted he had priors and fucked other men in the past, and he had always pleaded guilty to all charges. He wasn't scared. I think he came face to face with his demons a long time ago. So if he had raped and killed Steven Donnelly, he would have told me upfront."

"He could be a psychopath, you ever considered the possibility? With psychopaths, you can't really tell. They're bred to lie and make it sound like they're telling the truth."

"Yeah, well, I don't buy this shit. See, in the transcript he pleaded not guilty. But it's not exactly the way it happened. When I came to him, he wanted to plea bargain because he said he didn't stand a chance with his criminal record, and with all the shit happening in the Gulf War, it wasn't like a jury was

16

going to think he was Jesus resurrected and believed every word pouring out of his mouth was holy water."

"Go on."

"I told him there was no such thing as plea bargaining in Australia, so if he had not done it, he should just plead not guilty. I said to him if he was innocent, then there was no way a jury was going to find him guilty. See back then I believed the whole point of a court system was to seek the truth. I made a mistake. He knew he wasn't going to get away with it, and he was right, and I fucked up. I sent an innocent man to jail because I believed in the system, and the system fucked me over."

The waiter came back with my sandwich and Murray's cold beer. He smiled a lovely smile, and brushed some of his chestnut locks behind his right ear. It was nice to see someone who seemed happy at his job, no matter how mundane the job might seem to the outside world.

The sandwich was succulent and I knew I had made the right choice.

I spent a few seconds thinking about what Murray had just told me. I said, "You can't really blame yourself. You've said it yourself: the State wanted Mohammed locked away, and it's the reason they chose you."

"It's what pisses me off. I mean who the hell do they think they are? They think they can hand-pick recent graduates from law school to do their dirty work and fill in their political agenda? It's bullshit."

It was a dog-eat-dog world out there, and after all these years, Murray still reacted like a spoiled puppy.

I said, "Peter, you're not giving me much to go on here. You think he didn't do it, and you want revenge because the State screwed you over some ten years ago? What the hell am I supposed to do with this information?"

"Okay, look, he got convicted for killing a white boy who lived in Toorak, right? And he's from Broadmeadows, and all the previous rape victims were from the northern suburbs, all within a five-kilometre radius from where he lived. And in addition he always went for coloured guys, never for whites. He said he didn't have a thing for whites and never would. The pattern doesn't fit. I've done some research, and he's right. Rape outside one's race is uncommon, no matter what you've heard out there."

"Did he own a car?"

"No."

"Trains go all the way to Toorak from Spencer Street or Flinders Street. He could have stopped in Toorak, South Yarra or Prahran?"

"To rape someone? Come on. Why would a coloured man go all the way to Toorak to rape a white boy when he doesn't know shit about the area? Rapists like to work in an area of comfort, a zone they're familiar with."

"Maybe he borrowed someone's car."

He looked at me as if I had just spat in his face. "Stealing is more like it."

I took a sip from my light beer. "All right, you've got half a point. Did he happen to have an alibi on the day Steven Donnelly got killed?"

"Yes, but he can't remember his name, and he doesn't know where he lives."

"Well, rather productive. And he wanted to plea bargain with a nameless alibi?"

"Exactly my point. If Mohammed had concocted a story about an alibi, don't you think he would have got at least a name? The prosecutor's case would have crumbled before it reached the courts."

Murray wasn't half as stupid as Bain had made him out to be. He had done his homework, and no doubt because this little story of his had been keeping him awake in the small hours of the morning when guilt kicks in like a slap in the face.

I finished my sandwich and called the waiter over for a coffee.

Murray ordered another beer.

The waiter was back in less than two minutes.

I drank my coffee. "Why didn't you bring this up in court ten years ago?"

"Because I didn't know what I was doing. I majored in tax law, not criminal justice, so it took me a few years to think back and study everything that had happened back then. I spoke to criminal lawyers who'd been in the system for a long time, and they told me I got done from day one. I asked them if they would back me up if I sued the State Government and the prosecutor's office, but they threatened to *sue me* if I even mentioned their names to anyone out there. Everyone knows the system's fucked, but no one is willing to do anything about it."

It was hard not to feel compassion for Murray, especially when I could see how distressed he would have been when he finally realised the legal system was designed to do you over when you're young and eager to make your mark in the world. He had been a graduate hopeful who believed the lies he had been fed, and in return he got kicked in the teeth and pushed into the streets like an incompetent hustler with a fake university degree.

I said, "Okay, then how the hell did they pin him for it?"

"I thought you read the transcript?"

"Yes, but I want to hear it from you, there are always twenty sides to every story."

"Two eyewitnesses picked him out of a line-up."

"Who?"

"Two friends of Steven Donnelly."

"Two friends saw Mohammed with Steven, and they didn't do anything?"

"They saw Steven being dragged away, and by the time they caught up with them, both men were gone in a car."

"I thought he didn't have a car?"

"I said he didn't *own* a car, I never said he didn't have one."

My mind did a somersault. "Did they call the cops?"

"Yes, and someone else did, but it was a separate reporting. Mohammed's name was leaked by an anonymous caller."

"Rather convenient, don't you think?"

He didn't reply.

Outside the rain had stopped.

I gulped down the rest of my coffee. "So what else did they have to tie him to the rape and murder?"

"Steven's soiled underwear at his flat with seminal fluid all over them."

"What about the DNA test?"

"Inconclusive."

"The rest of his clothes?"

"A St Albans University sweater, that's it."

"So what did Mohammed say happened?"

"He said he got framed, and the cops planted the evidence in his flat. He said they could have done it easily because the back door of the flat was broken and anyone could get in."

"Did he say why he thought the cops might have framed him? I mean the police are not in the habit of framing people for no particular reason."

"No idea. I guess it's the reason John Bain recommended you, so you can figure out this whole mess, and tell us what we've got here."

A couple of large suits two tables from us seemed to be eaves dropping. They looked like young corporate types whose peak excitement for the day consisted of watching company stock go up or down by half a point. They seemed harmless enough, so I choose to ignore them.

"Can I ask you a personal question?" I asked Murray.

"Shoot."

"When you first took on the case, did you think Mohammed had committed the crime?"

He thought for a few seconds while taking a sip from his beer. "Yeah, I guess I did, but then, so did everyone else."

"Because he was gay?"

"Maybe, I don't know, I mean what does it really matter anyway? I'm trying to do something about it now."

"Yes, I can see, but I'm just wondering why it took you so long to change your mind." I paused for effect. "When did you first come out of the closet?"

Murray blushed and shook his head. "You read people pretty well, you know."

"I'm a woman."

"I come from a small country town where gay people are regarded with suspicion, so it took me a while to trust my own thinking. I guess I was angry at gay men for a long time, but in the end I figured out I was just angry at myself. Until I learned to accept who I was and where I fitted in this world, I would always be angry."

"You're doing the right thing, Peter. Life can be confusing when you're young, but it's good you've come full circle."

"Thank you, your understanding is appreciated."

20

I nodded and thanked him for his time
He retrieved his wallet from his jacket.
"No, I'll get it," I said. "The pleasure was all on this side."
I called the waiter over, paid the bill and left a generous tip.

CHAPTER SIX

I was at home going through Mohammed's trial transcript for the fifth time when Gérald came in. He was wearing his white doctor's uniform and looked as refreshed as if he had just stepped out of the shower. I didn't know how he managed to look so good after a twelve-hour shift. He was a tall blond with blue eyes and a friendly attitude. We had been together for ten years, and I wouldn't have traded him for anything, even with my wandering eyes. His French accent made all my friends jealous to death, and he was the most trusting person I have ever known. Sometimes he had more faith in me than I had in myself.

"Rough day?" he asked when he saw the piles of transcript lying on the coffee table.

"Interesting, let's say."

Without asking me, he opened the fridge and pulled out two light beers. He came to the couch and tossed one on my lap.

He said, "How's your friend John doing? He's still got the hots for you?"

"Never had."

"But you did."

"It was a long time ago. It's water under the bridge."

"But the boat is still floating."

We laughed gently and sipped our beer.

"You're going ahead with the case?" he asked.

"The money is good, and we could use it for our holiday. I'm going to find out what the hell happened to Mohammed."

"You're going to set him free?"

"I'm going to find out who killed the young student."

He nodded in approval.

The sound of the waves came through the open window like ambient music. Sunlight painted the room a summer canvas. I loved this place. It was so far away from all the absurdity of everyday turmoil and distant enough from the half day I had spent in the city.

"How's your patient doing?" I asked.

"Not so well."

"Have you figured out what's wrong with her yet?"

"She's got Churg-Strauss Syndrome."

I looked at him puzzled.

He sat next to me and rested his head on my shoulder. His warm breath was tickling the nape of my neck, but I remained still. He smelled like ammonia and hospital. His hair was soft like clean flannel sheets.

He locked his green eyes into mine. "We had to remove three quarters of her small intestine, all rotting from the inside. Her immune system is attacking her own cells. It's a very rare disease. There's only been twenty-five cases diagnosed worldwide in the past thirty years. She's had four laparotomies and a small-bowel resection. She's all stitched up, a real mess. She's been drip fed for seven weeks, lost twenty-five kilos. And she's only twenty-four."

I took a large gulp of beer. "That's rough. What brought it on?"

"No one knows, one of those mysteries in life. It might be asthma related, but no one's certain."

He finished his beer. "I'm going to have a shower. Why don't you come and join me in the bedroom? You've been working too hard, and so have I."

"Sure thing."

He disappeared, and sixty seconds later I heard the water

from the shower like rain on a tin roof.

Carefully, I piled up the sheets from the transcript in the right order and placed them back inside a maroon manilla folder with the embossed Smith & Gordon company logo printed on the front flap. I tossed the lot in a large, soft briefcase sitting next to the coffee table.

Ten minutes later, we were both lying naked on the white sheets of our queen-size bed, like a couple of Antarctic seals making the most of the sun. It had been espresso lovemaking, but good nonetheless.

"Ever think about getting married?" he asked.

"Why?"

"We've been together a long time. Maybe we should try the next level."

I stared at the ceiling for a few seconds.

"It's a serious decision to make," I finally said.

"I know, I know, and I wouldn't want you to go through with it unless you're absolutely certain."

I turned around and faced him. He was so gorgeous, I could have just said my vows right at that moment. "You know I love you more than anything in the world, but I don't know if marriage is right for us. I think it might ruin everything."

"Maybe you're right, I don't know. People are just asking why we're not getting married."

"What do you care what people think?"

"I know, why fix it if it's not broken?"

I smiled and stretched the length of my naked body on the bed.

He rested his head on my chest.

"But you want to get married, don't you?" I asked.

"Not unless you want to."

"But you would like to?"

"It wouldn't hurt."

I played with a strand of his blond hair between my thumb and forefinger. "I'll think about it."

CHAPTER SEVEN

Constable Gibbon had decided he was willing to talk to me, but he didn't have time to sit at a desk to do it. We were walking at the back of the Broadmeadows train station, where a bunch of kids hung around a Brotherhood of St Lawrence charity bin like blue flies around a corpse. The police station was just around the block and highly visible to anyone driving past to get to the shopping centre or the Broadmeadows Magistrate's Court. The air smelled of Pascoe Vale Road traffic and fried food from a takeaway shop nearby. The sun was high in the sky, but grey clouds were making their way from the Dandenong Ranges. The Brotherhood of St Lawrence kids saw us, but they didn't seem to care.

At first glance the suburb did not seem as bad as I had expected it with its recently-built, impressive Community Learning Centre, which took over what was once a council car park.

But as I stood there, oppressiveness filled the air like summer rain, and there seemed to be far too many people hanging around for the middle of the week. What ever happened to working for a living?

I had read about people knifing one another at the very train station we were standing in, but there was no real evidence of violence. Maybe I had to come back at midnight to see the reputed dark side of Broadmeadows.

"That's Mohammed's turf," Senior Constable Peter Gibbon said. "I grew up here. Thirty years ago, there wasn't an Arab around. Now the place is filled with them. Some people don't like it, but you learn to live with it."

"What about you?" I asked.

"What about me?"

"Do they bother you?"

"No more than the Asians or the Indonesians. In my line of work, you can't afford to get too personal about race. After a while, you start to learn there are good and bad people everywhere, and race means little. Most of these kids know they don't stand a chance. They go to the worst government schools available because nobody wants them."

Gibbon was a chubby guy in his early fifties with a soft voice and watery eyes that had seen it all. He sported specks of grey on his temples, and kept his thinning hair short and easy to manage. He seemed to be the type of regular guy who would retire in a coastal town one day and indulge in some serious fishing.

"What about the parents?" I asked.

"Too busy making ends meet to worry about their kids. Low-paid wages, cash in hand and undeclared, mostly supplemented by Centrelink allowances of one kind or another. But then, who would bother declaring three dollars per hour? I know I wouldn't."

"Did Mohammed finish his schooling?"

"Do they ever? Okay, a few of them make it and change their family situation around in one generation, what would normally take three or four generations to do. But the majority of them don't bother. The parents don't speak English, so it's not like anyone is going to correct them on their homework. The teachers have given up a long time ago; they'd rather invest quality time on kids who can communicate and who are high achievers. They know kids of recent refugee immigrants are never going to go to university or amount to anything. If they're lucky, they might get a job at the local Ford manufacturing plant doing repetitive, boring tasks. But there are more of these kids unemployed than jobs available. And when you add a juvenile record to your CV, well, you can pretty much kiss goodbye to the chance of ever getting a job in any form or shape. Work-For-The-Dole projects pretty much sums up your work history."

A city outbound train stopped at the station. People poured out of it like escapees from the Woomera Detention Centre. Many women had their heads covered in veils, and kids were loud and filled with domineering confidence. A young man with baggy pants and an oversized T-shirt jumped the fence to avoid having his fare checked. Constable Gibbon saw him but didn't move an inch.

"Have you met Mohammed's parents?" I asked.

"The mother was a teenager when she got pregnant with Mohammed. Nothing unusual. Some of these people marry at the age of twelve back home. Teenage pregnancies are as common there as divorces are in Australia. It's hopeless from day one."

"It's a pretty bleak way to look at things."

"It's reality. You can romanticise all you want, in the end it's not going to matter much. There's a lot of racial tension since the September 11th Twin Towers attack and the Bali bombings. Most Arabs don't support terrorist actions, but they cop flak just the same. Arab kids get abused at school, and veiled women are spat on in the streets."

The train station cleared, and people headed towards the shopping centre. We walked into a newsagent next to the entrance of the train station and picked up a couple of vanilla Cokes. We pulled the rings on the way out.

I said, "Do you think Mohammed killed Steven Donnelly?"

"Who gives a fuck? He is where he belongs. You've seen his priors? It was bound to happen one day or another. He's not a victim here, like some of the other Arab kids. That faggot paved his own way. He's just an arsehole, full stop. Gives his entire race a bad name."

"There's a rumour going around he got framed."

"Maybe he did, maybe he didn't. It was ten years ago, so nobody really gives a shit anymore. Point is he's dangerous, and even if he didn't kill anyone, he would have continued to rape young men, so he's better off where he is, for him and for everyone out there."

We looked at the kids we saw previously going through the Brotherhood of St Lawrence charity bin. An older one in white-striped, black tracksuit pants was helping a younger one in dirty jeans to get inside the bin by holding him by the legs. The younger one tossed back whatever he grabbed, and then they sorted the items out on the ground.

"Can you believe this?" Gibbon said. "Then they go and sell the stuff at the Sunday market."

"They're just kids. Something should be done to get them out of this mess."

"Yeah, I hear you, and so does everyone around. But no one really knows what to do. Multiculturalism doesn't always go hand in hand with harmony. Don't believe all the shit you read in the local papers."

"What about the city council? Don't they have some type of youth program to catch those who risk falling between the cracks? "

"They do what they can. Most of them are white folks with bleeding hearts. They organise meetings other white folks attend, and nothing ever comes out of them, other than wasting taxpayers' money. To make it look like they're doing something, every year they throw a multicultural event where every wog has his day. Frankly, it's all a big waste of time, if you ask me, nobody understands anything any more."

"Your enthusiasm is inspiring."

He looked at me almost with contempt but changed his mind. "When you've lived here as long as I have, it's easy to understand where I'm coming from. If you really want to know what it's like, you've got to be in the streets, you've got to feel the people, talk to them, understand what makes them tick, and then maybe, and only maybe, you'd be able to do something worthwhile."

"And you think you're doing something worthwhile?"

"I do what I can, and it's more than most people around here." He passed one hand over his bristled, grey hair. "Anyway, don't get your hopes too high on Mohammed. The court case is old and trying to dig all this shit from the past is like trying to steal from the dead. The young man is never going to come back to life, and I don't think his parents want to be reminded all over again about the nightmare they had to go through."

I finished the rest of my vanilla Coke. "I understand, and I certainly don't want to be a time bomb hanging over everyone's head, but if someone else killed Steven Donnelly, then he doesn't deserve to be walking the streets now, does he?"

"You're right, but still, I don't think you should get your hopes too high."

"I never do when I'm chasing leads."

"Good because I'd hate to see you going home disappointed."

"Yeah, so would I, so I'll keep your advice taped to the back of my skull."

"You do that, and watch your arse. You don't really know who you're dealing with."

"Who?"

"Just trust me."

He left me by myself and went to have a friendly chat with the kids recycling stuff from the charity bin.

CHAPTER EIGHT

I parked the car in one of the five visitors' spots reserved for those who didn't live or work there. The other four spots were free. It was just on 2.30 p.m., and although visiting hours were not currently scheduled, the governor agreed to make an exception since this was business and not pleasure.

"Fuckin' car," Tyron said to me. "Can't you get something bigger like everyone else?" He struggled to shift his heavy frame out of yellow MR2 Spyder.

I only purchased the roadster two weeks ago.

"Not unless I intend to pop a kid in the near future."

"And what's the deal with the XXX MR2 number plate?"

"I'm a producer of erotic films after hours."

He smiled. "Very funny."

"Seriously, no idea, the plates came with the car. "

Tyron headed for the front entrance.

I followed.

The sky was overcast and rain had been predicted for late afternoon.

Someone told me once jail is where you go when you don't belong anywhere, a place you call home when you don't have a proper home. I don't know if it's true because most people don't really go there in the first place, they are sent. Prison is a form of punishment disguised as rehabilitation because revenge isn't palatable to most people.

From behind, Tyron looked like the Exhibition Building, the kind of bloke you pass in the street and your jaw drops two inches just from the sheer size of him. He grew up in New Zealand in a Maori family and came to Australia when he was a child because prospects were better here in those days before Australia fell into the recession it had to have.

He turned around to face me. "He knows we're coming?"

"Far as I know, yes. I haven't spoken to him directly on the phone, but the governor assures me he knows."

"Speaks English?"

"Who?"

"Mohammed."

"Better than he did ten years ago. Prison life has forced him to communicate in one language only."

We walked casually towards the front entrance. The earth smelled of spring flowers and recent gardening.

It was kind of reassuring to have a friend as impressively built as Tyron because you never worried about your personal safety when he was around. Only a lunatic would try to provoke someone built like a tank and as mean-looking as a snake. But Tyron was just a little boy in a man's body. I had known him since high school, long enough to build the kind of trust you only see in couples celebrating their diamond anniversary.

My gentle giant had obeyed me and neglected to shave for three days. He looked messy enough to give the impression he might have escaped from a zoo during a full moon. He wore an oversized, red-and-black, chequered shirt, baggy jeans and soiled trainers. And as a bonus, he reeked like someone who'd just crawled out of a sewerage processing plant.

I wore my favourite pair of faded jeans and a white tank-top. My brown hair was tied with a red elastic band, and the fake Ray Bans clipped to the front of my top were just for show.

We passed the high-steel security gate, where our names were checked against a list with the names of other guests who would drop in within the next 48 hours to visit society's finest citizens in this overrated country club conveniently tucked away in the middle of farmland.

We entered the foyer, bare walls with four security guards armed to the teeth. We were searched thoroughly, short of being stripped naked and fondled. A sleaze-bag in uniform spread his electronic device down the length of my legs three times while eyeing one of the other guards. If he had tried a fourth time, I would have knocked his teeth out with my elbow.

The body search continued with Bobby, the spaniel cross, sniffing our crotches for the carrying of illegal substances, including Tim Tams, which were banned from the prison since a couple of inmates nearly gouged each other's eyes over the last remaining chocolate biscuit *accidentally* left in the plastic in-tray by one of the correction officers. Of course, it was a complete coincidence the two inmates involved in the bloody battle were known by everyone on the premises to love one another like David and Goliath. The story was told to everyone who cared to listen to Bobby's master in case someone did try to smuggle the highly hazardous chocolate biscuits inside the maximum security area. It was reassuring to know our tax dollars were hard at work.

Our photos were taken with a high-resolution digital camera, and personal information, including contact numbers and residential addresses, were logged into a security database.

"You take this stuff seriously," I said to the middle-aged correction officer whose saggy eyes told me he should have gone home five days ago.

"Have to, you wouldn't believe the amount of shit people try to get through these gates. If it hasn't been done yet, someone is inventing it right this minute."

"A matter of national security, uh?"

Saggy Eyes looked me as if I were a chimp, which escaped from her cage, and chose to ignore my comment. He wore a dark, brushed moustache, and his skin discolouration told me after a long-working day, drinking was his favourite pastime.

We proceeded into a web of corridors reeking of commercial floor polish and ended up in a room with a table and two orange chairs. One of us would have to remain standing up. The furniture was round-edged just in case someone decided to use it as a weapon and insert the corner of a table into a visitor's eardrum.

A correctional officer, who was fresh-faced enough to be the son I didn't have, led Bah Sheh Mohammed into the room and made him sit at one end of the table.

I sat opposite him.

Tyron stood to my right like a traffic light at an intersection.

Mohammed wore the compulsory orange prison uniform enhanced with a photo-ID card and his own personal bar-code, which would never see the laser-beam of a checkout register.

The atmosphere was oppressive, kind of what you would expect in a place like this. The room was bare of decorations, and there was no natural light. The walls were painted a monotonous green, an obvious failed attempt at capturing the great outdoors.

"Any problems I'm just outside," the correctional officer said.

Two black cameras with flashing red lights were mounted at the two opposite corners of the room and captured every move and sound. So much for lawyer-client confidentiality.

Mohammed's hair was the same length as his beard, number one all around. His eyes and expression reminded me of a hawk, and his eyebrows met somewhere in the middle of his face. He had a natural tan, which was more likely to have come from his cultural inheritance than the solarium at the prison's gymnasium. A bare-chested man was tattooed on his forearm with a chiselled jaw line and outrageously defined muscles, which can only be seen on morning cartoons. He must have had the tattoo done in Australia because back in his home country, he would have been stoned to death just by thinking of getting it.

"What do you want?" he said instead of greetings.

"I'm Patricia Lunn and I'm here to help you."

He took one look at Tyron. "And who's he? Your bitch sister?"

I glanced at Tyron, and he shrugged.

"A gift for you in case you get bored," I said.

"No shit, you're a funny woman."

"He's going to help us on this."

"Us? What the fuck is this? Are you cops or something?

Hey, I'm already doing my time here, so I don't know what the fuck you want from me."

"I've been hired to find out whether you really killed that young man ten years ago."

"Really? And who's interested?"

"The lawyer who took your case."

"Murray? Little redneck motherfucker who can't find a nail in his own arsehole even with a search party and a metal detector?"

CHAPTER NINE

Tyron said, "Mohammed, why don't you do us a favour, and stop being such a dick? We know life is hell in here, but you don't have to remind us. We're here to help you, so show a little respect."

Mohammed eyeballed Tyron for a full ten seconds. "All right, but I've already told the cops everything I know. What difference is it going to make now?"

I leaned forward. "Why don't you cooperate, and we'll see where it leads us? You've got nothing to lose; you're in for twenty already."

Mohammed's facial muscles relaxed. "What do you want to know?"

"Tell us your side of the story."

"Aren't much to tell. The bastards framed me, that's it."

"How?"

"Fuck if I know. I was asleep, and a whole army of them turned up one morning and took me at gunpoint, scared the shit out of me."

I didn't tell him I was one of them. "Why do you think they chose you?"

"Do you guys read the papers or follow the news?"

I did a face that told him to go on.

"Well," he said, "Arabs are not exactly the toast of the town. And it's been like this way for ten fuckin' years, which means if you want to find a guilty party and satisfy the public, find a middle-eastern motherfucker, just like me."

"I don't know if it's all there is to it, Mohammed. Not everyone in jail is of middle-eastern origin. We're not in America and you're not a black person. You've been found guilty of raping a white, heterosexual male, so how else did you think it was going to end?"

"Well, then, it's this fuckin' homophobic society we live in."

"Doesn't tell me why they chose you and not someone else."

"It was my turn. Three prior convictions, they wanted to get me off the streets and into the slammer. Opportunity knocked and they took the door down with a sledgehammer."

"Who's they?"

"Cops."

"Lots of cops out there, can't you be a little more specific?"

"Nope. But there's a security guard at the university campus where the body was found. You should talk to him. He was one of the first people at the scene."

"Okay. Anything else you can tell us?"

"Can't think of anything."

"If you do, call me."

I passed him one of my business cards.

He stared at it for a few seconds, looked at Tyron, and then back at me. "You better watch your arses."

"We know how to look after ourselves," Tyron said.

"If they want to get you, and if they find out you're trying to help me, they're going to get you, no matter how tough you think you are."

"You let us worry about our safety," I said.

He stood from his chair. "I'm just saying, no one's gonna help you then. No one gave a fuck about me when I got framed."

The correctional officer walked back in the room and led Mohammed away.

We were escorted out of the room, back down the maze of

corridors, and to the foyer. When we got outside the building, sunlight was blinding like a torch in your face.

"What do you think?" I said to Tyron.

"Don't like him, but I won't let my opinion cloud my judgement."

"Same here."

CHAPTER TEN

The northern campus of The University of Highton, where Steven Donnelly had been found dead, covered some twenty hectares of historical buildings, lawns, trees, and gardens, all perfectly maintained for the pleasure of the academics and the students who spent a great deal of their waking hours there. The campus was a city within a city, and it would have been easy to spend a whole week there without feeling the need to mingle back with the uneducated.

I didn't want to look suspicious, so I dispensed with the skimpy skirt and tank-top. I wore jeans and a white cotton shirt fitted tightly around my frame. Although I was much older than the average student, there were a few mature-age students parading the grounds, I could have been one of them. No one asked any questions, unless you wore camouflage gear and carried a large gym bag that could house a rifle, which for some reason looks oddly out of place at a university campus.

The sun was high in the sky, and today was the first day of spring that lived up to people's expectation—warm and inviting. Melbourne's weather was a potpourri of four seasons in one week, but after twenty years of total immersion, I had come to appreciate it.

I had managed to find the security office at the corner of Swanston Street and Mitford Road in the Dickinson Jerry building. I parked the roadster in a spot marked *Security Only – All other vehicles will be towed away at the owner's expense*.

I stepped out of the roadster and walked straight to the front desk. I told the reception clerk at the counter about my business.

"Is Mr. Leeson expecting you?" he asked. He was in his mid-twenties with gel-spiked hair and seemed to be taking himself far more seriously than the rest of the world did.

"Not really."

"I'll see if he's not busy."

He was talking to my breasts.

He made me wait for a full minute before announcing Mr. Leeson will see me in the office *now*.

Mr. Leeson's office consisted of a large desk with set of drawers on both sides, a couple of grey filing cabinets, a computer and a set of four monitors attached to the west wall and clearly visible from where he was sitting. He was a relatively large man in his mid-fifties with dark hair and a prominent forehead. He shook my hand with his beefy fingers. His skin reminded me of raw hamburger. His eyes were set so close together, it was as if he was looking right past me.

"Please, take a seat," he said. "What can I do you for?"

"The Steven Donnelly case. Rings a bell?"

His mind digested the information for a few seconds. "Sure does. We don't get bodies found every week on the campus. Are we talking about the young man who was found behind the Old Arts Building in—"

"—nineteen-ninety-two."

"Right. Yeah, I remember the case, all right. So what are you, a cop or something?"

"Private investigator hired by Smith & Gordon to look into the case."

I pulled my ID card.

He glanced at it but didn't seem really interested in knowing whether I was who I said I was. "And what's your interest in this case ten years later?"

"Something's come up. There's a chance the wrong man has been sent to jail."

"Really? Wasn't he an Iraqi or something?"

"Something."

"Okay, whatever. How can I be of help?"

"Were you the one who found Donnelly?"

"Nope, some Arts student who came early for a lecture. I think he needed to take a whole month off after his little discovery. Not exactly surprising. I was second at the scene, and I tell you now, it wasn't a pretty sight. A decade later, I'm still having nightmares."

"Can I see the location where the body was found?"

"Sure thing."

He moved from behind his desk. He was more bulky standing up than when he had been seated. "Just follow me."

He told the young man at the reception he would be away for twenty minutes or so, and unless it was an emergency, he didn't want to be disturbed.

We walked west up Mitford Road until we reached Patterson Hall, and then turned left and aimed for the South Lawn. Just up the steps to our right was the Old Arts Building almost hidden by foliage.

"You get many problems on campus?" I asked.

"Nothing major. Of course, everyone fears one day we're going to get something similar to the Rowville shooting."

"There's always the risk of having a copycat around."

"Tell me about it. Everyone is getting really paranoid a half-brain with some kind of attention-seeking disorder is going to shoot fellow students, just for the sake of getting his face splattered all over the front page of the dailies. Instant fame. I've got no doubt it's going to happen one of these days."

Four young men barely out of their teens were sun baking and studying near the Old Arts Building. They gave me the once-over and smiled.

I smiled back.

"It's certainly a perfect place for a crazy person to hang around," I said.

"Yep, and there are plenty of crazy people out there." He stopped just in front of the building and turned around. "There, it's where he was found."

There was a row of bushes behind us, thick enough to

camouflage a body without anyone noticing.

Leeson was pointing at a specific point. "Right here, I remember as if it just happened yesterday."

"Did anyone touch him when you got there?"

"Nope. He was found the way he'd been killed. No underwear, and his chest fully exposed. There was bruising too, especially around the neck."

"Happens a lot when you get strangled."

"Never seen a strangled person before, so it kind of shook me up a bit."

I looked at the once-was crime scene, and it didn't tell me anything.

There were students everywhere around us, and most of them had most likely been attending elementary school when the horrific deed took place. In fact, other than Leeson, there was a good chance the majority of people on campus had no idea an undergrad had been murdered right here at this spot, in the midst of a legion of young minds who would one day become leaders of this world. The killer could have gone one better and dumped the body in front of the criminology building. That would have really got everybody jumping around like fleas on a dog's back.

I glanced to the right and noticed the four students we walked past a minute ago. It broke my heart knowing Steven Donnelly could have been one of them, and some bastard ended his life in such a perverted way.

"Do you know if Donnelly was a good student?" I asked.

"Come again?"

"Was Steven Donnelly a hard-working student?"

He looked at me puzzled. "What makes you think he was a student here?"

"He wasn't?"

"Nope."

We returned to Leeson's office.

"Wanted to become a cop, but he never made the grade," Leeson said, referring to the reception clerk who had nothing new to announce when we got back to the office, other than it was time for his break. Leeson let him go and told him to stay away from the student union bar. "Got a hell of an attitude, though. If it was up to me, I would have sacked him by now."

41

"A lot of those around," I said.

Leeson sat back at his desk. "Yeah, tell me about it."

I toyed with everything Leeson told me and what I already knew about the murder of Steven Donnelly. "Any ideas why the killer would have come all the way to The University of Highton to dump a body?"

Leeson rubbed his beardless chin. "Wish I could help you, but criminology is not my department. I was hoping you were going to be the one to tell me."

"It just seems odd to me why someone would come all the way from Broadmeadows to kidnap a boy from Toorak, and then drives all the way to Carlton to get rid of the body."

"You're right there, given it's rather difficult to access the Old Arts Building by car without being noticed."

"And I doubt he carried the body in his backpack."

He pinched the bridge of his nose with his thumb and forefinger. "You know, come to think of it, we do get a lot of contractors driving in and out of the campus, especially first thing in the morning. The gates are often left up, so he didn't really need an access code or a permit to get through."

"I guess it's a possibility."

I paused for a few seconds to look at the surveillance monitors attached to the walls, four black-and-white screens showing various sections of the campus in ten-second intervals.

"You got someone here twenty-four hours a day?" I asked.

"Now we do. Ten years ago, no way. There was no need for it." He played with the collar of his shirt and added, "Want a cola? Keep my own supply right here."

"No, thanks. I'm going to get moving. Do you know where I can get a list of students who were in the class of the student who found Donnelly?"

He removed a Coke from a bar fridge near his desk and pulled the ring from it. "That's going a bit far back. Most of them would have graduated or dropped out by now. In fact, there's a good chance many are living interstate or even overseas."

"Who would keep a list of those students?"

"Student Admin." He pulled a photocopied campus map on green paper from under his desk. "We're here. Just walk up

42

Mitford Street, turn at Gate 6 and continue down Stanhope Road. Student Admin is at the end to your right, facing the Old Science Building, right here." His pudgy finger landed on a rectangle just below the union lawn.

I took the map. "Do I need to bribe them?"

"Well, let's just say you got to have a pretty damn good reason to want to comb through the records. I doubt they'll give you anything unless you have some sort of warrant."

"Yeah, I kind of anticipated this level of cooperation."

"Either way, you're not going to get any today because they've closed for now. You can always come back tomorrow."

He took a gulp from his Coke and made a gastric sound similar to that of an orgasm.

I folded the map and pocketed it in the back of my jeans.

He said, "You know, I'm thinking about what you said before, and how Arab bloke must have known the campus pretty well to dump the body where he did. If he had never been on the campus, how would have known were to dump it?"

I nodded.

Leeson drank the other half of his Coke. "Strange planet, I tell you. If I had been the father of the young man, I would have gone berserk."

I left Leeson with his Coke and monitors.

My little visit would undoubtedly cause him to have a new bout of nightmares.

CHAPTER ELEVEN

Tyron and I were killing time at the Laundry on Johnston Street. It wasn't quite a pub, or a club or a bar or a café, but a bit of everything. It was the kind of place you rendezvous with real friends, the types who were not necessarily impressed by the price of the drink but more by the depth of your conversation. We liked to come around on Jazz night, but tonight was poetry reading, and celebrated poet Paola Bilbrough was going to indulge us with her latest work. Gérald was working most evenings, which was something you have to get used to when your lover is in the healthcare industry. But I didn't mind because it gave me the freedom to be myself.

Tyron said, "I spoke to Bud yesterday, and he said Mohammed is a bad arse."

Bud was one of Tyron's connections from the seedy side of Melbourne.

I turned to face him. "Bud knows Mohammed?"

"Did time with him a while back."

"And?"

"Reckons Mohammed didn't kill the boy but he is a fucked-up bastard either way."

"Well, it's Bud's word, which doesn't mean it's gospel."

"Hallelujah."

We were sitting at the bar, close to the pool table and a red couch, drowning ourselves with the Beer of the Week. The place smelled of alcohol and cigarettes. Two blokes in flannel shirts and bleached jeans were playing pool. A girl in a short yellow dress and a white tee was eyeing Tyron so indiscreetly she might as well have just come up to him, pulled down his pants and given him a head-job. We guessed she must have been with the pool sharks, but she seemed bored and completely disinterested in the game. She must have sensed I wasn't Tyron's girl. There was nothing intimate about the way we carried out our conversation, and together we looked more like two trees in someone's yard than boyfriend and girlfriend.

Tyron didn't miss a beat. "What do you think is going on here?"

"She wants something, and she doesn't want it from me or her boyfriend."

"Yeah, I kind of figured out that was what was going on."

While the pool sharks were too busy concentrating on the game and calling each other names, the girl discretely circled the table and landed half a metre in front of Tyron.

"Busy tonight?" she asked.

"Depends," Tyron said.

"Want to meet around the corner?"

"Maybe."

"Well, I'm going for a smoke. I might see you there."

"Sure."

Then she walked up to one of the pool sharks, the one who could pass as handsome from a distance, whispered something in his ear, and left the place.

I put my drink down. "You're not serious?"

"Why not?"

"She's young enough to be your daughter."

"Don't have a daughter."

"She's someone's daughter."

"They all are."

"True."

I ordered another round. It was fine beer combined with a great atmosphere. Ben Lee was playing in the background, but not so loudly we couldn't hear ourselves.

I said, "Did I tell you Gérald asked me to marry him?"

"Nope."

"Well, he did."

"And?"

"Nothing."

He emptied one third of his glass. "You want to?"

"Not really."

"Did you tell him?"

"No really."

"Why not?"

"Don't know."

He finished the rest of his beer. "You ought to tell him."

"I know."

"Well, I'm going to take a gulp of fresh air. Don't go away."

He left ten dollars on the counter and departed through the front door. His shoulders were so broad he had to turn sideways to get through the entrance.

I finished my beer and called it a night.

CHAPTER TWELVE

Patrick Wood, Dean of Administration at The University of Highton, was a painfully thin man in his late fifties who stuttered noticeably enough to be annoying. A variety of degrees and certificates decorated the back wall behind his chair, and judging by the neatness of his office, he appeared to be a man who took great pride in doing his job. One of the windows was open, letting the sweet fragrance of landscaped gardens fill the room.

Wood's office was located exactly where Leeson had showed me on the map, facing the union lawn. It was just on 10.00 a.m., and most students were in the middle of lectures or tutorials. Those who weren't enjoyed a dry spring day with a clear sky as far as the eye could see. Summer was still a few weeks away, but students had already purchased hot weather clothes, tees and shorts for boys, and short dresses and tank-tops for girls.

Apparently I had been lucky to see him because under normal circumstances, he would have been far too busy to talk to me without making an appointment. The front desk clerk had told me so when I made my inquiry.

"Are you a student here?" Wood asked.

Being thirty-five and looking like a twenty-five-year old had its advantages.

"No, I'm actually looking into the death of Steven Donnelly."

"I'm sorry, is that supposed to mean anything to me?"

"Ten years ago, a young man was found strangled near the Old Arts Building."

He struggled with his memory for a few seconds. "Of course, I remember now. It was such a long time ago, but it does feel like yesterday. I don't know why I couldn't place the name immediately."

"Not many people can after such a long time."

He stood up and we shook hands. "Exactly what is it you're after? I thought the killer had already been brought to trial and found guilty? Isn't he still in jail?"

"Yes, he is, but someone thinks there might have been a miscarriage of justice."

"Who? The killer?"

"Well, not as such. His lawyer."

"I see." He sat back at his desk. "Please take a seat. I'm not sure how I'm going to be able to help you. The police handled the case, and we certainly had nothing to do with it. He wasn't even a student at the university."

"Well, it's why I'm asking. One of the students at the university found the body. I was wondering if you could give me a list of students from the classes that student attended?"

From the look on his face, I felt as if I had just asked him to hand over his credit card and pin number.

He said, "Exactly what's your interest in the case?"

"I'm been hired to look into it and review the facts."

"Are you a criminal lawyer?"

"Not exactly, I'm a private detective."

"Right, so you're not working for the police?"

"Not as such, but I'm licensed by the government."

"It doesn't mean anything. And it certainly doesn't give you the authority to access the documents you're requesting."

"Well, I was hoping, given the circumstances—"

"There are no circumstances here, it's a closed case."

"But you have to understand, we're talking about a man

who's spending the next twenty years in jail for a crime he might not have committed. I'm sure if this man was one of your students, you would have done everything in your power to help him."

He raised one eyebrow. "You don't know anything about me, Ms. Lunn, and I certainly don't like to be patronised. I'm a fair man, but it's not something I should even feel obliged to explain. I know the boundaries of civilian jurisdictions, and I have a duty of care and privacy to the students at this university. I'm afraid I'm going to ask you to let this one go."

"Well, I'm afraid I won't be able to do so."

"Suit yourself, but you're certainly not going to get any information from me."

"I can ask around."

"It's not something I'll be able to prevent. Just be careful whom you choose to harass. Some of our students have parents in high places, and you wouldn't want to be dipping your toes in muddy waters."

I stood from my chair. "Thanks for the cliché, Mr. Wood, but if it's all the same to you, I think it might be time for me to leave."

"A very good idea indeed." He rose to his feet. "I'd hate to be in the position of having to remove you from the university on the grounds of trespassing."

"I'll be on my best behaviour."

He circled the desk and walked me to the entrance of the office, his eyes on my breasts. "But by all means, if there is anything *else* I can assist you with, feel free to contact me."

He passed me his business card with the university logo embossed and checked me out from head to toe.

I gave him mine in return. "You've been more than helpful. If you ever need a private detective, you know where to find me."

He looked at the card like a kid reading a candy wrapper.

I left the room, and he shut the door behind me.

Bastard.

CHAPTER THIRTEEN

The Donnellys lived in Grange Road, Toorak.

I had left the car outside the two-story mansion, which was surrounded by elevated walls and could only be accessed by a high steel gate. Two s-series Mercedes Benz and a BMW 4WD were parked in the driveway leading to the front entrance. German car manufacturers had really managed to suck in those with too much disposable income. I noticed a double garage attached to the house and wondered why it was not used to house the expensive cars. The owners were either too lazy or just loved to showcase their possessions.

The Donnellys were expecting me, although I had managed to not mention exactly what the purpose of my visit was, other than telling them it had something to do with their son.

I walked up to the front door via a gravel driveway adorned with rose bushes on both sides and garden lights that stopped drivers from running over the freshly-cut lawn by accident. The air was mild and clean, and the sky a bright blue.

I pushed the button of the doorbell and waited for a good minute.

The heavy wooden door held by thick iron hinges opened and a tall man appeared before me.

"You must be Patricia Lunn," he said. "I'm Joseph

Donnelly, but you can call me Joe."

We shook hands and he let me into the hallway. An aroma of vanilla and baked bread filled my lungs as if I were at a shopping mall. The whole length of the hallway was polished floorboards and original oil paintings the size of kitchen tables.

Joe wore beige slacks with a marine blue shirt and tortoise shell glasses. His hair was non-existent at the top, but he made that up with a generous hazel crown that stopped below his ear lobes. He reminded me of a cop in a TV series I had seen recently.

The Donnellys owned a chain of chemist shops, including one in Chadstone, Melbourne Central, the Bourke Street Mall, and near the Hyatt on Collins. From my own research I had found out Mr. Joseph Donnelly had inherited his wealth from his father, who had got his from his father. To this day, everyone had astutely managed to double their inheritance money every ten years or so. There had been no mental illness in the family, and no one had any prior criminal record of any sort. On paper, the Donnellys looked like the perfect family, and if it had not been for the sudden, brutal death of Steven Donnelly, life would have been almost faultless.

Mrs. Donnelly was waiting in the lounge room by a floral couch. She wore a white blouse and pleated skirt. Her hair was dark and cut into a fringe. She wore her lipstick a little too red, but for some reason, it blended nicely with her general appearance.

"Would you like something to drink?" she asked.

"A glass of water would be nice."

She vanished and thirty seconds later she reappeared with a clear tumbler filled with ice and a 600ml plastic bottle of spring water. She twisted the top and filled the glass three quarters full.

"Please, take a seat," Mr. Donnelly said. "You said you had something important to tell us about Steven."

They were both seated opposite me, scrutinising my features, as if I were someone applying for a nanny job.

"I've been hired by Smith & Gordon to look further into your son's death."

They turned to each other and then back at me.

"Isn't the killer in jail?" asked Mrs. Donnelly.

"Well, yes, he is, but there are now doubts as to whether he was actually the person who killed Steven."

"Whose doubts?"

"Peter Murray, the lawyer who represented the defendant."

The colour drained from Mr. Donnelly's face. "What does this have to do with us?"

"He was young at the time, and now he's not sure his client received a fair trial."

"So he wants a re-trial?"

I shifted slightly forward, my hands folded together like an Avon lady closing the sale. "Well, no, but I've been asked to go over the facts once more just to make sure there hasn't been a miscarriage of justice."

They both sat silently for a full thirty seconds.

"So what exactly do you want from us?" Mrs. Donnelly finally asked.

"I'd like to run through the details again."

"To what end?"

"Well, to establish if justice has been done."

Without warning Mr. Donnelly jumped from his seat. "You've got a fuckin' nerve coming into our house and asking us to help get this sonofabitch out of jail! Who the hell do you think you are? You work for—?"

"Smith & Gordon."

"Well, I'm going to make sure you don't work for Smith & Gordon again, you arrogant bitch!"

The words coming out of Mr. Donnelly's mouth didn't match his appearance. Other than looking like a cop, he would have blended nicely at a conference table with other suits, all sharing their profit making suggestions for maximum capitalist gain and minimum loss. He certainly wouldn't have spoken to anyone the way he was speaking to me right this minute. I was taken aback but not entirely surprised. There is nothing like the grief of a lost child to make you lose your composure.

Mrs. Donnelly grabbed her husband by the sleeve and tried unsuccessfully to get him to sit down next to her.

"I'm sorry," I said, "I know this is a delicate situation, and I know exactly how you feel—"

He fired his words like a machine gun. "No, you don't! Your son wasn't raped and killed by some homicidal faggot! You have no idea what this family has been through, no idea whatsoever, and for you to come here and insult us to our faces, you've got a lot to learn about respect and manners."

"I'm so sorry you feel offended, but it wasn't my intention to hurt you."

"You're lucky you're a woman, or I would have knocked your lights out by now."

Mrs. Donnelly was now up and tried again to grab her husband by the arm. "Joe—"

"I'm not going to let them walk all over us," Mr. Donnelly said. "They've done that once already ten years ago, and now they're coming for the second blow. Get the hell out of my house before I call the cops!"

I refrained from commenting further.

When I stepped outside the entrance of the house, Mr. Donnelly pointed his finger at my face like someone threatens a victim with a knife. "You come back here with your sorry ass, and you'll need an ambulance just to get home."

He slammed the door in my face.

CHAPTER FOURTEEN

I dropped in at the St Kilda Road Police Complex. An old friend still worked there, and I needed to bounce back and forth some ideas with someone who wasn't too close to me. I also needed a lead on the case.

The roadster was parked in a tow-away, police-only parking zone. The security officer at the front desk cleared me after I left all my metallic belongings—car keys, coins and a TAG Heuer copy I picked up on a trip to Indonesia on a tray and walked past a metal detector.

"Is she in?" I asked.

"Let me check." He tapped something on his keyboard and watched the monitor at the same time. "Yes. Tenth floor. Should I tell her you're on your way?"

"No, thanks. I'll surprise her."

Cops were coming in and out of the building like shoppers during a mid-summer sale. A couple of them waved at me. After last year's little accident, when one of their own nearly broke my spine, I had become what I would like to refer to as an honorary cop, and it wasn't a bad position to be in when you're a private detective. The advantage was I didn't have to wear the badge and didn't have to obey the rules, all the perks without the bureaucracy.

Sheila McGregor was a third-generation Australian who had been in the force since she turned nineteen. Her father had been a cop, and so had her grandfather. Her two daughters were currently at the Police Academy in Mount Waverley. She walked like a man and spoke like a man.

When I entered the tenth floor of the complex, I saw Sheila in the distance. Her curly, red hair was fleecy and ran all the way down to her buttocks. She was hunched over her desk like a garden gnome lost in a mountain of paper work. The office smelled of paper pulp and plastic.

I adjusted the visitor's pass attached to my shirt and walked straight up to her.

"Sheila, you're getting wilder with the years. Love your hair. Do you think they're going to cast you as an extra in a new series of Xena?"

She looked up and grinned from ear to ear. We had worked many cases together during my early years in the force and had kept in touch since then. She was not a very close friend, but she was reliable and respectful. I tried to be the same in return.

"Well, if it isn't Miss Private Eye herself. What have you been doing with yourself? Still having time off for your back injury?"

"Gone and buried. I'm back on the job and only one month away from a well-deserved holiday."

"Tell me the name of anyone who doesn't deserve a holiday having worked all year round in this nuthouse."

We laughed at our attempt at humour.

"So, what brings you around this time?" she said. "Need some prints checked, or you've just dropped in to tell me you're joining the force again?"

"I'll pass on both offers. It's a case I'm working at the moment. How good is your memory?"

"How certain is it you're going to find my arse back on this chair tomorrow morning?"

I took a chair opposite her desk. "Does the name Steven Donnelly mean anything to you?"

She knitted her brows, and then her eyes lit up. "Yes, that's the young man who got done by some Arab guy. It was a while back, wasn't it?"

"Nineteen-ninety-two."

"Yes, I remember, his body was found on the grounds of The University of Highton."

"Well, I'm looking into his death again. The lawyer who represented the defendant claims his client didn't get a fair trial."

"Everyone's client is innocent."

"This one believes it."

"How so?"

"He reckons his client got done because he's gay and middle-eastern."

Sheila tapped her silver pen against the tabletop. "Everyone's got an axe to grind these days about homophobia and racism. Have you checked his priors?"

"Yes."

"Well, there you go, no point pissing in the wind. Cops are not much into the racism thing these days, don't give a shit if it's an Arab, a Vietnamese or an albino. If he's got a list of priors longer than a monthly credit card statement, then he's going to cop some flak, and there's nothing that can be done. Cops are humans too. They don't like to send back onto the streets some rapist who's going to do more damage. As far as I'm concerned, whether he killed the Donnelly kid or not, he deserves to be where he is."

"It seems to be the general consensus amongst everyone I talk to."

"Ask yourself why."

"He's Islamic."

Sheila shifted in her seat. "Well maybe it has a little to do with it too, I don't know. After September 11th and the Bali bombings, what do you expect?"

"Except he got convicted in 1992, and the terrorist acts you're referring to are only recent."

"Well, ten years ago it was some other bullshit. These people are always fighting one another and blaming the whole planet for it."

I could see I wasn't going to change her mind on the subject, so I moved on. "You wouldn't know if the detective who was on the case is still around?"

"Hurst? Yep, still around and a hell of a good cop. His work is tidy, his record clean and his continuity the best in the business."

"Do you think he's the kind of cop who would have framed Mohammed if he thought he was guilty?"

She seemed startled. "Well, Patricia, I don't know, and maybe he did and maybe he didn't. Why don't you do yourself a favour and speak to him? You're more likely to get some straight answers from him than from me."

"You see him often?"

"Comes around now and then. Works a lot with the Crime Investigation Unit these days."

"Do I have to make an appointment?"

"I'll give him a buzz and get him to get in touch with you. How does it sound?"

"Like a gift from heaven."

"Almost. He's a little cocky with a touch of arrogance, but don't let his charm stop you."

"I'll be on my best behaviour, scout's honour."

We chitchatted about her daughters and my forthcoming holiday in Broome. I told her about Gérald wanting to get married, and she suggested I should press ahead before he changed his mind and married someone else. Being French and a doctor, she reckoned, he wouldn't exactly have to smash his head against a brick wall to get other women interested in him.

She picked up a stack of sheets from her in-tray. "Well, thanks for dropping by. I would love to chat longer but I got a lot of paperwork to go through. Remember paperwork? No, I suppose you don't get much in your line of work."

"Don't bet on it. I'm developing RSI, and it's not from firing a gun."

"Yep, I hear you."

I waved at her and moved away from the desk.

"Hey, Patricia," she called out.

I turned around.

"Yes?"

"Watch your back on this one. I think you're going to piss off a lot of people by sniffing around a corpse."

"So everyone keeps telling me."

"Maybe there's some truth in it."

"Maybe."

CHAPTER FIFTEEN

Gérald and I were sitting at the end of the St Kilda Pier, watching the sun dive into the sea and colour it amber like oil on canvas. His head rested on my shoulder, and it helped me to ease life's little problems for a while. His five o'clock shadow tickled the nape of my neck, and it made me feel so close to him. His blond hair was finger brushed like a schoolboy, and he wore light, cotton summer chinos with a bright orange shirt.

I was in a short summer dress with printed flower motifs.

We were drinking a couple of light beers concealed in brown paper bags. The beer was clean and cold and the air warm and thick like cream, just the way I liked it.

"How's the Bain thing progressing?" Gérald asked.

"Not too good. Everywhere I turn, people tell me to watch my back."

"So maybe you should."

"I'm thinking about it."

"What's your opinion on the warnings?"

"Don't know, still trying to join the dots and see the big picture. If you come up with any theories, feel free to contribute."

He said, "What does Tyron think?"

"He thinks Mohammed is where he is because everyone else thinks he deserves to be. Seems to be the case, and it makes me wonder who am I to think otherwise. What Mohammed did before he went to jail was wrong, there's no doubt, but he shouldn't have to pay for someone else's crime."

"Hey, you don't have to try to convince me. I don't agree with incompetent justice."

"I can't help thinking he got framed because he was gay and of middle-eastern origin, no matter what everyone else is trying to tell me. Racism is rampant, and too many people close their eyes to it. They have this ideal of a harmonious multicultural society, but the planks underneath the bridge are so rotten, everyone is going to fall through someday."

"Is this your cheer-up theory for the day?"

"This whole thing is getting under my skin."

"Well, maybe you should let it go."

"Can't do. Someone might be doing time for nothing, while someone else is as happy-as-Larry for getting away with murder."

A father and mother with two daughters walked past us. They seemed as bright as the sun on the horizon.

Gérald turned to face me. "Don't you miss having a normal life?"

"What's a normal life?"

"Like these people." He pointed discreetly at the couple with the kids.

"Never had one, so I can't really miss something I've never had."

"But you could have."

"Maybe I don't want to."

He said nothing further and took a sip from his beer.

I said, "Is this your way of asking me if I've been thinking about getting married?"

He looked up again. His eyes met mine. "Well, since you're bringing it up…"

"I've been thinking about it, and I don't think it's a good idea."

"Why not?"

"It wouldn't suit our lifestyles."

"Why?"

"The next thing you know, we're going to have kids, and then I'll have to change jobs because mine is too dangerous, and you'll want to give up your job to spend more time with the kids, and we'll be broke and forced to take jobs we hate and leave the kids at a child-minding centre."

"It's all part of life, everyone's doing it."

"I've never been like everyone."

"I know."

"The reason why you fell in love with me."

He smiled and took another sip from his beer. "But sometimes it's not enough, sometimes people need to take a relationship to the next level. Don't you?"

"I don't see how marriage is going to help. I'm comfortable and satisfied with what we've got here. Aren't you?"

"Of course I am, but you're missing the point."

A boat went past and splashed a bit of water our way. The water was cold but felt good nonetheless. He was beginning to annoy me, but I didn't want to become hostile.

I said, "Why do you want to get married?"

"I want to experience everything. I don't want to look back at my life and have regrets."

"It's a valid point, I guess."

"Of course it's valid, Patricia. Chasing arseholes is not a natural part of life; being married and bringing up a family is."

"An interesting philosophy."

He emptied his bottle and wrapped it back in the brown paper bag. "Can you promise me you're going to give it some more thought?"

I looked at him. "It's all I've been thinking about lately, and the case I'm working on."

"You're not going to give up on me, are you?"

"Is that a trick question?"

"You're not, are you?"

"You'll be the first to know if I do."

CHAPTER SIXTEEN

I was in the middle of calculating my first fortnightly invoice for Smith & Gordon, and for a few seconds I had no idea what was happening. Detective Hurst had not knocked on the door or tried to announce his arrival. His outrageously strong musky aftershave slapped me in the face and forced me to look up.

"You want to see me about something?" he barked.

I looked up. "Excuse me, but who might you be?"

"Hurst. You left a message with McGregor to get in touch with you, and now I'm here."

Detective Hurst wore an Italian-cut, designer suit and a signet on the fourth finger of his right hand. His hair was implacably styled and his tie held together with a brushed silver pin. His nails were manicured like a film star, and if he had not flashed his ID, I would have thought he worked for the mob.

He took a chair opposite me without asking permission and began fiddling with a desk calendar I had left sitting at the top right corner of my desk.

I put my pen down. "You spoke to McGregor?"

"Sort of."

"So you know what this is about?"

"Donnelly. You're trying to get that Islamic fag out of the slammer."

"I wouldn't exactly put it in those terms"

He spread his hands. "Well, then, let's hear your version of the fairytale."

McGregor had been right about Hurst being arrogant.

I said, "I've been hired by Smith & Gordon to look into the case on behalf of the defendant's lawyer. I'm more or less familiar with the case, but I would like to be enlightened by the detective who was in charge of the initial investigation."

"That's it? Sounds identical to mine, apart from phrasing." He lit a cigarette in spite of the no-smoking sign at the door and on the desk.

I said, "Except I'm not looking at getting Mohammed out of the slammer. I'm more interested in finding out if justice has been carried out."

"Oh, it's been carried out, all right, I'm the one who was in charge of the whole investigation."

"I'm not doubting your level of expertise here, on the contrary. I'm interested to know if you've left anything off-the-record. Like maybe some tiny bit of information that might make a hell of a lot of difference."

He stopped flicking through the pages of the desk calendar. "You're full of confidence, aren't you? What makes you think I'm going to sit here and waste my time with someone who's trying to undermine work I did ten years ago?"

"Cause I was told you were a good cop, and good cops don't like miscarriages of justice."

He laughed.

I didn't.

He stared. "Is that what they teach you at the academy of private investigators?"

"That and some more. All I know is that Mohammed is in jail convicted of a crime that holds together on nothing more than circumstantial evidence."

He crossed his legs and tossed his cigarette in an empty cola can sitting on my desk. "The boy's underwear was found in Mohammed's flat."

"No witnesses."

"Two witnesses saw him drag the boy away."

"But not rape or kill him."

"Fibres on his clothes matched those on the boy's missing sweater."

"Like I said, all circumstantial."

He cracked the joints of his fingers. "Where are you going with this? He's been proven guilty and convicted, so what exactly is *your* problem?"

"I want to know if you've put Mohammed in jail because he's gay and Islamic."

"You've got to be fuckin' kiddin' me? Is this why you've made me come all the way here, to call me a racist to my face? Is that what this is all about?"

"I just want some straight answers. I'm getting a little tired of all these little warning bells telling me I have to watch my back."

"Then maybe you should stop knocking on the wrong doors."

"Why? What's going to happen if I persist?"

"You're going to get a lot of people pissed off, including me."

"Well, I guess I've already managed to piss you off. Who else are we talking about?"

"Donnelly's parents to begin with."

I smiled. "I wouldn't worry about that, it's already done."

He seemed puzzled. "You spoke to Joseph Donnelly?"

"It's not illegal?"

"You've got no idea what you're getting yourself into."

"So everyone keeps telling me. Would you like to educate me on the subject because I'm at a loss here?"

"Go fuck yourself, Lunn. You think you're on some kind of higher mission here. The only thing you're going to achieve is to get your PI license suspended."

"I wouldn't bet too highly on that one. I know my way around the legal system, and I'm not easily intimidated."

He stared at me for what seemed like an eternity. "I don't particularly like you, Lunn, but you've got balls for a woman, and it's a trait I admire. You remind me of myself when I was young."

"I didn't know you had a sex change."

He didn't laugh. "Okay, I'm going to give you some solid advice here, and you better keep your ears open."

"They're flapping in the wind."

He jabbed his index finger to my face. "Get off this case before you end up dead."

"Is that a threat?"

"No, it's advice you'd better listen to."

"I've never been good with advice, that's why I left the force."

"Donnelly's got a shit load of money, and money makes the world go round. It's all you need to know."

We paused for a few seconds.

He pulled another cigarette from his packet.

I pointed at the sign on the desk. "No smoking in here. I'm an asthmatic, so if you feel the need to poison yourself, do it in your own space."

The cigarette remained in his hand for a few seconds before he slid it back in the pack. He stood up from his chair. "You just remember what I've told you. You keep sticking your nose in other people's business, and the next time I'll see you, it will be at your funeral."

"Yeah, how's that? Donnelly's going to pay you to do his dirty work? Is that what happened the last time?"

"Fuck you."

And then he left.

I opened all the windows of the office to get rid of the stench of cigarette smell and his musky aftershave.

CHAPTER SEVENTEEN

Finding the people you need to solve an investigation is tricky, and sometimes you have to resort to what some people would refer to as unethical tactics. As a private investigator, I generally try the usual outlets—telephone directories, banks, Medicare database, utility bills, electoral rolls, Vicroads, Centrelink and the Internet—before turning to tricks involving a great deal of role playing with a hint of deception.

In many cases, it's relatively easy to find someone, unless the person happens to be a woman who got married several times and has changed identities more often than some people brush their teeth. The other chief enemy is trying to locate someone after a great length of time has elapsed, from the moment of the crime to the moment you're trying to find the person. The Steven Donnelly case was ten years old, and in ten years, it's not just water running under a bridge, but a flood.

I was working from home because I had enough of the office and didn't really feel like having Hurst bursting in again unannounced and chain-smoking like an nicotine-addicted teenager.

In the morning the sky was a crisp blue, and for a while I though it was going to be a splendid walk-along-the-beach kind of day. But by mid-day, it became clear the temperature wouldn't climb by a single degree past twenty.

Gérald was on day-shift, so I knew I wouldn't get disrupted until at least five o'clock. I made a pot of fresh coffee and took the phone off the hook.

I was looking for two names that had appeared on the transcript of the trial of The State vs Bah Sheh Mohammed; the two characters who had witnessed Mohammed kidnapping Donnelly in Toorak and throwing him into a car. Doug Carlton and Crystal Gartenberg.

Carlton was such a common name, when I searched the White Pages online, the directory told me *There are too many listings to display for your search criteria*, so I narrowed it down to five after discarding names that didn't match his initials. I then searched the Medicare database and found only one Doug Carlton and matched it to an address in Malvern from my White Pages listing.

For Crystal Gartenberg it got more complicated. When I entered the surname into the White Pages online search engine, all I got in return was *There are no listings matching your search criteria*, which told me she must have got married or changed her name. I knew VicRoads kept records of maiden names and change of names.

Half an hour later I was at my local VicRoads branch.

I took a number and waited for my turn.

When number 74 was called, I walked up to the counter and placed my private investigator ID on the counter.

"Hi, I'm working on a missing person case, and I was wondering if you could do a quick search for me."

The man at the counter was tanned and had dark locks down to his neck.

"Can't help you. You'll need some type of warrant or a letter from the police."

"Look, I'm in a kind of a jam here, and I wouldn't be coming here unless it was an emergency."

"I understand, but it's against regulations, sorry."

I pulled a crisp one-hundred-dollar note from my purse and slipped it on the counter. "Here's my warrant. It's really important I get an address."

He glanced around to make sure no one was watching him and slipped the one-hundred-dollar note in the pocket of his shirt. "What name did you want to check?"

I passed him a bit of paper with the name Crystal Gartenberg on it.

"Give me a sec."

He tapped into a computer and made me wait a few seconds.

He looked up. "Sorry, nobody with that name."

"What about a change of name, can you find out?"

"It will take a little longer. Take a seat and I'll call you."

I returned to my seat and flicked through a copy of *Royal Auto*. I read an article on how most road accidents were caused by rude drivers and not by people who sped. I was half way through the article when the VicRoads clerk called me to the counter.

I walked up to where he was standing. "What have you got?"

"Crystal Gartenberg changed her name eight years ago. My guess is she must have got married. Happens all the time." He scribbled something on a piece of paper and slid it over the counter.

"Thank you."

"I didn't give you this, and I've never seen you before."

"Happens all the time."

He smiled and called up the next number.

When I stepped out of the building, I unfolded the piece of paper he scribbled on.

Crystal Carlton.

CHAPTER EIGHTEEN

Malvern is not exactly Toorak, but the houses are relatively expensive and the suburb has its own charm with its old Victorian dwellings and picket fences. Old money lives in Malvern, and many generations have stayed there because they've become used to it, and also because the area was considered a good investment.

The Carltons lived in Claremount Avenue, near the Malvern Railway Station. The street was leafy and quiet with no teenagers hanging around with their skateboards and caps put on backwards. It was the kind of place you'd expect conservative, middle-class people to live in, those who never really had to worry about where their next dollar was coming from.

My car was parked opposite the Carlton's household, from a 4WD and a two-door, late model S-series Mercedes Benz parked in their driveway. It was just on 6.00 p.m., and Doug Carlton had been expecting me.

When he opened the front door, I said, "Patricia Lunn, I called you half an hour ago."

"Please come in."

He didn't bother shaking hands and made me follow him down a dark corridor and into a room on the left. The place smelled of recent cooking and a little mildew.

"I understand you want to talk about Steven Donnelly," he said. "I'm not sure exactly what you want from us. It was such a long time ago, and we've already told the police everything we know. This is long buried."

He wore bone-coloured chinos and a pink polo shirt that displayed a toned frame. His eyes were blue and deep set in a face as close to flawless as humanly possible. His chestnut hair was impeccably styled, like those of a model in a fashion magazine.

Crystal Carlton was waiting for me in the room. She was sitting on a large, modern red sofa costing more than my laptop. She was the female version of Doug. Perfect figure, inviting smile, and dressed in a gorgeous yellow summer dress, which made me feel self-conscious in my faded jeans and white tank-top. She wore her blonde hair tied into a short ponytail like so many young women did these days.

She said, "Hi, I'm Crystal. Would you like something to drink?"

"You've got light beer?"

"Yes, we do."

She brought back a bottle of Cascade on a silver tray with a chilled glass.

"How do you get the glass so cold?" I asked.

"We put them in the freezer," she said so proudly you'd think she had invented an elaborate method and patented the rights to chilling a common beer glass.

We talked shop for a little while, and I found out Crystal worked at the Esplanade Hotel during the day. This bit of information took me by surprise given the hotel was a dump, and she looked so middle-class. I just couldn't imagine her working there with people who were into tattoos, body piercing and four-letter words.

Doug was sitting opposite me on a single reclining chair. He was having a short black, even though he was probably going to go to bed in the next few hours.

He turned to me. "Well, now that we're all sitting here comfortably with our beverages, would you care to explain what's on your mind?"

"I would like to go over the details of Steven Donnelly's

abduction."

"What is there to go over? Haven't you read the police report?"

"Yes, but I've got this habit of checking out things first hand. I'm getting paid generously to look into this, so I would like to ensure I'm giving my client value for money."

"An honest private investigator? I guess if I'm ever in need of a PI, I'll know who to call."

"Thank you." I took a sip from my glass. The beer was icy cold. "What do you remember about that day?"

They eyed each other for a few seconds.

Crystal toyed with a glass of water.

Doug said, "I don't know why someone would want to go over all these details again ten years down the track. Who did you say you worked for?"

"Smith & Gordon."

He nodded in approval, although I was certain he had never heard about the firm but didn't want to come across as ignorant.

He crossed his legs. "You know, it's not exactly fun for us to go over these details again. It's something we've been trying to forget for years. I don't know if you've ever had a death amongst your friends, but it's not the kind of memories you want to stick in the family photo album for reminiscing."

"True, but I guess it wasn't really Steven's wish to make it so unpleasant for the rest of us. He didn't choose to get murdered."

Silence.

Crystal swallowed. "We were doing some shopping on Chapel Street, and then we saw Steven arguing with some guy. He grabbed him by the arm."

"What time was it?"

"Around eight-thirty, nine."

"In the morning?"

"Evening."

"And what did you do?"

Doug raised his hand. "Nothing. We thought they were arguing about something trivial."

"And the man who grabbed him was the same person you

identified in the police line-up?"

"Of course."

"Are you sure?"

"Yes, I am sure."

I turned to Crystal. "What about you?"

"Yes," she said without hesitation.

"And was it dark when you saw him being kidnapped?"

Doug answered, "Well, yes, but there's plenty of light in the area. It was him no doubt about it."

"How far were you from the incident?"

They looked at each other.

Doug said, "I don't knowmaybe fifty metres."

I sipped from my beer glass and directed my next question at him. "So how did Steven react? I mean, you said it looked as if they were fighting. What exactly was happening?"

"Mohammed grabbed him by the arm, Steven tried to resist, and then the Arab forced him into the car."

"And then what? He just walked around to the driver's side and took off?"

"Yes, basically, that's it."

"And Steven didn't try to jump out of the car?"

"It happened so quickly."

"It must have."

"What's that supposed to mean?" Doug's tone changed.

"Oh, nothing, just that the kidnapper was very quick, he must have known what he was doing."

"Well, yes, I guess he did know what he was doing."

I turned to Crystal. "What about you? Is that what you saw?"

She was going to answer, but Doug leaned forward. "She saw exactly the same thing as I did. We saw the *same thing*. We already told the police."

I said, "I was just interested to hear what she had to say."

"I told you she saw the same thing." His tone of voice was firm and bordering on aggressive. He threw Crystal a menacing glance.

I decided to let that one pass. "How well did you know Steven?"

Crystal answered, "Very well. He was my best friend."

I nearly spilled my beer. "Steven was your best friend?"

"Yes."

"So you must have known who his friends were? I mean, he *was* your best friend, wasn't he?"

Crystal finished her glass of water instead of replying.

Doug stood from his seat. "I don't know where you're going with this. Mohammed was charged and convicted. What does it matter whether Steven was our friend or not?"

"You're right, I think I've taken enough of your time."

"Yes, you have," he said. "We have to meet some friends in half an hour, so if it's all the same to you, could you please leave now?"

"Sure. You've been very helpful. I'm impressed with your recollection of the events."

They suddenly looked pleased with themselves.

Crystal stood up. "Thank you."

"You know, you can call me any time if you remember something," I handed Doug my business card.

"Will do."

I knew he had no intention of calling and never would.

CHAPTER NINETEEN

The University of Highton had many bars and takeaway shops. You have to be pretty strong-willed to walk into the Student Union Building and resist the temptation of pizzas, freshly-cut sandwiches, French fries, hamburgers, oriental food and hundreds of drinks. Not gourmet food by any means, but enticing nonetheless.

I was in the bar on the first floor and had made myself at home. There were at least one hundred students in there. Some were trying to get some homework done in the middle of the blasting TV and the conversations, while others looked as if they had given up on the real world. Three young men were sharing a plate of chips drowned in ketchup, and some female nursing students were giggling over enormous textbooks like a gaggle of teenagers. It wasn't a bad place to be, even if you weren't a student. The atmosphere was alive and smelled of sweat and sticky carpet.

I bought myself a light beer and moved to the outdoor balcony. The air was crisp and my beer was beautifully cold. There was a splendid view of the campus, where students lounged around, unaware this might in fact be the best time of their lives. What a glorious way to spend a Tuesday afternoon. Maybe I should have become a university lecturer instead of a stick-your-nose-in-what's-not-your-business investigator.

I was seeking someone old enough to have been around when Steven Donnelly was killed. I wasn't following a particular lead, so it wasn't going to hurt me to find a fresh one.

I spotted a man in a brown tweed jacket and a pair of jeans. He had grey around the temples and seemed disinterested in everything around him. He was rather good-looking, if a little too old for my taste. He didn't seem like the kind of person who was going to give me much trouble, so I decided to make a move.

I tucked my shirt tightly inside my jeans, pushed my chest forward and walked straight up to him. No need to beat around the bush.

I said, "Can I buy you a drink?"

"Me?" He eyed me suspiciously.

"Yes."

"I think you're making a mistake. Is this some kind of prank or something? Because if it is, I'm not interested."

"Well, no, it's not a prank. I'm a private investigator." I pulled my ID out and placed it in front of his face.

He studied the laminated ID card. "I thought you were a student here, you look so—."

"Young? I wish, I'm thirty-five, but thanks anyway." I slipped the ID back in my jeans pocket. "So, you want that drink or not?"

"I guess I will, same as what you're having."

I went to the bar and brought back another bottle of light beer. He told me his name was Dr. Thomas Burrad, but everyone called him Tom.

"It's a fascinating job you have," he said.

"Keeps me happy."

"Good." He took a sip from his beer. "Happiness is all that matters in this world." He looked at my right arm. "What's with the bruising? You don't go and beat up people, do you?"

"Oh, no, I do a bit of taekwondo to keep fit. I placed third in the Australasian Championship last year, so it's inevitable I get some minor injuries."

"Impressive. I guess I better watch my language."

We laughed wholeheartedly.

Initially, I had imagined him to be rather introverted, but now I realised I had been wrong. His hazel eyes sparkled with excitement, and his composure was that of someone relaxed and confident. His hands were face-up on his knees.

I moved a little closer. "You work at the university?"

"Lecturer in philosophy."

"For how long?"

"Fifteen years longer than most."

"Have you ever heard of Steven Donnelly?"

His eyes became glassy. "Why does that name ring a bell?"

"Nineteen-ninety-two. He was found dead near the Old Arts Building."

He clicked his fingers. "Right. Some Arab got jailed for it."

"Bah Sheh Mohammed."

"Yes, I remember now. It was one of our students who found him."

"Is the student still around?"

"Oh, I don't think so. It happened such a long time ago. Funny thing I remember: two students who saw him being dragged away knew him pretty well. It's a small world, I tell you."

"Two students?"

"Yes, they were going out with one another at the time, and they ended up getting married."

"Doug Carlton and Crystal Gartenberg?"

"Correct. She had a German-sounding name. How did you know?

"Paid them a little visit yesterday. How well did you know Crystal Gartenberg?"

"She was in a couple of my classes, but I wouldn't say I knew her well. She took first year philosophy like many students just to get the credits. Most think it's a slack subject, but then they're in for a nasty surprise."

I could see the barman eyeing me from a distance, probably wondering why I was trying to come on to someone old enough to be my father.

"Did she have many friends on campus?"

"Oh, yes, she was popular. Both of them were. Apparently Steven Donnelly was often on campus with them, even though he wasn't a student."

"Really?"

"Yes, he liked to pretend he got in. He missed out on an offer the year before he got killed, so he just turned up to some of the lectures."

"Happens often?"

"What?"

"Outsiders sitting on lectures?"

"It's hard to tell. Lecture theatres can accommodate hundreds of people at once, so you can't keep a headcount on everyone who attends."

"I see."

"His boyfriend was studying on campus, so it gave him another reason to hang around there."

I spilled some of my beer. "He was gay?"

"Oh, yes, everyone around here knew. He kept it a secret from his parents. I don't think they know to this day."

"Do you know his name?"

"Can't help you there. But Doug or Crystal might be able to point you in the right direction."

He took a gulp from his beer.

I said, "How do you know so much about Steven Donnelly's private life?"

He smiled. "So, you didn't just offer me a drink to ask me questions, did you?"

"What do you think?"

He finished his beer. "Where do you want to go?"

"Are you asking me if I want to have sex with you?"

He was taken back. "Well, I wasn't going to put it in those words."

I smiled. "Thanks for the offer, but as much as I find you attractive, I'm kind of old-fashioned. I'm saving myself for the groom."

"Oh!"

"I wouldn't want to rush into anything I'll regret later."

"I see."

"It keeps me happy."

He smiled. "And happiness is all that matters in this world, right?"

We laughed.

CHAPTER TWENTY

I was in my office going through some of last year's case files when Tyron walked in unannounced. I had not expected to see him until six o'clock at the gym. Three times a week we pumped iron together at Terry Bennett's and pushed ourselves beyond what we would normally do if we worked out solo. He was a great spotter. The companionship also provided the extra motivation I needed on days when I would rather go to bed than to the gym for a hard workout.

Outside the sky was a deep blue. The air smelled of seaweed. It whisked in from the open window to my right and circled the room until the indoors felt like the outdoors.

Tyron held a brown paper bag in his right hand. The aroma from inside the bag filled the room and took over the smell of the ocean. Cheeseburgers and French fries, the two evils of society's contemporary diet.

I said, "You know I'm trying really hard to cut down on junk food. And aren't we supposed to go to the gym tonight?"

"Worrying about junk food is causing you more harm than eating the stuff," Tyron said to me.

"So you keep telling me, but I haven't found any medical research to back up your little hypothesis."

"I'm working on it. It's a well-known fact stress is more

directly linked to cancer than food consumption."

"I don't know what they taught you at high school about nutrition, but whatever it was, it wasn't on the curriculum."

He placed the bag on my desk and began to empty its contents. He took a bite from one of the steaming, hot cheeseburgers. "I'm not going to beg you to eat any. I'll eat the lot if you're not interested."

I tossed my good sense out the window and gave in to our gastronomical sin.

We shared three large fries and six cheeseburgers. We washed the lot down with two light beers from a bar fridge I had well hidden under my desk. I made a mental note I would have to do an extra set of each exercise that night at the gym to compensate for the zillion calories I had just gulped down.

"I like your shirt," I said and swallowed the last drop of my beer.

"Brand new. Picked up this morning in a men's shop on Elizabeth Street. I had the price tag removed at the counter because I wanted to wear it immediately."

It was a yellow, cotton blend shirt with tortoise shell buttons. It was a nice contrast to his coffee-coloured skin. He was quite a good-looking man, and I never understood why he was still single. He insisted it was his choice, and he didn't want to be burdened by a relationship. I felt being single was more of a burden than being attached.

I tossed the wrappers in the bin. "Any news from Bud?"

"Yep. What about you? Set a wedding date yet?"

"Nope. What's the deal with Bud?"

"There's a verbal contract on your life."

I locked my eyes with his. "Really?"

"Some guy contacted Bud and asked him if he was interested in making a quick buck, and your name came up."

"How much?"

"Didn't say."

"Shame. Be nice to know what I'm worth."

"Maybe better if you don't, you might get offended."

"Thanks for the vote of confidence. I'll remember not to send you a postcard from Broome."

"Damn, there goes my collection. Me and my big mouth."

He finished his beer and tossed the empty bottle in the recycle bin near the entrance. I could sense he wanted another one, but there was only one left in the bar fridge, and I chose to keep it for myself.

He said, "Donnelly's the only thing you're working on?"

"Yes. Didn't want to get loaded with too many cases before my little vacation."

"So, it wouldn't too far-fetched to assume whoever wants your head on a stick is the same person who doesn't think too highly of your investigation?"

"Could be someone from the past, but I doubt it. We'll have to assume the obvious at this stage."

"What's your theory?"

I toyed with my empty beer bottle. "If someone wants to get rid of me, it means there's something not right about the way Steven Donnelly got killed, and maybe Murray is right, Mohammed got set up."

"Kind of helps putting things into perspective, I guess."

"So Bud never mentioned why someone wants me out of the picture?"

"Nope. But then, he might know, but he hasn't bothered telling me because in his line of work, you don't want to be known as a snitch."

"He's got a reputation to maintain. Good work ethics."

"It's the only way to keep the business coming your way."

The junk food was rumbling in my stomach, and I wondered if it might be a good idea to run to the washroom and stick my finger down my throat. Life was so uncomplicated for Tyron. If he was hungry, all he had to do was pick up anything from anywhere, and somehow the calories didn't show up as badly on his body as they did on mine.

"You know," I said, "I've spoken to a lot of people in the last few days, and some of them are really unhappy about Mohammed scoring a get-out-of-jail card."

"Can't blame them, especially if he did kill Donnelly."

"True, but I did get some death threats and plenty of warning, which kind of makes me think there's more to it than people getting mildly upset."

"Warnings don't mean shit. To have a contract killer, you

need to have contacts. It's not something you can arrange with the friendly Indian guy at the local Seven-Eleven."

"Never assumed it would be." I looked out the window. I was restless and felt like going for a walk. I turned my attention back to Tyron. "What about getting in touch with Bud's contact? If Bud's not willing to talk, maybe his guy will."

"Bud won't give you a name. And even if he did, what makes you think his contact will?"

"I was afraid you were going to say that. It's a merry-go-round with no stop in sight."

"Bud's not taking on the job, but if the money is right, there'll be a few takers."

I smiled. "Thanks. Remind me not to leave my windows open at night."

"And if the money is crap, there are plenty of junkies out there who'll do it for next to nothing." He smiled this time.

"I guess we better start thinking seriously about my personal safety."

"That's 'we' as in Gérald and you?"

"And you, if you want to keep your job."

"Why, you're going to sack me?"

"No, but dead people don't pay well."

"Good point, I knew I was hanging around you for a reason other than friendship."

He touched his lips with his fingers.

I felt sorry for him so I opened the bar fridge and pulled the last light beer from the top compartment.

He gulped half of it in one go.

"Thanks," he said.

"You're welcome."

CHAPTER TWENTY-ONE

Gérald's brother came over at the weekend. He brought his Australian wife with him. They got married last year, and Gérald kept telling me how well the marriage was going and how much more committed they were now in the relationship. They had taken it to the next stage, and it was clear, according to Gérald, it was the only thing to do if a couple were committed to the growth of a relationship.

Gérald's brother was called Dominique. Gérald told me how in French Dominique was spelled the same for both men and women. Dominique's wife was a petite, fake blonde with freckles and a cancerous tan. Her name was Tammy. She was originally from Perth and had met Dominique when he was touring Australia during a three-month holiday. Dominique had set himself up as a documentary filmmaker, and in spite of the language barrier, was very successful at his job. He occasionally dabbled in commercials, but his forte was French-narrated documentaries about Australia, which he sold year after year to French and Canadian television stations.

Gérald and Dominique were watching a soccer game on SBS while commenting in French. Neither Tammy nor I understood a word they were saying or shared their passion for soccer. Europeans had an obsession with soccer, which was just as silly as Australians with football.

Tammy and I were in the kitchen fixing a meal for supper. I wasn't the cooking type. Gérald was usually the one who spent a great deal of time in the kitchen after a long day at work. But he didn't mind because he liked cooking, and he considered himself a bit of a gourmet chef. Given the inadequacy of my culinary skills, I had to agree. It also gave him a chance to put his mind on something other than his patients at the hospital.

Tammy was showing me how to make lemon tartlets. She said they were good because they could be eaten as an entrée or a desert, depending on whether you served them with salad or cream.

I watched her unwrap a frozen pastry sheet from a packet. She was quick and efficient, like a master chef trying to impress the young apprentice.

"So, how's the marriage?" I asked. I wanted an opinion other than Gérald's on-going monologue on the subject.

She glared at me as if I had just said the four-letter word.

"That good?" I said.

"It's not what it's cracked up to be."

"You're not going to divorce him, are you?"

"I don't know, it's like going back home to your parents, you lose all your sense of privacy and dignity. You're always referred to as the wife of your husband."

"Well, I've lived with Gérald for ten years, and we don't have that problem."

"That's because you're not married to him."

"Good point."

She cut the pastry into squares and used a brush to coat them with cooking oil.

I went on, "But marriage is just a formality, a paper, it shouldn't change anything."

"Yeah, well, it's what I thought too when Dominique asked me to get married. We'd been together five years, so it didn't seem like a big deal. But then you begin to notice some subtle differences."

"Like what?"

"Can you pass me the lemons?"

I handed over two lemons sitting on the bench.

She continued, "Before marriage, you still treat each other with some respect, like two separate individuals. Once we got married, things began to disintegrate."

"What things?"

"Like leaving his stuff around and expecting me to pick up after him; going to the toilet with the door open. And money. See, before we got married, we took care of our own finances. What I earned was mine, and as long as I paid my share of the rent and bills, I could do whatever else I wanted with my money."

"And how is it different now?"

She shook her head. "Oh now, he's Mr. Auditor. I have to account for every dollar I spend. Every time I buy something, I get this lecture on how I should really put the money into our joint savings account for the house. We haven't even bought the damn thing yet, and already I have to stop living just to pay a non-existing mortgage!"

I smiled secretly at her open confession. I guessed Dominique was either blind to what was happening, or he had embellished his marriage experience to impress Gérald.

Tammy used her fingers to press the pastry firmly against the tart moulds.

"You know," I said, "if you're not happy, you should tell him."

"Not so easy."

"Why not? You're husband and wife, and if you can't even communicate what's on your mind, then what's the point of being together in the first place?"

She stopped what she was doing. "Dominique doesn't know I'm pregnant."

"What?"

"I got tested. I'm two months in."

I didn't know what to say.

She continued placing the pastry into the moulds.

I said, "You should tell him, you know."

"I know, but I can't bring myself to do it."

"Do what?" a male voice said.

We both turned around.

It was Dominique.

85

Gérald stood still behind him with the look of someone waiting on death row. It was obvious they had been standing there the whole time Tammy had been talking.

"*Merde!*" Dominique shouted. "You're pregnant, and you haven't said a word to me. And yet you go and tell a complete stranger?"

Tammy backed two steps.

Gérald was holding Dominique by the arm. "It's okay, it's okay."

"No," Dominique yelled, "it's not okay. Why the hell didn't she tell me? I have the right to know, I'm the father!"

Tammy said, "I was going to tell you, swear to God, I was going to tell you."

"When? During the delivery?"

"Well, I couldn't tell you because of the state you get in all the time."

"What state?" He turned to Gérald. "What is she talking about?"

Gérald shrugged.

I exited the kitchen and grabbed Gérald on the way. I whispered, "We should leave them alone to sort it out."

"They're going to kill each other."

I pulled him by the sleeve. "Maybe it's what they need."

Gérald and I retreated to the lounge room. I tried to get myself interested in the soccer game on TV, but the shouting coming from the kitchen was as painful as cuts with a razor.

I said, "Do you think we should go back in there and save someone's life?"

"I'm a doctor. Let them do the damage first."

I smiled but felt uneasy. After all, it was me who got her to talk.

When they left, I opened the fridge and pulled out two light beers. I pulled the tops off and passed one on to Gérald.

"Jesus," I said, "what a nightmare! How can people live this way?"

"Habit, I guess."

"I hope this will never happen to us."

"What? Fighting or marriage?"

"Both."

CHAPTER TWENTY-TWO

I had been waiting at the St Kilda Road Police complex for a Frank Pestana to join me.

All morning, I had been going through my file notes, and I realised I still had not figured out who made the anonymous phone call to the police and gave Mohammed away as the killer. Pestana was the cop who received the call according to the trial transcript and the police record on file. At the time, he was young and wet behind the ears, and probably didn't know much about police procedures. He had been twelve years in the force now, and had been working at the St Kilda Road Police Complex for the past five years.

The lobby was busy as usual with cops and evidence experts walking in and out of the place as if it were a takeaway joint.

"Patricia Lunn?"

The man before me was in his early thirties with jet black hair and olive green eyes. There was something very Southern European about him, but I had expected it from his name.

"You must be Frank Pestana."

"In the flesh. Please, follow me."

We made it to the elevator and waited for our turn.

I said, "You're specialising in something these days?"

"Fingerprinting. We're going up to the ninth floor. We've recently renovated the whole place and got ourselves state-of-the-art digital equipment. I can check fifty thousand prints in one hour. Beats the card system."

"High tech everywhere, the bad guys don't stand a chance."

"Don't bet on it. The bastards are getting software engineering degrees these days, so it's not unusual for one of them to know more than the whole department."

I smiled.

He didn't.

The elevator door opened and we entered.

He pressed the button for the ninth floor. We were the only ones on board. I was wearing my jeans and a push-up bra under my tee. He glanced but had the decency not to stare.

"So what's this thing with the Donnelly boy?" he asked. "The case is re-opened?"

"I've got an interested party who wants to find out if the killer is really the killer."

"What makes you think he didn't do it?"

"I don't think anything, I'm just doing my job."

"I see."

The door of the elevator opened. I followed him like a bitch on heat. We entered a large office filled with computers and desks. Other cops were working frantically at their individual tasks. The room smelled of new plastic. No one looked up when we walked past the desks.

"Come this way," he said. He stopped at a desk next to a large window with a view of the West Gate Bridge and beyond.

I said, "Nice view."

"Took me ten years to get it. It's not bad." He sat at his desk and with his hand invited me to take the chair opposite his. "It was an Arab guy who did it, wasn't it?"

"Bah Sheh Mohammed."

"Yeah, the bastard had it coming. Can't say I'm sorry he got done for it."

"Seems to be a popular opinion. I guess he didn't have many friends in high places."

Pestana threw me a look. "You want something to drink. Coffee? Tea? Orange Juice?"

"I'm fine."

"Suit yourself." He picked up a pack of fingerprinted cards from his desk and flicked through them as if they were collector's football cards. "So what is it you want to know?"

"You're the one who got the anonymous call about Steven Donnelly's killer?"

"How do you know?"

"It was in the trial transcript."

"I see. Yes, I got the call. It took ten seconds in all."

"What did the voice sound like?"

He looked up. "Lady, it was ten years ago. You can't expect me to remember the voice from a ten-second-phone call from ten years ago. I'm a person, not a machine."

"Just asking, some people have photographic memories."

"Well it might be the case, but I don't have a sound recording device surgically attached to my brain. And even if I did, the batteries would have run out a look time ago."

I shrugged.

He said, "All I can tell you is I called Detective Hurst straight away. Everyone knew he was in charge of the investigation."

"What did Hurst say?"

"Nothing. He just took the name down."

"And?"

"What else did you expect?"

"It was you who called Hurst?"

"Like I said I called him immediately."

"Does this happen often?"

"What?'

"Getting anonymous calls that lead you straight to the killer?"

He placed the fingerprinted cards back on his desk. "I guess it doesn't. But every case is different. Where are you going with this?"

"I'm just wondering if Mohammed got framed."

"It'd be one fuck of a set up." His skin picked up colour. "Excuse the language."

"It's all right. But it's possible?"

"I doubt it, but, yeah, anything is possible. I mean the bastard deserved what he got. Did you read his priors? Far from being an angel, so in a way, everybody is happy he's behind bars."

"And Hurst wasn't surprised you got an anonymous phone call?"

"I guess not."

He picked up the cards and began shuffling them like a dealer. "Now that you're mentioning it, he never asked me the name of the person who made the call. He just took the details down and hung up."

"Not even a few days after you called him?"

"Nope. I let it go because it didn't seem very important, particularly after they got him for thirty years." He stopped playing with the cards and looked straight into my eyes. "You seriously think it could mean something?"

"Yep."

"What?"

"Hurst already knew who made the call."

CHAPTER TWENTY-THREE

My laptop was switched on, and I was typing a preliminary report on how the Donnelly case was unfolding. No one asked me, but I knew John Bain would eventually come and visit or make a call to ask me to elaborate on my progress. I had already worked on a generous invoice for Smith & Gordon justified putting in a bit of extra paperwork.

Tyron was sitting opposite my desk, going through today's *Herald-Sun* headlined with the Melbourne and Sydney raids on suspected terrorists. We'd been working out at the gym that same morning, and both our bodies were hard like steel. Since I complimented him on his yellow shirt the other day, he had even slept in it. Tyron wore the same clothes for days when he knew he looked good in them. Just as well no one told him he looked good in a dress, otherwise he might have turned into a transvestite.

"Gérald's still bothering you with lifetime commitment?" he asked.

"We had his brother over, and things sort of worked themselves out."

I told him what happened the previous night.

He said, "Guess your life's got a way of taking care of itself. I wish it was that simple for me."

"Tyron, your life is not complicated. You get up, you eat something, you take a dump, you go to sleep."

"And I workout."

"Sorry, I forgot the overtime."

He shook his head. "If I hadn't known you since high school, I'd think you're being a smartarse or something."

The window of my office was open. Traffic noise was flooding from outside. The sun was high in the sky, and it was warm enough to parade around in a skirt and tank-top. I wasn't wearing any shoes, one of the many perks of being self-employed and not having to account to anyone else at the office.

I was about to make another smart remark but never got the chance.

Three men twice my size but half that of Tyron walked into the office.

"Which one of you is Lunn?" one of them asked. He was tall and mean looking with a mono brow that forced you to stare. He was dressed like a nightclub bouncer with a gold chain around his neck that reminded me of a dog in a collar.

"I am," I said.

Tyron did this twitch with his left eyebrow, and I knew immediately how this unforeseeable meeting was not going to end in a group hug.

Mono Brow went on, "Okay, I'm going to tell you this once and once only."

"Why, you've got a short term memory or something?"

He chose to ignore my comment. "You're working on the Steven Donnelly case?"

"You already know the answer since you're here."

He looked at his two friends. One wore a crew cut and manicured beard that made him look like a rap gangster. The other had more hair on his arms than a monkey.

"She's a smart bitch that one," Mono Brow said.

Crew Cut grunted.

I said, "You must be confusing me with your wife. Whatever it is you want, I'm not interested, so you can take yourself and your two gorillas back to the zoo."

Crew Cut and Hairy Arms couldn't refrain from smiling.

93

Tyron stood up from his chair. He looked like a Greek column in the middle of my office. "You blokes think this is funny? Why don't you get out of here before I crack your heads like walnuts?"

Mono Brow did a swift move of his right arm to reveal the butt of a concealed handgun tucked between his belt and his belly. "I'm just doing my job here. Consider yourself warned."

I said, "I'm shaking as we speak. Who sent you?"

"Doesn't matter."

"Does to me."

"You don't want to fuck with these people."

"They're already fucking with me, so what's the difference? They might actually enjoy it."

Mono Brow threw me a hard stare.

Tyron moved one step to his side.

Mono Brow moved back. "We're done here. Hope we don't have to come around again."

I said, "Damn shame, I was beginning to develop a crush on you."

He turned around and nodded to his two friends.

When they left the building, Tyron peaked through the open window.

"Anything?" I asked.

"Econovan. White."

"Can you read the plate from here?" I grabbed a pair of binoculars from my desk drawer and tossed them to where he was standing.

He looked through the binoculars and scribbled the number in a little notebook he kept in his shirt pocket.

"I should have snapped his fingers," he said. "Bastard didn't even have an appointment."

"I'm sure you'll get another chance."

"I hope so."

CHAPTER TWENTY-FOUR

I was back at The University of Highton.

While going through my notes that morning, I recalled Steven Donnelly had been in a relationship when he was killed, but there was no mention of the boyfriend in the trial transcript or the police report. In fact the only person who told me he had a lover was Dr. Thomas Burrad, the philosophy lecturer I met the other day at the university bar. He had not given me a name because he didn't have one to give, but since he was the one who mentioned the boyfriend, it was common sense to go back to the source.

I managed to find Burrad's office on the second floor of the Old Arts Building. He was sitting at his desk when I knocked on the door and walked into his office without waiting for his reply.

"Dr. Thomas Burrad? Remember me?"

He looked up, and from the expression on his face, he was obviously trying to place where he had seen me before. He glanced down to my chest and his eyes lit up.

"It's the private detective, Patricia Lunn. I didn't think I was ever going to see you again." He stood halfway up from his chair. "Please take a seat."

I sat opposite his desk, and he sat down again.

His office was dark but well furnished. There were bookshelves wall to wall, filled with modern philosophy hardcovers and paperbacks—Kant, Rousseau, Byron, Nietzsche, Dewey—and of course all the classics, such as Plato, Socrates, Aristotle, and many volumes of Christian writing. A copper-and-green banker's lamp on his desk, the same type which can be found at the State Library, added a scholarly serenity to the room. There was a computer with a flat screen occupying the right corner of the desk. The room smelled of printed paper and ink and reminded me of my school days, when I used to hide between the rows of bookshelves at the library and read true crime books instead of attending classes.

"Any luck with the Donnelly case?" he asked.

"Bits and pieces, nothing concrete."

"Anything I can do to help?"

I could see from the look in his eyes he hoped my visit might have been of a personal nature rather than a work-related one.

I said, "You remember how you told me Steven Donnelly used to date someone who studied at this campus?"

"Yes, and I also said I didn't know his name."

"Okay, but I really need to find out who he is. Can't you at least point me in the right direction?"

He played with the cap of a plastic biro. "I heard Steven's boyfriend was majoring in acting. I can put you in touch with the theatrical program manager. He might be able to dig up something. Donnelly's death was big news on campus when it happened. Everyone knew about it. I'm sure he would have paid attention to the ruckus given one of his students was going out with the victim."

"And how do I get in touch with this person?"

He checked his watch. "I've got a lecture in forty-five minutes. If you want to go now, I'll take you there."

"Great."

We left the office and walked across the campus. Students were rushing in all directions as if the world were coming to an end. Others were just sitting and talking, seemingly not in a hurry to do anything or go anywhere, the last pit stop before joining the rat race.

Burrad said, "I don't know if Steven's boyfriend ever ended up doing anything with acting, but if he had been successful at it, I guess we would have seen his name in print somewhere."

"Good point, but since neither of us knows his name, he could be starring alongside Tom Cruise in the latest Hollywood blockbuster, and we wouldn't be any the wiser for it."

"Of course, you're right."

We passed the Engineering building, circled the water fountain and took the stairs alongside the Alexander building.

"It's here," Burrad said. "I better go and introduce you so he takes you seriously. H\e tends to dismiss people who are not part of the university. He's got his own little philosophy about university time, and how it should only be used for people who work or study there. The rest of the world can take a ticket and wait until the cows come home."

"Thanks."

We walked down a spiral staircase and entered a room that was almost entirely concealed from the main corridor. Inside there was a group of six students, two girls and four boys, and a man in his early forties wearing an out-dated goatee and a yellow polo shirt one size too small. Unlike most of his peers, his chest was wider than his gut, and his arms the size of my thighs. This was a man who diligently committed himself to a few hours of workout at the gym, and it showed. He was losing some of his chestnut hair at the top, but other than that, physically, he seemed to be the kind of guy who would have made all the girls wild at high school.

"That's Robert Fisher," Burrad whispered close to my ear. "Not the friendliest person in the world, but if you annoy him long enough, you might just get what you want."

"Annoying people is my speciality, so it shouldn't be too much trouble."

The students were in pairs and obviously undergoing some type of acting exercise. One student was miming, the second repeated the same moves, as if the first student happened to be looking at his own reflection in a mirror.

"Bob," Burrad interrupted, "this is a friend of mine I'd like you to meet. Patricia Lunn, she's a private detective, and I think you might be able to help her."

Fisher's face didn't show any surprise. His deep blue eyes were hard to read, his pupils so small, they were almost non-existent.

"What can I do for you?"

"I'm looking into the murder of Steven Donnelly, ten years ago."

Fisher glanced over to Burrad.

Burrad said, "His boyfriend used to be in your acting classes."

Fisher hesitated for half a second. "Yes, I know the student you mean. May I see some credentials?"

"Sure," I said.

Burrad stepped back. "Look, I've got to get to my lecture. I'm sure the two of you will be able to work it out." He turned to me. "If there's anything else I can assist you with, please don't hesitate to drop by." He winked on his way out.

"Thanks."

I pulled my ID from my jeans pocket and handed it over to Fisher.

He examined it as if it were a fake. "What exactly do you want from me?"

"Just the name of the young man who used to go out with Steven Donnelly before he got killed."

"I don't know if I can give you that."

"A matter of national security I gather?" My favourite little taunt.

"No, but there is such a thing as privacy, even at a university campus."

"Thanks for the lesson on students' rights, but I think that whomever Steven was going with ten years ago is most likely to be an adult who doesn't need the protection of the university."

"I understand that, but still, it is not my duty to reveal private information on past students."

"All I want is his name."

"That's what the other man said too."

"What other man?"

"Another detective came to see me two days ago."

I was genuinely surprised. "What was his name?"

"Don't remember."

"Hurst?"

"Couldn't tell you. I wasn't paying much attention at the time. It's only now someone else is asking me the same question that I am asking myself questions."

"And he wanted what?"

"Same as you, to get hold of Peter Weinmann."

"Steven's boyfriend?"

He turned red and flexed his biceps like a nervous tick. "Well, I guess it was. Now you know. Happy? He'd spoken to Weinmann ten years ago when Steven got killed, and he wondered where he was now."

"You wouldn't happen to know where I could find him?"

"Who? Weinmann or the cop?"

"Weinmann." *What an idiot!*

"Even if I did, I wouldn't tell you."

"You're really charming, aren't you?"

"I don't have to be."

"I know, but you're an actor, you could at least fake it."

He turned his attention back towards his students. "All right, that's good, break it up" Back to me: "You've wasted enough of my time. You can leave now."

"It was nice to meet you."

"My pleasure."

I walked away.

Another day, another arsehole.

CHAPTER TWENTY-FIVE

Gérald was working day-shift, so I was all by myself. I finished my report to John Bain and stapled my invoice to it. I hoped to God I was going to get to the end of this case soon because summer was just around the corner, and I had yet to make arrangements for my holiday in Broome. Of course, I couldn't just dump the case, go on holiday and come back later. With the element of surprise still in my court, I could catch some people off-guard, and it would be less likely that they'd have time to arm themselves with elaborate lies. I had not figured out why I was getting warned from every side, but it only made me more determined to push ahead.

By the time Gérald had come home the previous night, I had been fast asleep. In my dream I met someone whom I didn't know, and we began having an affair. I had never cheated on Gérald, so when I woke up the next morning, I couldn't figure out why in the world I had had such a dream and whether in meant anything at all. Somehow, I had felt as guilty as if I had had committed one of the seven deadly sins.

Over a steaming cup of freshly-brewed coffee, I dialled Weinmann's number. I had found his contact details in the online directory. I was greeted by the humourless sound of his voice on the answering machine.

"You've called Peter Weinmann's. I can't attend to your call right now, but if you care to leave your name, number and what time you've called, I'll get back to you as soon as possible."

I left a message to tell him to call me urgently.

I hung up.

By midday, I had not heard from him. I dialled again.

"You've called Pe—"

I hung up.

I dialled up immediately after that and left a second message after the beep.

On the third day, I got lucky. He picked up the phone.

I recognised the voice from the answering machine.

I told him who I was.

"Look," he said, "I'm sorry, but do I know you?"

"I left two messages but you haven't returned my calls."

"Well excuse me, but I do happen to be a busy person, and telephone messages from complete strangers don't happen to be on my priority list. What can I do for you?"

"I'm looking into the death of Steven Donnelly."

There was silence at the other end of the line.

"Mr. Weinmann? Are you still there?"

"What could you possibly want with Steven Donnelly? It was an open-and-shut case, I really don't have time for this."

"It's not going to take long."

"I'm sorry, I have to be at the National Theatre in one hour. I'm going to have to let you go."

"I—"

He hung up.

I pulled on a pair of jeans and a yellow tank-top, and headed for St Kilda.

CHAPTER TWENTY-SIX

The National Theatre is located on the corner of Carlisle and Barkly Streets, approximately one hundred and fifty metres from St Kilda foreshore, Luna Park and the Palais Theatre. I had a hell of a time finding a parking space. After driving around Irwell, Belford, Carlisle, and Barkly Streets, I ended up parking in Greaves Street, a walking distance from the theatre.

I had no idea what Weinmann did at the theatre, but I guessed that it might have something to do with acting since acting had been his main interest from a long time back.

I entered the theatre, which I had never bothered to visit, and was surprised at the grandeur of the establishment. While trying to locate Weinmann, I treated myself to a small tour of the foyers, grand staircase and the auditorium. The whole place was spotless and smelled like freshly-vacuumed carpet.

I managed a conversation with the cleaner, a tall, gangly, twenty-one year old, blond lad with three earrings in each ear. His name was Alex, and he told me he would take me to Weinmann, who happened to be one of the contracted acting teachers at the theatre.

Alex explained how the theatre was originally built in 1920 with a three-thousand seat capacity for the showing of films. But soon after the opening of the nearby Palais Theatre in the mid 1920's, the theatre was closed for extensive renovations, and the seating capacity was reduced to 2500, which still seemed a large number to me. But that was back then, and currently the theatre only had a 783-seat capacity. He went on explaining how the original stalls had been converted to Drama, Opera and Ballet Studios.

He invited me for an entire tour of the theatre, but I suggested another time. He pointed down a corridor and told me I would find Weinmann two doors to the right.

Weinmann was in his office by himself. It seemed as if his urgency to leave home had not been such an emergency after all. I could only see the back of his head and his shoulders. He had salt-and-pepper hair and a blue shirt with a seventies oversized collar.

I knocked on the open door. "Peter Weinmann?"

He turned around, took one look at me and said, "I'm sorry, but we're not taking any new students at the moment. I can put your name down for an audition in February."

His nose was straight, and he had a George Clooney chin. He had the looks of someone who'd probably thought he deserves to be an actor because physically he was a cut above the rest, as if acting depended on nothing but looks.

I said, "I'm not here for acting classes. We spoke earlier on the phone."

He blinked quickly. "Excuse me?"

"I'm Patricia Lunn. I'm the private investigator who wants to talk to you about Steven Donnelly."

"I thought I told you I was busy? What is wrong with you people?"

"Well, Mr. Weinmann, now that I'm here, we might as well get it over and done with."

He glared at me as if I were contaminated with an infectious disease. "Look, Steven Donnelly wasn't even my boyfriend. He was just a casual fuck, so there's really nothing much I can tell."

"Then you don't mind if I ask you a few questions?"

"Do I have a choice?"

"You could tell me to go, but a little cooperation would be appreciated. I'm sure Steven would be grateful you're trying to help if he had the chance to put in his five cents' worth."

He chewed over my comments for a few seconds. "You've got five minutes."

"How long had you known Steven for?"

"I told you, I only went out with him a couple of times."

"Some people at The University of Highton think you were an item."

"Like I give a fuck about what some people at Highton Uni think."

"Ever heard of Detective Hurst?"

"Who?"

"Hurst, the detective who was in charge of the case ten years ago."

"Doesn't ring a bell. Why?"

"Just asking."

He moved forward and crossed his arms. "You know, you should really think your questions over before you annoy the shit out of everyone you come across. Having a PI license doesn't give you the right to interfere with people's lives You're walking on thin ice here, no one likes what you're getting yourself into."

"How do you know?"

"Let's just say I made a call after you rang me."

"To whom?"

"None of your god-damn business. Now, I've got some paperwork to do and a class starting in twenty minutes." He turned his back on me.

I took one step closer to him. "You gave me five minutes —"

"But I've got nothing else to tell you. Goodbye and close the door behind you."

"Well, it was nice to meet you."

"Yeah, and don't come back. You're not welcome here."

"So I guess your offer for an audition in February is no longer applicable?"

"Please leave before I lose my temper."

"Well, we wouldn't want to see that happen now. I might end up like Steven."

He stood from his chair, pushed me out of the room and slammed the door.

Ouch!

CHAPTER TWENTY-SEVEN

I figured since Weinmann was an actor, he had to have an equity card, so I rang the MEAA from my office and asked if they could provide me with some information.

"And who might you be?" The woman on the phone was polite but firm.

"I'm an independent producer. We're casting for a feature film for early next year, and Peter Weinmann seems perfect for the role of one of the principal characters."

"Well, I can't give you any information on Mr. Weinmann. We protect the privacy of our members. But what I can do is give you his agent's name and contact. I'm sure she'll be interested in your offer."

"That would be great."

"Just hold the line for a moment."

I was patient for what felt like an eternity. I was sitting in my office, the door locked and the windows wide open. I didn't want another unexpected visit from Detective Hurst or Mono Brow and his two gorillas. Tyron was running an errand for his nephew in Shepparton, and I didn't expect to meet with him until later in the day for our regular workout at Tony Bennett's.

The MEAA woman came back on the line. "Here we go,

Mr. Peter Weinmann is with an agency called Prestige Actors Management." She gave me the agency's contact details.

I thanked her and hung up.

I rang up Weinmann's talent agent. I told her the same fib I told the MEAA woman, and she was very eager to send me a copy of her client's acting resume. Five minutes later, Weinmann's laser-printed, one-page CV came through my fax machine. A clean 300-dpi head-shot followed.

Weinmann had appeared in a lot of student short films earlier on in his career, most likely from his contacts at the University of Highton and its associated film school at the State Institute of Performing Arts. He had a small part in a Judy Davis's feature film, which never amounted to anything, a bit part in a low budget science fiction rip-off of Star Trek, and half a dozen commercials. He did some work for the Melbourne Theatre Company, La Mama and the National Theatre, for which he was now one of its principal teachers. He was a financial member of three co-op theatre companies and on the board of management at the Centre for Moving Images. All in all, and in spite of his lack of fame, he had succeeded well in the cut-throat business of the entertainment industry. Too bad they didn't teach manners at drama school.

I spent the rest of the afternoon looking through my files and entering Weinmann's name through Internet search engines. But nothing productive came up.

I stretched and pulled a light beer from the bar fridge. It was just as well I was into light beer and not full strength, or I would have been a drunk by now. I wanted to go home but had promised Tyron I would be waiting for him.

By 5.00 p.m., I was going to call it a day and thought of calling Tyron on his mobile to cancel, but his gigantic shadow suddenly appeared through the smoked glass of my office door. He tried to open the door but didn't succeed.

"Hey, it's me."

I stood from my chair and let him in.

He gave me the once over. "What's the matter? Expecting someone undesirable?"

"Let just say I'm looking over my shoulder these days. I might not be in my twenties, but I still take pride in my dentures."

"Damn, you fooled me, I thought they were your real pearlies."

"Very funny."

"Guess you won't be having any of this then." He pulled a brown paper bag from behind his back. "Chinese, hot and ready to go."

"Tyron, you're going to have to stop feeding me junk food. The day I get my first heart attack, I'm going to make you pay the medical bill."

"Not if the bounty on your head goes according to plan. Better eat up and enjoy it while you're still alive."

I pulled two cold, light beers from the bar fridge and popped the tops off.

He grabbed one and half-emptied it, and then he removed the Chinese from the take-away bag.

Tyron ate his fried rice with chopsticks.

I resorted to an old favourite of mine, the fork.

I said, "Nice," and gulped another mouthful.

"Felt guilty enjoying all that good food by myself."

"Glad your conscience is in the right place."

He patted his stomach. "Yeah, right here."

We both laughed.

I pulled Weinmann's acting CV from my in-tray. "Check it out. This is the young man Donnelly used to go out with. Well, he's not a young man anymore, but it's him nonetheless."

He studied the Weinmann head-shot. "Casanova. Where did you get this from?"

"Got himself a talent agent who was more than happy to send me all his little details since I'll be shooting a feature film early next year."

He eyed me and looked back at the photo. "You're going to get caught one day. You've bullshitted so many people, it's a miracle there's still a pool of them to draw from."

"Then I'll move to Sydney—uncharted territory."

"If you buy a condo by the Harbour, I'll keep you company."

"I'll have to charge you board. On your salary, you wouldn't be able to afford it."

"Thanks for reminding me you pay your employee

minimum wages. And on the subject of wages—"

"No pay rise until this case is wrapped up."

He rolled his eyes and handed me back the head-shot. "So what did Weinmann have to say for himself?"

"Nothing much. In fact he was rather defensive and evasive. If I didn't know any better, I'd say he's the one who killed Donnelly. And if he isn't, he's certainly hiding something."

"What happened?"

"Gave me the run-around with his answering machine for three days, and when I finally caught up with him, he was as charming as a doorknob."

"Sounds like my type of guy."

"He didn't know anything about anything, but it sounded like a fairytale because his acting teacher from uni said Hurst might have been talking to him some ten years ago, just after Donnelly got killed."

"So?"

"Well, what beats me is why was Weinmann's name not on the transcript or the crime files. When someone gets killed, the first suspect is always the spouse or the lover. If a detective interrogated Weinmann, something should have been on paper."

Tyron finished his Chinese and washed it down with the rest of his beer. "Well, someone's fucking someone behind someone's back, and no one knows who started the whole copulation process."

"That's one way to put it. But now I'm wondering if there's a connection between Weinmann's name not appearing in the crime files, and the three tough guys who came to visit us at the office the other day."

"And Hurst."

"And Hurst, of course."

Tyron crossed the room to the window and peaked through the open glass. The sky was bright blue, and the traffic was humming like bumblebees. He said, "I haven't run those plates from the Econovan yet, but it should be looked into."

"You know what other thing bothers me?" I tossed the empty take-away containers in the bin next to my desk.

"Everything."

"Yeah, well, other than that, the two people who witnessed

Donnelly getting kidnapped were both students at The University of Highton. Weinmann was also a student at The University of Highton. Mohammed wasn't and yet he chose to dump Donnelly's body on the grounds of the university even though he abducted him in Toorak. Wouldn't you call it a little bit coincidental?"

"And why didn't anyone pick abnormality up before?"

"Maybe no one had a reason to." I swallowed a mouthful of beer.

"What about Murray?"

"Depends what information the cops were feeding him, probably far less than he needed to mount a good defence."

"Jeez, Patricia, this case is starting to feel like a poorly-scripted episode of Blue Heelers."

"Yep, where all the innocent by-standers could be the murderer."

CHAPTER TWENTY-EIGHT

Dr. Dickenson was a forensic pathologist at the Victorian Institute of Forensic Medicine in Southbank. The VIFM was the statutory body in charge of Forensic Pathology, Clinical Forensic Medicine, Forensic Toxicology and other forensic scientific services in the State. The Institute was also responsible for education in forensic medicine, and thus incorporated the Department of Forensic Medicine at Monash University, delivering quality undergraduate and postgraduate courses for medical and legal students. The blue-grey building complex was also the home of the Coroner's Court.

Outside the sky was covered in a grey blanket, and there was a cold wind coming from the sea with the smell of rain in the distance, not the type of weather I expected at this time of the year, but it was why Melbourne was such a fun place to live in.

I had worked with Dr Dickerson on many occasions when I was in uniform, and we'd maintained a good relationship since then. He was in his early fifties and wore his hair short. His nose was long and pointy, and his eyes had the softness of a cocker spaniel. He had been working at the institute for as long as I could remember. He was polite, immaculate and loved his job. I had great respect for a man who had great respect for others, dead or alive.

"Patricia, so good to see you," Dr. Dickenson said. "How's your back?"

"I'm working out again, so it must be almost perfect."

"You've got to watch it, if the back goes, everything goes."

"Tell me about it. How's the kids?"

"The young one is bumming around, trying to figure out if she should go to university or work for a year. Tracy's getting married."

"Really? God, but she's only—"

"Twenty-one. I know, but it's her choice. What can you do?" Then: "I suppose you want me to look up a file for you."

"It's kind of old."

"How old?"

"Ten years."

He looked puzzled for a few seconds. "We might still have it on record."

I gave him all the details, which he wrote on a notepad.

He said, "Why don't you wait for me in the cafeteria, and I'll bring you the file over."

"That would be great."

Five minutes later, I was drinking vending machine coffee from a paper cup so thin it burned my fingertips. I was alone in the quiet room.

Before I finished my coffee, Dr Dickerson walked into the cafeteria with a bone-coloured manilla folder in his hand. "Got it. I've got everything classified neatly in boxes. It pays to be organised."

"I wish I could say the same for me."

He looked at my coffee. "How can you drink this coffee? It tastes like paste. I've got Moccona in the office drawer."

"It's okay. I didn't want it in the first place, just for something to do."

He sat opposite me and opened the file. "Steven Donnelly. An open-and-shut case, I believe. The culprit got thirty years or something. What exactly are you after?"

I told him how Bain and Murray got me on the case and what they expected me to achieve.

He flicked through his files. "Here's the autopsy report. Let's take a look."

"Can you tell me what he died of?"

"Well, officially his heart stopped beating. But there was another reason. He was choked to death."

"With the killer's bare hands?"

"Nope. A rope or belt, or something tough enough to leave a straight mark around his neck."

"Did we find the weapon?"

"Nope. And probably never will now."

"Did he have any defence wounds?"

He flicked through some pages. "None whatsoever. Scrapings from under his fingernails were inconclusive, and there was no bruising or cutting anywhere but around his neck."

"Was he conscious when he got killed?"

"Well, it's really impossible to tell."

"It's rather strange, don't you think?"

"Which part?"

"Well, the victim has no defence wounds or bruising of any sort, and the killer has none either. And yet, two witnesses said they saw him being kidnapped. Surely, if someone grabbed you and tossed you in a car, you wouldn't just sit there like a rabbit caught in headlights."

He chewed on my comment. "Good point. No one really thought about it when it happened. The killer got caught straight away, so there was no need to dig any further than necessary. You know what it's like, you were a cop once. Too many cases going on at once, and not enough hours to spend quality time on them."

I was about to finish my coffee until I remembered how foul it tasted. "It's kind of weird how someone gets raped and killed, and there's no bruising whatsoever."

Dr Dickerson frowned. "Raped?" He flicked through his report. "No evidence he was raped here."

I put my coffee down. Didn't Mohammed kidnap the young man to rape and kill him? Didn't they find Donnelly's soiled underwear at the killer's place?

"Are you sure?" I asked.

"I performed the autopsy myself. I know back then I didn't have the experience I have now, but I would never have missed something so important. There was no evidence of rape whatsoever. No bruising, no bleeding, and no semen found inside his anus."

"What about Mohammed?"

"What about Mohammed?"

"Any trace evidence? If he had sex with Steven, wouldn't he leave something behind?"

"Well, no semen, but I would have expected some exchange of pubic hairs or something. Absolutely nothing connected to Mohammed."

"And justice has been carried out?"

Dr Dickerson played with his fingers. "I guess everyone missed that one."

"Did they? Or was it convenient?"

"That's a possibility, but it's for you to figure out."

"Yeah, and I don't like what this whole thing is telling me."

He shook his head. "It's going to make a whole lot of people look as competent as arseholes."

"Why didn't you put that in your report?"

CHAPTER TWENTY-NINE

It was Monday morning, and Tyron dropped into my office.

"How you doing'?" he said and tossed a brown bag filled with hot doughnuts on my desk. "Thought you might need a bit of energy. First day of the week is always a ball breaker."

I grabbed the bag from my desk and tossed it back at him. "No, thank you. You're not going to be around to help me when I'll need to call the fire brigade to pull me out of the door frame. Now, I'm sure you didn't come around just to ensure that I have my daily intake of sugar and hot jam."

He shrugged. "I've run the plates of that Econovan. Some prick called Garry Morgan. Does the name mean anything to you?"

"Nope."

"And I got a little something else."

"What?"

"Sonofabitch's got a record for spousal abuse."

"Damn, now we've got a genuine reason to break his head open with a cricket bat."

Tyron read from his notebook. "Two years ago, the cops got a 000 call and turned up at his place. Morgan's wife was black and blue, apparently she asked for it."

"Don't they all?"

"Yeah, well, it's the story I got anyway. I've never been married, so I wouldn't know what the deal is, but I gather beating your spouse is not in the marriage contract."

"And yet every bastard seems to think it is."

"Is that why you're not getting married?"

I threw him darts with my eyes. "Hey, come on, Gérald is not an arsehole! It's got nothing to do with it."

"I'm sorry, I was out of line."

"Forget it."

He chewed on his jam doughnut.

I said, "Oh, hell, give me one of those."

He tossed the bag over my desk, and I burned my lip with the first bite, but it tasted good nonetheless.

I told him what I had found out from Dr Dickerson.

"So what do you think it means?" he asked.

"Murray is probably right, Mohammed got framed."

"Well, isn't it what we suspected all along?"

"Yep, but now it looks as if someone with an upper hand is playing a game here. I mean Donnelly wasn't even raped or assaulted, and Mohammed got twenty years for it. Doesn't it change the whole scenario?"

Tyron tackled his third doughnut the way an under-age kid goes through his first packet of cigarettes. "Do you think Hurst's got anything to do with it?"

"If he doesn't, then he's the most incompetent detective around."

"What's your impression?"

"Everyone thinks highly of him in as far as doing his job properly goes, so I guess we can rule out he is classified under the cops-without-brains category."

Tyron finished his last doughnut. "Got something to drink?"

"Coffee?"

"You know I don't drink coffee."

I pulled two light beers from the bar fridge under my desk. He pulled the top with his teeth.

I said, "You're going to crack a tooth one of these days playing Mr. bottle-opener with your pearlies."

"Nah, they're thick as bricks." He took a mouthful and said, "So you think Hurst is the one calling the shots?"

"Maybe someone's paying him to turn a blind eye. It's the impression he gave me when he dropped in for a little visit. Somebody's covering up for whoever killed Donnelly, and whoever it is, he's got the cops on his side."

"Uh-huh, and the cops do whatever they want."

"Read the paper this morning?"

"Yeah, fifty cops in the state got suspended for criminal activities."

"Justice for all."

"I thought it was a myth."

"So did I."

CHAPTER THIRTY

The Econovan was parked in the driveway of a Glenroy realtor, which looked like a one-man shop, complete with dirty windowpanes and faded-colour photographs of houses selling to desperate first-home buyers and immigrants on low-income or social welfare.

The plates on the van matched the numbers Tyron gave me. There was a nasty dint on the driver's side, just by the blinker. Another king of the road who probably pushed his way into traffic without indicating and believed brakes are fashion accessories.

Tyron had decided to come for a joyride and for a chance at getting back at whoever had sent Mono Brow, Crew Cut and Hairy Arms to pay us a little visit.

We stepped out of the roadster, looking somewhat conspicuous because of Tyron's statue-like frame. He moved like someone who carried a backpack filled with quarry stones. To anyone seeing us it would be pretty obvious we were not a couple looking for their first home to bring up our infant.

"Why the hell is a realtor getting himself mixed up in a murder investigation?" Tyron asked.

"Maybe the shop is a front for some other types of illegal activities, probably makes more money from dope dealing and scaring the living daylight out of law-abiding citizens than selling house-and-land packages."

"Sonofabitch has got it coming to him one of these days. And today might just be his lucky day."

To the right of the realtor was a milk bar and to the left a second-hand shop stocked with over-priced junk anyone could pick up for free at the local tip. There was not a living soul in sight, like the day after a nuclear fallout.

"Friendly neighbourhood," Tyron said.

"Yeah, I heard there are retirement condos just around the corner for sale. Might be time to think about our future."

I opened the front door of the shop. A little bell announced my arrival to the fools who chose to spend a good part of the day in this dump.

There was a reception desk to the left, the standard cheap-as-matches, plywood model, with no one attending it. The place smelled like an old-fashioned country pub, dust and beer. The last receptionist had probably committed suicide on a Monday morning rather than turning up to work for another week.

I pointed to the empty seat. "Position vacant, if you're interested."

"My butt wouldn't fit in the chair."

A male voice said, "Can I help you?"

I turned around.

The man's eyes shifted from me to Tyron. He was a big guy, but not as big as Tyron, and could have done with a full membership at his local gym. His suit was too small for his frame and his eyes bloodshot from drinking or lack of sleep. His hair was oiled and as slicked as a seal that had a brush with an oil tanker.

I forced a smile. "We're interested at looking at beach-front properties, preferably with a raised patio and a rumpus room for the kids."

He pulled on his tie. "You folks are not from around here, are you? There's no beach in the area. You're in the wrong suburb, so why don't you get the fuck out of here!"

"Garry Morgan, right?" I asked.

"Yeah, and what is it to you?"

"So, you *are* the man who owns this thriving business?"

119

He paused for a few seconds. "Are you with the REIV?"

"Nope, but I wish we were."

"Then state your business or get the hell out. And if you're cops, I want to see some identification now."

Tyron stepped up beside me. "Why don't you chill out, we haven't even started yet."

Morgan grabbed a baseball bat from the entrance of his office, but he was way too slow. By the time he levelled the bat to his waist, I had already knocked out one of his teeth and nearly pushed his nose inside his skull with my special taekwondo double-jump kick.

Morgan folded over in half, his kneecaps making contact with the grey industrial carpet. He held his face with both hands, blood dripping on his white shirt.

"You broke my fuckin' nose!" he managed to cry out.

I stood above him. "What interest have you got in Bah Sheh Mohammed?"

"Who?"

I kicked him in the ribs, and he fell sideways, making a thumping noise like a laundry bag filled with dirt.

Blood and saliva was ruining the only clean spot on the carpet.

"I don't know what you're talking about," he said. "Who the fuck is Bah Sheh Mohammed?"

"Did you send three guys to my office last week?"

Morgan looked up.

Tyron stepped forward.

Morgan rolled back. "All right, all right, I send people around all the time. Who are you?"

"Patricia Lunn."

He looked at me and back at Tyron. "And who the fuck is he?"

"He's my next of kin. Now, did you or did you not send three thugs to my office last week?"

"It wasn't my idea, someone asked me to do it."

"Who?"

Morgan tilted sideways and pushed his back against the wall. His nose was swelling by the second.

I made a step sparring move.

"All right, all right," Morgan said. "Some cop I do business with. We go back a long way. He does me favours, I do him favours."

"What kind of favours?"

"Closes his eyes when it suits me, and I provide him with helping hands whenever he needs them."

"You wouldn't happen to know the name of that cop, would you?"

"Nope."

"And you go back a long way? Strange. The cop's name wouldn't be Hurst by any chance?"

Morgan hesitated for a few seconds. "Yep, it's him. He's a good cop, but sometimes he gets in little jams."

"Yeah, I heard he's a good cop, everyone keeps telling me. Then why do I find it hard to believe?"

"I'm sure he didn't mean anything."

"Oh, really?"

"He said not to hurt you, just to make it clear you get the message." He massaged the bridge of his nose with his right hand.

"Well, I got a message, but it wasn't really clear since I didn't know where it came from. And if you see Hurst, tell him to have the balls to call in on me next time he has a message to deliver instead of sending the grease squad."

"I certainly will."

"I bet you will, unless you're stupid enough to want full facial reconstruction."

I turned around and aimed for the door.

I heard Morgan say to Tyron: "Hey, what's this shit she's into?"

"Taekwondo, placed third in the Australasian Championship last year. Trust me, you don't want to mess with her."

CHAPTER THIRTY-ONE

Gérald and I had just finished watching a double feature at the Astor Theatre and decided to take a stroll up Chapel Street. Even though it was past ten thirty at night, there were still many people walking the streets and enjoying the night life the many cafes and bistros encouraged.

We came out of Borders and entered a café with table-and-chair patio-sets and people dressed to impress. The night was pleasantly mild, and going to bed didn't seem like the right thing to do.

I ordered a light Cascade and Gérald a short black. We sat at a table and watched the night crowd go by. Most were young and enjoyed too much free time and disposable income. It was a striking contrast to the down-and-out suburbs I had visited recently while investigating for Bain.

"We should be doing this more often," Gérald said.

I said, "I agree, but between your shifts and my lifestyle, it's an impossibility."

"Maybe if we were married, things would be different."

"Maybe."

"We'd be more committed to one another."

I took a gulp from my beer. "Gérald, I couldn't be any more

committed to you if I tried."

"Oh, I wasn't complaining, but if we were to get married, well, it wouldn't be anything like Dominique and Tammy."

"Of course it wouldn't, I mean, why would you even try to compare us to your brother and your sister-in-law? We're nothing like them."

"True."

"To begin with, you're far more handsome than he is. Look at you, you work out three times a week despite your hectic schedule, and, I'm sorry, but your brother has no sense of fashion whatsoever."

"Are you saying I have a good sense of fashion?"

He was wearing a Kenji Urban black shirt with grey chinos and black shoes. He had a wide chest, and his arms were the type you wanted to hang on to. Gérald was the only man I had ever met who took so much care of his appearance, which I perceived as a form of great respect for the person he was going out with—me.

"You're a walking billboard on how to dress properly," I said.

"Well, thank you." He smiled and sipped his coffee.

"You're welcome." I paused for a few seconds and added, "When this is all over, we're taking this two week vacation in Broome, and I don't care what comes up, this time nothing's going to stop us."

"I look forward to it."

"I'm going to spoil you rotten."

"Even after I've annoyed you so much about marriage?"

I took his hand in mine. "Nothing you can say will make me want to be away from you—ever."

I was looking at Gérald when two men appeared on my sides. They were both dressed in black suits and long coats, and it would have been almost comical if they didn't look so scary. The one to my right had a scar running from his chin to the top of his left eyelid. He was the youngest, but his grey eyes expressed fearlessness and no sense of morality. The one to my left wore a gold signet on his right hand and his hair cut short like an army recruit. He was tanned and didn't look like a local. They both obviously suffered from watching too many episodes of the Sopranos.

The older man closed in. "Don't do anything stupid. I have a gun tucked in my coat, and if you try any of your taekwondo moves, I will shoot you right in front of all these people."

The dry tone of his voice and the seriousness of his stare told me he meant every word he said.

I couldn't see Gérald because the younger one was blocking my view.

I said, "What did I do? Take your parking spot? Hey, I'm sorry, I'll move my car right away."

He didn't twitch or smile, or indicate in any form or shape he found me amusing.

He said, "You're a nice looking woman, so it would cause your husband great distress to find you in a situation requiring major medical attention. And since he's a doctor, after we're done with you, he'll probably recommend euthanasia."

"I'll make sure to leave you something in my will."

"I've heard a lot about you Ms. Lunn, and I admit I'm rather impressed by your persistence, and a little in awe at your foolishness. So I'm going to make this very clear. Drop the Mohammed case you're working on."

"Let me guess, Detective Hurst asked you to pass on a message?"

"If you persist with this investigation, the next time you see me will be the last."

Before I had time to reply, he and his younger friend disappeared as swiftly as they had appeared.

"God," Gérald said, "they scared the living daylights out of me. Who the hell were they?"

"Men in black, probably from outer space."

"No, but seriously, weren't you scared?"

I drank from my beer. "Yes, I was, sweetie, but that's just the way the world is when you're involved in my line of work."

"I don't know, Patricia, maybe you should drop this case. I mean, is it really worth it? What exactly are you getting out of this?"

"Money to start with, but I know we don't need the money desperately with your job and everything."

"Then why?" The colour drained from his face. He seemed genuinely scared.

"I don't know why, Gérald. Maybe it's because I started something, and I don't like people telling me to stop. It usually means I'm on the right track. And think about the person who killed Steven Donnelly. Shouldn't he be in jail right now instead of Mohammed?"

Gérald looked at the crowd and creased his eyes. He had the right to be concerned about our safety.

I took his hand in mine. "Look, we can always move to another place for the time being. I'll talk to Bain, tell him what's going on and get him to pick up the tab on all the expenses."

"Better than being shot in the back of the head and dumped in someone's front yard, I guess."

"I'm not going to argue with you on that point."

CHAPTER THIRTY-TWO

I was sitting in my office, feet propped up on the desk, the telephone receiver tucked between my neck and right shoulder. The room smelled of freshly-brewed coffee from a pot I had made ten minutes ago. My mug was already empty, and soon I would have to go back to the kitchen for a refill.

"And who are these people?" Bain asked. His voice was not smooth like it had been when he surprised me with a phone call a few weeks ago. It felt as if I were a child being interrogated by a parent who had to set the record straight.

I said, "How the hell would I know? If I had the slightest clue, I would have called the police by now."

When I told him how the investigation was going, and how my life had been threatened, he became very angry. "But you just told me the police might be involved in this?"

"Well, it's only a calculated guess. All I know is Detective Hurst asked someone to make it clear to me I should drop the case."

"Did he also send these *men in black?*"

"Not sure. They wouldn't tell me. But one thing's certain, these men are not amateurs, and they sounded as if they meant every word they said."

There was a pause at the other end of the line.

"John?"

"I'm here," he said. "I'm just wondering if it's safe for you to continue with the investigation. I don't want to put your life in danger."

"Well, it's kind of a little late, but I do have a favour to ask you."

I told him to find Gérald and me alternative accommodation until the case was solved.

"There's no problem there. I've got a furnished, two-bedroom town-house in Port Melbourne up for rental. The current tenants don't want to renew their contract, so it will be free as of next Wednesday. Why don't you move in there for now? I won't charge you a cent, of course, and at least it won't be too far for Gérald to get to work at the hospital."

"Sounds good."

"It's a lovely place, and I wouldn't sell it for anything, which is why I decided a long time ago to put it on the rental market."

"You know what they say."

"What do they say?"

"A change is as good as a holiday."

CHAPTER THIRTY-THREE

On Wednesday morning, Tyron and I arrived at Bain's retreat. It was magnificent, just as he had described it. We had a full view of the ocean, right up to Williamstown and beyond. No wonder Bain didn't want to give up the apartment. The walls were painted white inside and out, and the furniture was minimal and mainly black leather and chrome. The air was crisp and smelled of saltwater.

Gérald was at work, so Tyron helped me to bring everything in. Tyron would be moving in with us for the time being. We had no idea who the men in black were, but one thing was certain, they knew a lot about me, which meant they probably knew Tyron was on my books. It didn't take a genius to figure out if I was in danger, so was Tyron and everyone associated with me. We had to stick together if we wanted to survive the ordeal. I had hardly slept the previous night, and obviously the men in black had got to me more than I had liked to admit to myself or my entourage.

Tyron took the room at the end of the hall because it was the smallest and the only one offering him a clear, unobstructed view of the front door. He had an unlicensed, sawn-off rifle under his bed, just in case things got out of control. He would be able to shoot the bastards without getting out of bed.

I was unpacking groceries in the kitchen when Tyron came back from his room.

"Nice pad," he said. "Wouldn't want anyone to come in and wreck this place. It would be a damn shame."

"Well, as long as nobody traces our movements back to Bain's little hideout, then I guess we should be pretty safe here."

"Don't bet on it. If Hurst is involved in this, sooner or later someone's going to figure out where we're hiding. You'll have to move out of the country to be safe, and even then, the sonofabitch probably has contacts with Interpol."

I removed a six-pack of light beer from a paper bag and put it the cold compartment of the fridge. Tyron was looking at the beer the way a child looks at a bag of lollies.

"Won't be cold for another hour," I said.

"Uh-huh." He cracked the joints of his fingers. "So, you've never seen these bozos before?"

"Nope, and I know just about every arsehole in the vicinity."

"I thought you said he wasn't a local?"

"True. His tan was deep and rich, probably from Queensland or WA."

"Seems a long way to come just to bury some sin from ten years ago." He paused for a few seconds. "Do you want me to check some IDs with Bud?"

"Sure, it won't hurt. At least we might find out what we're up against."

Tyron helped me put the rest of the groceries in the pantry.

He said, "You're not thinking about giving up, are you?"

I locked my eyes with his. "I don't know if I should be offended or just punch you in the mouth."

"Just want to make sure you know that if you ever want to back away from all this, I understand."

"Why? Because I'm not muscle-bound like you? Come on, Tyron, you'd still be selling door-to-door insurance if it wasn't for me."

He shrugged. "All right, I'm going to have a shower now."

"Hey, Tyron?"

129

"What?"

"Any chances of getting someone to watch Gérald's back?"

He searched his memory bank for a few seconds. "Sure, but it will cost you."

"Don't worry about the money. Bain is covering all the expenses. Gérald just seemed very concerned yesterday, so I wouldn't be able to live with myself if anything happened to him."

"I'll talk to Bud."

"Thanks."

"You're welcome."

CHAPTER THIRTY-FOUR

If I couldn't get any information out of Peter Weinmann, I thought it might be wise to inquire with his next-of-kin. I made the call to his parents from Bain's retreat, and briefly told them what it was about without getting into too many details. Based on past reactions I've had from people about my supposedly trying to get a convicted murderer out of jail, I didn't feel it wise to spill all my beans at once.

The Weinmanns lived in South Yarra, one of Melbourne's most exclusive suburbs, only a couple of kilometres from the Donnellys. Tyron decided to come with me, but because of his sheer size, I thought it best if he waited in the car.

"What do you think I'm going to do?" Tyron protested as I parked alongside the curbside. "Beat the information out of them?"

"That's not the point, these people will get a heart attack just by looking at you."

"Well, you're the boss."

I handed him over the keys to the MR2. "Here, just in case you need to make a quick getaway for jam doughnuts."

"You're funny. Anyone ever told you that?"

"All the time. Maybe I should get a job as a circus clown."

I stepped up to the front gate and rang the bell and waited thirty seconds.

"Yes?" a voice said though the intercom.

"Patricia Lunn. I'm here for Lindsey Weinmann."

"Oh, yes, please, do come in."

There was a buzzing noise, and I pushed the gate open.

The house was a Georgian Mansion with Corinthian columns and sash windows with delicate wooden glazing bars and panes of glass all the same size. The front yard was most likely maintained by an army of gardeners, or someone employed full time. Rows of prized rose bushes dotted the white gravelled pathway to the front entrance.

A man in his early to mid-fifties came out to greet me. He wore green, corduroy trousers and a yellow cashmere cardigan. His hair was brown from a bottle, and you could tell because he had not a streak of grey, and yet his face was cross-hatched with wrinkles like a scrunched-up shirt.

"Lovely house you have here," I said by way of ice-breaking.

"Yes, it's quite impressive, isn't it? Revival of Classical Roman architecture by the Italian architect Andrea Palladio, very popular design in Britain during the reigns of Kings George I, II, III and IV. It has it all, symmetry, simplicity and classical details."

"It must be worth a fortune."

"Close to two and a half million dollars. These types of property are a good investment."

"I'm sure they are." *If you have a few hundred thousand dollars sitting in your bank account for a deposit.*

"Do come in, we've been expecting you."

We were Lindsey and Sharon Weinmann. She was a petite, bottle redhead with freckles and heart-shaped pink lips. Unlike her husband, her wrinkles were virtually non-existent, and under her freckles her complexion was china white. She reminded me of an prisoner who had been sheltered from the rays of the sun for thirty years. At least she had zero chance of developing skin cancer.

They walked me to the living room with all the bare essentials of good ol' Aussie battlers—full-size grand piano, original works of art in oils and watercolours, marbled floor

132

lavished with Arabian rugs, expensive couches with matching footrests, state-of-the-art home theatre system with a 50-inch wall-mounted plasma screen, and a stocked-up personal bar that put the local liquor shop to shame. The whole place smelled of leather and floor polish.

"Care for something to drink?" Mr. Weinmann asked.

"I won't take much of your time."

"No, really, it's no problem." He turned to his wife. "Sharon, why don't you bring Ms. Lunn a glass of water?" To me: "Unless you prefer something else?"

"Water is fine." I didn't want to start a fight over a drop of water, even though we were experiencing the worst drought in thirty years.

Sharon vanished somewhere past the lounge room.

Lindsey Weinmann circled the coffee table. "So, what brings you around? You wanted to tell us something about Peter? He's not in trouble, is he?"

"Not at all. I'm investigating the death of one of his old university friends, Steven Donnelly."

He gave me a blank look.

I said, "You don't know him, I gather?"

"I can't say his name means anything to me."

Just then moment, Sharon walked back in the room with a crystal class filled with water and ice.

"Thank you," I said.

Lindsey turned to his wife. "Have you heard of Steven Donnelly? Apparently he was an old friend of Peter back during his university days."

Sharon looked as if she was pulling cobwebs from her brain, but her eyes gave away that whatever she was going to tell me would be a far stretch from the truth.

"The name doesn't mean anything to me," she finally said.

I stared at her. "He used to go out with him ten years ago."

The Weinmanns looked at each other.

"Apparently they were very close," I said.

"Well," Lindsey said, "Peter was a very handsome and intelligent young man back in those days, he had a lot of friends."

"That's what he told me."

"Then it's the truth. What are you exactly getting at with this questioning?" There was a tone of slight irritation in his voice like sandpaper on metal. "Is my son a suspect in this murder?"

"Absolutely not. There's just reasonable doubt the man convicted for Steven's murder did not kill him. I'm trying to establish some leads so the real killer is brought to justice, and an innocent man doesn't have to spend the rest of his life behind bars."

They were silent for a moment.

"Well," Lindsey said, "if you've spoken to my son, then I guess he's already told you everything you need to know."

"As a matter of fact," I said, "he wasn't very co-operative, which is kind of frustrating when you investigate a crime that took place such a long time ago."

"Sorry to hear. I'll have a chat to him and ask him to be a little more considerate. Is there anything else we can help you with?"

"Yes. Have you ever heard of Doug Carlton and Crystal Gartenberg?"

Sharon looked startled.

They both shook their heads.

"Are you sure? They witnessed the abduction of Steven Donnelly before he was murdered. Crystal Gartenberg married Doug Carlton, and she goes by the name of Crystal Carlton these days. I think they did their undergraduate studies with your son."

They thought for a few more seconds.

"And I think you're wasting your time," Lindsey said. "We didn't know Peter's private life in minute details. In fact, we didn't know Peter well at all back in those days. He was young, and he had his own problems, we had our own problems. We let him have plenty of freedom."

"I see."

"Sorry we can't be more helpful. I can sympathise with the difficulty of your work, but there's really nothing we can do for you."

"Well, then I'll be on my way." I pulled two business cards from my bag. "In case something comes to mind, or if one of your friends does remember something about Steven

Donnelly, Doug Carlton or Crystal Gartenberg, then I would be very grateful if you'd call me."

They both took a card and examined them as if they were fake one-hundred-dollar notes.

Lindsey said, "You work for yourself, do you?"

"I do a lot of contracted work."

"Do you investigate white-collar crime?"

"If it's illegal, I'll look into it."

"Well, my company is sometimes in need of a good investigator. Then you don't mind if I get in touch with you sometime in the near future?"

"By all means, I'll be glad to see what I can do."

I didn't particularly like the Weinmanns, but I didn't want to let my judgement get in the way of billing an absurd amount of money to anyone who was willing to pay.

Lindsey walked me back to the front door.

"You know," he said, "I'm not exactly sure what you're looking for here, but something tells me you're going to make a lot of people angry."

"Why exactly?"

"I don't know, but digging up things from the past has ever led to anything good in my experience. Let bygones be bygones, it's my motto."

"Seems to be everybody's motto these days."

He smiled, but I couldn't figure out if it was out of malice or sympathy.

When I returned to the car, Tyron had one arm hanging out the window, his head pulled back, and he was snoring like a beat-up lawnmower.

I put my index finger to his temple and said, "Bang! You're dead."

He opened his eyes. "I wasn't sleeping, just thinking. How did you go?"

I stepped in the car and switched on the engine. "Nice, self-righteous people, as you would expect in a neighbourhood like this. Tried to smooth me out by offering work somewhere in the unseen future. Still, I think they belong with the Donnelly gang."

"Why?"

135

"They're all a bunch of fuckin' liars."

CHAPTER THIRTY-FIVE

I worked out three times a week at Terry Bennett's gym on High Street in Prahran, most of the time with Tyron. But on that particular Wednesday evening Tyron was running an errand for a client of mine whose son had been charged with shoplifting. Apparently the kid couldn't produce a docket on his way out of the shop, but he claimed he had paid for the item, and if the shop manager bothered to check the security tapes, it would clearly show the teenage boy was telling the truth. For some unknown reason, a 'technical' problem occurred with the security camera at the time the teenager bought the item, and nothing had been recorded. Tyron was making a personal visit to the shop manager to get to the bottom of the problem.

Everyone had gone home, and I had all the equipment to myself, just the way I liked it. The gym smelled of sweat and rust.

I had finished my forty-five minute set, which consisted of a mixed combination of bench presses, triceps pull-downs and curls. My muscles were hard like rolling pins, and the workout made me forget about the Donnelly case for a while. I had no idea where this investigation was going, but my leads were few and far between, and the billable hours would make an accountant's head roll uncontrollably.

I stepped down from the first floor of the building to a dark, narrow set of stairs. The light wasn't working, so I was extremely careful not to break my neck in the process.

When I entered the street level, the air was mild and pleasant and the traffic trickling. All in all, I felt somewhat good to be alive, but it was more likely from the adrenalin still kicking in my bloodstream than from naively believing my life was relatively under control.

I headed towards my car, which I parked next to a pizzeria further up near Chapel Street. Just when I reached for my keys, a dark figure appeared from the side of a white van parked two spots from mine. The figure was in a long coat and looked masculine in appearance, and somehow, I knew our nocturnal encounter wouldn't end up in a bear hug.

The muscles at the back of my neck tensed up when I noticed a pistol in his right hand.

He lifted his arm and aimed in my direction.

Instinctively, I dropped to the floor and rolled towards the back of the car.

Pop! Pop! Crunch!

The bastard got the fender of the MR2.

I didn't have a gun, so that automatically placed him in an advantageous position.

There were only two choices. Either I waited for him to come and take a chance at giving him a good belting before he perforated my vital organs, or ran like a synthetic rabbit chased by a pack of racing greyhounds.

I decided today was a good day to be a synthetic rabbit.

Before my assassin got to the back of my car, I was up on my feet and running back to Terry Bennett's. As soon as I entered the staircase, Pop! Pop!—splitters erupted from the door like fire crackers on a movie set.

I reached the first floor and turned all the lights off. I knew the gym well enough to walk around in the dark. I knew my killer was efficient, but it didn't mean his eyes were night goggles.

I ran halfway across the gym and squatted behind a lat pull-down machine.

Footsteps were coming up the stairway, but my killer was in no hurry.

I searched for a weapon within my reach. There had to be a dumbbell left somewhere on the floor by someone who had not bothered placing the equipment back on the racks.

Moonlight coming from the high windows in the east wall illuminated the back of the gym. I could make out the shadow of every piece of equipment—the bench press, the rowing machine, the lat machine, the leg extension. I had used each and every one of those machines, sometimes until it felt as if my muscles were going to tear through my skin.

The killer's silhouette appeared against the back wall.

He was still holding his gun.

He didn't say a word.

I tried not to move, but my squatting position was beginning to hurt the small of my back.

He came towards me.

I could move fast and take him by surprise.

I rolled to my right side and landed next to a rack of cast-iron dumbbells. Instinctively, I grabbed a two-pound one with my right hand.

My would-be killer was moving in.

If I was going to hit him with the dumbbell, it would have to be hard and fast. A second of hesitation would most likely result in a bullet between the eyes.

He stood still.

I stopped breathing.

Then, without warning, he turned around and walked back to the entrance of the building.

I stayed in the dark for a full ten minutes. He might have been waiting for me on the staircase, and as soon as I re-appeared, he would use my head for target practice. It's what I would have done if I were him rather than venture blindly into unfamiliar territory.

There was no back exit in the gym, other than a door leading to an apartment where the owner lived. I decided it might not be such a good idea to tell the owner I had a gunman on my trail.

I left the building through the high windows on the east wall and nearly broke my neck in the process.

When I got home, I ran straight to the bathroom and stayed under a hot shower for thirty minutes.

CHAPTER THIRTY-SIX

Tyron had arranged with Bud to provide Gérald with some protection. While Gérald was at work, there was someone looking over his shoulder, an ex-cop who carried more ammo than a weapons manufacturer. Everyone who came into close contact with Gérald had to be checked and double-checked by Mr. Ammo and the security staff at the hospital. Because I had been close to getting killed, the police were now involved. A marked patrol car was parked in front of the hospital entrance on the lookout for anyone with a long, black trench coat.

I was with Tyron at the hospital canteen. He was gorging on two vanilla slices and drinking a large chocolate milk shake. The canteen smelled of coffee and fried food.

"Given the doughnuts the cold shoulder?" I asked Tyron.

"Couldn't get them passed the security check." He swallowed half a vanilla slice in one go. "Not that I'm complaining, these things taste damn good."

An old couple was eating breakfast at the end of the room, eggs on toast and orange juice. The canteen lady was re-shelving the chocolate section by the front counter. No one else was around.

There was a visible bulge near Tyron's ribcage.

"You're carrying a weapon now?" I said.

"This one's licensed, if it's why you're asking."

"I don't doubt you. Still I'm just not sure if it's wise to carry a weapon with you all the time."

"Well, you nearly got killed last night, and I'm sure your killer isn't struggling with his conscience about whether he should be carrying a weapon or not."

There was nothing I could.

"You know, there's something really wrong with the Mohammed case."

"Jeez, Patricia, you're very perceptive."

"Someone is not asking me to stop investigating anymore. He's going to make sure I do."

"Who?"

"I have a suspicion the killer from last night is one of the men in black who paid Gérald and me a little visit at that coffee shop in Toorak. The height and width of the bastard is similar. And he moves the same way, calm, collected and sure of himself."

Tyron grabbed the other vanilla slice. "Want some?"

"No thanks."

He took a bite. "So what's the big plan?"

"Well, the sonofabitch is probably going to come back for me in the near future. That'll give me a chance to find out who he is."

"That sounds like a good plan." There was sarcasm in his tone. "And how are you going to proceed?"

"Keep my eyes open and jump on him the first chance I get."

Tyron washed down the second vanilla slice with his milkshake. "Uh-huh, well, maybe you should think about getting a weapon too. He doesn't sound like the kind of guy who's going to agree to put his gun down and jump in the ring with you to sort out your differences."

"You know I don't like guns, Tyron."

"You don't like car accidents, but you're still driving a car."

"But a gun is designed for killing."

"Or protection, it all really depends from which angle you're looking at it. If you don't know where to get one, I can arrange something."

Gérald and his bodyguard walked into the canteen.

"I'll think about it," I said to Tyron and then turned to Gérald: "Hey, sweetie, working hard this morning?"

He walked up to where we were sitting and kissed me on the forehead. "They're cutting me some slack because of our present situation. I have the option of taking my annual leave now if the need arises."

"I don't think it will be necessary. I'll get to the bottom of this in no time."

"You're confidence is reassuring. How are you anyway?"

"Good in spite of all that's happened."

Mr. Ammo was checking me out from head to toe.

I said, "You're going to introduce me to your friend?"

"Oh, yes, sorry," Gérald said, "this is Frank Garvy, he's going to be my closest buddy for a little while."

Garvy, alias Mr. Ammo, was dressed in a inconspicuous black suit and gun holster clearly visible from under his jacket. I had no idea if he was licensed or not, but as long as Gérald was safe, it's all that mattered. Garvy wore his hair short and brushed back and had an uncanny resemblance to a famous Australian-Italian actor who'd made it big in Hollywood. He carried himself like someone who had eyes behind his head.

"You've been doing this for long?" I asked him.

"Five years, and I wouldn't want it any other way. The money is good and the work is steady."

I nodded.

Gérald turned to me: "How are you progressing with the case?"

"Everyone's lying to me, so it's hard to figure out the snakes from the sticks."

"Snakes bite, sticks don't," Tyron said.

I ignored the comment. "My guess is Steven Donnelly was killed by someone who knew him and not a total stranger. There are too many people trying to protect something or someone. If I didn't know any better, I would say they all believed he deserved to die and the truth should remain buried."

They all nodded, apart from Garvy who blinked twice instead.

"You know," Tyron said, "I don't know where this is all

going, but if I get my hands on one of these bastards, I'm going to do something very illegal, and it involves a lot of pain."

"Like pulling nails with a pair of pliers?"

"I was thinking more about something involving the soothing sound of crushing bones."

"You've always been quite a poet."

"Funny, I always thought myself more of a rap artist."

"Isn't it the same thing nowadays?"

"Yeah, except rap artists have a monopoly on the word 'motherfucker'."

I smiled and everyone else looked away.

CHAPTER THIRTY-SEVEN

I wasn't going to wait like a sitting duck for the next bullet to hit me square between the eyes. Crystal Carlton had always been a good lead, but then I didn't particularly want to go behind her husband's back. Doug sounded like the type of jerk who'd cram some chauvinistic bullying attitude down her throat if I pressed her too much.

But it was before someone tried to fill my body with lead. Since my life was hanging in the balance, I couldn't be bothered with the courtesy calls before making an appearance.

I remembered Crystal worked at the Esplanade Hotel—known as the Espy to the locals—from the conversation I had with her and Doug the other day.

There were only a handful of people so early in the morning because most people were either busy making a living or preferred a cup of coffee to a glass of beer for breakfast. The place was a mismatch of old couches, coffee tables and chairs reeking of beer and cigarettes.

Crystal had her blond hair up in a ponytail and wore a black, silk-like top and a pair of jeans. Her push-up bra did a good job of making her look like a woman who knew how to use her femininity to her advantage. She looked nothing like the woman I had met the other day in the privacy of her home, other than being ridiculously easy on the eye. She didn't notice me until I walked right up to the bar. She was busy putting some beer glasses away from a rack.

"Well, hey there," she said when she caught my eye, "you're still around."

"Hello, Crystal. Did you expect me to have skipped the country?"

She forced a smile. "No, no, I just heard something about you getting shot at."

"Yeah, I heard the same story, but my marksman's got the skill of a child with a water pistol. He never had a chance."

"So, what brings you here?"

"Thought it might be a good idea to finish the conversation we started over a week ago. I have the feeling you haven't told me everything you know."

She looked at me for a whole ten seconds. "Can I get you something to drink?"

"Bit early for me, but since you're offering, I'll have a light Cascade."

She turned to the bar fridge, removed a beer and pulled the top off. "Doug's at work, and I'm stuck in this shithole for the rest of the day."

"I kind of like this place, actually." I lied.

"Yeah, well, you're not the one working here. You wouldn't believe the number of arseholes who think everything behind the bar's up for grabs."

"I can imagine." I sipped from my beer. "Why don't you quit if you don't like it?"

"Doug's not bringing enough home to keep us both alive."

"I thought you came from privileged families. Hasn't his father got a connection who could land him a job on twice the salary with half the workload?"

"I wish, but Doug's never been one for begging. Too much pride. He's really hard to get close to."

"Some men can never fully satisfy a woman."

She smiled. "I liked you the first time I saw you. I'm so sorry Doug was such a jerk the other day. Are you here to ask me about Steven?"

"Well, yeah, actually this is a business call, but I've got all the time in the world. We can talk shop if you want."

She looked around. "Let's go down the back. We'll have more privacy."

There was no one else at the bar.

I said, "What about the customers?"

Crystal shrugged. "They can wait, it's not like they're going to die of thirst."

She stepped from behind the bar, and I followed her downstairs to another room with a stage. A man in a white tee and jeans was setting up the stage with mikes and speakers.

"They play live music in this room?" I asked.

"Fridays and Saturdays we feature double live acts. It gets pretty packed, I tell you."

We sat at a table far away from Mr. Soundman, next to a speaker big enough to blow anyone's eardrums in half a second.

I sipped from my Cascade. "You know, something still bothers me from our conversation the other day."

"What's?"

"You told me you and Steven were best friends, right?"

She stood still for a few seconds. "Yeah, well, but it was a long time ago."

"Okay, okay, I'm not saying it wasn't a long time ago. I'm just curious because you've never mentioned he had a boyfriend."

"Why would I mention this?"

"Well, Doug said when you first saw Mohammed and Steven together, you thought they were having a lovers' quarrel. But surely, if you were Steven's best friend, you would have known who he was going out with at the time?"

Crystal went red from the neck up. "This happened such a long time ago. And Steven, you know, he swapped guys like some people swap football cards. I don't know, maybe he'd just changed boyfriends, and he had not told me about it."

"I see…kind of strange if you were best friends, though."

She said nothing and just stared at Mr. Soundman.

I said, "How long had Steven been going with Peter Weinmann when he got killed?"

"A couple of months." She wasn't looking at me when she

147

answered.

"Then why did you think Mohammed might have been Steven's lover when you saw them fighting next to the car?"

"I never said he was. Doug did."

"Did you really see an Arab kidnap Steven?"

"Yes, I did." She was still avoiding eye contact.

"I think you're lying."

She stood from her chair. "Well, then, it's your opinion and there's nothing I can do about it. I better get back to work."

"You know Crystal, I think you all knew one another, Peter, Doug, Steven and you. And all I have to do is talk to a few people to find out if you were close-knit. So why don't you save yourself further embarrassment and tell me what's going on?"

She stared at me. "So, yes, we all knew each other, where are you going with all this? Because we knew each other, it doesn't mean we had anything to do with Steven's murder."

"What bothers me here is how Steven's murderer supposedly dumped his body at The University of Highton, even though he had most likely never been there, and the four of you were hanging around the university on a regular basis. Kind of strange, don't you think?"

"You're the detective, so why don't you find out and get back to us when you've got some answers?"

"I very much intend to do so."

"Good, if you live long enough to figure it out."

She walked away from the table.

I stood up. "What did you say?"

"Go fuck yourself."

CHAPTER THIRTY-EIGHT

I was sitting in John Bain's office in Collins Street. He wore a sharp, Italian-made suit with a blue shirt and red tie. His black hair was brushed back—he had given up on the fashionable messed-up look—and his teeth were so white, they looked as if they didn't really belong to him. And since he was a smoker, it was nothing short of a miracle. His shoulders were broad and his stomach flat like a surfboard. He was like a good red. The older he got, the more sophisticated and appealing he became.

The aroma of freshly brewed coffee filled the room like at an Italian cafe.

"I'm sorry about all this mess," he said. "If I'd known things were going to turn out the way they have, I wouldn't have asked you to take up this case." He pulled a cigarette from his silver case and lit it.

I said, "That's okay, you weren't to know, and besides, I'm glad we ended up catching up with one another. If it had not been for Murray, maybe we would have never seen each other again."

He smiled, and my stomach churned. I don't know what it was about Bain that turned me into a moron with a schoolgirl crush. Given I was so in love with Gérald, it made me feel like the utmost deceitful bitch.

"Well, I'm convinced of one thing," I said. "Murray is most likely right. Mohammed didn't kill Steven Donnelly."

"I'm glad you've got that much sorted out." He stared at me for a few seconds. "Have you had lunch?"

"Not yet."

"I'll have something brought up from downstairs."

Five minutes later we were in the conference room eating avocado club sandwiches. I was dying for a beer, but cola was the order of the day.

"Okay," Bain said, "have you got some specifics?"

I told him everything I knew.

He masticated his sandwich as if it were the last meal he would consume.

When he finished, he wiped his mouth with a paper napkin.

"That's it?" he said.

"Well, yes, basically, it's as far as I've got. And the fact I nearly got killed really points out how something is not right at all."

"Okay, Patricia, I'm not going to disagree with you here. You're absolutely right in as far as someone is trying to bury this case so deep nobody is ever going to dig out the truth, but what you've given me here is all circumstantial. I can't go to the State Prosecutor with this and ask him to release Bah Sheh Mohammed because you think someone else killed Donnelly. I mean it's what Murray wanted to do, and look where it got him."

I drank half my cola and absorbed the impact of his words. The money he paid me was damn good, but I was getting somewhat tired of being pushed around by Melbourne's model citizens.

"I'd like to dig a little further," I said.

"You don't have to, you know."

"I know, but it seems to be one of those times where quitting would be like dropping out of your PhD one month before completion."

"Uh-huh, and what does Gérald think?"

"He hasn't said."

"Doesn't he want you to drop the case?"

"If he wanted me to, he would have told me by now."

He took a long drag from his cigarette. "Well, if you really want to stay on, I don't have a problem with your decision. I just want to make sure it's what you want, and you're not forcing yourself to do this because you think you owe me something."

My brows crossed. "Come again?"

"No, I mean since you've already been paid all this money, maybe you feel you have to find a resolution to this mess."

"Believe me, John, I never feel obligated to do something I don't want to.

"Fair enough." He pushed his plate to the side. "Coffee?"

"Sure. Make it short black and strong enough to strip the paint off a wall."

He left the conference room and came back three minutes later with two short blacks. He sat and pulled a new cigarette from his silver case.

"Want one?" he asked.

"Never smoke."

"Worried about your health?"

"I don't see the point of smoking."

"Each to his own." He inhaled and exhaled. "Here's what we're going to do; I'm going to arrange for Garry Morgan to be arrested and interrogated."

"The realtor? Why?"

"From what you're telling me, Detective Hurst is tied up in the case and Morgan probably knows more than he's saying."

"So how's Morgan going to help?" I sipped from my coffee. It was hot and strong like I asked him to make it.

"You told me Morgan and Hurst have done each other favours. Well, if we put the squeeze on Morgan, he'll be able to tell us where we're heading."

"Morgan's not going to give you anything on Hurst."

"I can get five lawyers around the clock on his back, and I'm sure we'll find a little something to pass on to the REIV and the Office of Fair Trading. He'll lose his realtor license and we'll toss in a $50,000 fine and a prison term as a bonus. He'll squeal about Hurst when faced with such a bleak future."

I shifted on my chair. "You're probably right, but it might

just end up being a waste of time."

John smiled, but I wasn't sure if it was with me or at me. "You know, Patricia, I'm trying to get the wheels in motion here. It doesn't look as if you've got a grand plan that's going to save the day."

"I'm sorry, I didn't mean to come across that way. You're right, we've got to start pushing forward instead of waiting for things to happen."

"I know you like working on your own, but sometimes you have to accept the help you're given if you want to get somewhere. Even as a cop, you used to be too independent. I thought you would have changed by now."

I stood up. "I know how to work with people, John, otherwise I wouldn't have lasted in this business as long as I have."

"Okay, just don't put yourself in a compromising position. I don't want to grieve for the rest of my life."

"You won't, trust me, I know how to look after myself."

He smiled again and pulled another cigarette from his silver case.

CHAPTER THIRTY-NINE

Bain gave me a call at his hideaway in Port Melbourne that same evening. Morgan had been visited by a couple of uniforms, and he was spending the night in lock-up after getting a little more aggressive than was legally tolerated. He got his nose broken again for his trouble, and I couldn't bring myself to feel sorry for him. He had been so standoffish when we visited him the other day, whatever beating he received since then, he clearly earned it.

Early the next day Gérald left for work with Garvy and his collection of handguns. Mr. Ammo had been staying at our apartment with Tyron. They played cards in the kitchen until around one in the morning.

Tyron was still sleeping. His snoring sounded like one of the garbage trucks that woke up the neighbourhood at the crack of dawn. After Garvy went to bed, Tyron stayed up all night with the TV switched on to some cable sport channel that broadcast live college football from the States. I didn't have the heart to wake him up since he had been keeping vigil when the rest of us were sleeping like white mice in a college lab. When I peeked in his room, it smelled musky. His muscles were bulging from under the white sheets, and the barrel of his sawn-off rifle pointed in my direction like an accusing index finger.

Back in the kitchen, I washed down a multivitamin with black coffee, and half an hour later I was sitting in my office on Chapel Street. I shouldn't have been in at work alone, given that someone had already been using me as target practice.

The front page of the paper told me that the troubles in Iraq were still in full swing. I was flicking through the real estate section when the door was kicked open without warning, sending the deadlock flying to the middle of the room.

Hurst stormed in and slammed the door.

"Who the fuck do you think you are?" he screamed. He wore a burgundy shirt and black trousers that made him look more like a crook than a detective.

"I'm sorry, but did we have an appointment?" I flicked through the pages of my desk calendar. "Not that I can see. Look, I'm kind of busy at the moment, so why don't you come back some other time?"

He threw darts with his eyes. "You fuckin' bitch, someone ought to teach you a lesson."

"I really don't give a damn whether you fancy me as some female dog or not, but unless you have something to discuss, then I suggest you pack your attitude and leave my office immediately."

He pulled a semi-automatic from the holster under his jacket and aimed it straight at my face. "I could kill you, and the world would be better off. Give me one good reason why I shouldn't shoot you right now?"

"Because you're the arsehole and I'm just doing my job."

"What's all this shit with Morgan? Did you arrange to have him arrested?"

"As a matter of fact, yes, I did. Apparently he hasn't paid his REIV membership for the past two years and was operating without a license. Now, that's really immoral, isn't it? People like him should be rotting in jail."

He circled my desk and shoved the barrel of the gun right up my nose. "I'm going to have Morgan released, and there's nothing you can do about it."

"Could you please not stick that gun up my nostril?"

"Fuck you."

"I'm sure you want to, but I'm already in a relationship and extra curricula sex is not on my agenda this morning."

He knocked my temple with the butt of his gun.

Before he had time to react, I was up on my feet, pushed his hand holding the gun up in the air and sank my knee into the pit of his stomach.

He went down on all fours.

I snatched the semi-automatic from the floor and removed the magazine, which I tossed straight in the waste basket.

I grabbed him by the roots of his hair and dragged him to the chair facing my desk. He was about to come up again, so I punched him in the temple.

Hurst held on to his ear. "Fuck, this hurts. Where the hell did you learn to fight like that?"

"The Academy of Private Eyeballs, and you thought we didn't learn anything there." I returned to my seat. "Now, are we going to talk, or do you want another clip behind the ear?"

He stood silent for a little while and massaged the side of his head. I didn't want to rush him because I knew that pain was something people needed to overcome before they got back their common-sense.

"You know, Patricia," he finally said, "you have no fuckin' idea what you're getting yourself into."

"I've been trying to find out, but everyone is tossing me the shit end of the stick. Why don't you tell me what you know, and maybe we'll discover that we both have a friendly side to our personalities."

He looked at me eye-to-eye. "You can't prove anything, anyway."

"You know Mohammed didn't kill that boy, don't you? You framed him for god knows what reason. What was it? Money? It usually is. Or there's women, sex and pornography involved in the deal, and I haven't worked it out yet. Please, feel free to join in whenever you're ready."

"You're wasting your time and putting your life in danger, and the lives of everyone around you. You can push all you want, no one's going to talk to you."

"Morgan will."

"No, he won't."

"Faced with a jail sentence longer than Martin Bryant's, he

155

will."

Hurst was still nursing his ear. I began to feel sorry for him.

"Want something to drink?" I asked.

He nodded.

I opened the bar fridge. "I've got beer or beer."

I pulled two bottles without waiting for an answer and passed one over to him.

He unscrewed the top and swallowed half the contents in one go.

I said, "Did you tell Morgan to send those clowns to my office the other week?"

"It was just to get you off the case, no harm intended."

"What about the men in black? And the guy who tried to shoot me on High Street? No harm intended either?"

This time he seemed genuinely puzzled.

He shifted on his seat. "I've got no fuckin' idea what you're talking about."

I let that sink in for half a minute. "Okay, then, you must have some idea of who else wants me out of the game, other than you, of course."

"You know, you're a real pain, Patricia, I'm sure a lot of people want you out of their lives. What makes you think that everything is related to Steven Donnelly?"

He had half a point, but I wasn't going to give him the satisfaction of acknowledging that.

"Let's just say that I don't usually have a firing squad on my tail when I'm doing my job."

"Proves my point that you should let this one go."

"Proves my point that I must be on the right track, and you're just trying to protect your own interests."

He stood up but had to steady himself against the back of the chair. "Yeah, okay, whatever you reckon, I'm out of here. When someone starts snapping your fingers off one at the time, don't come crying to me. I've warned you enough times."

"Shit, Hurst, now you're really scaring me. I think I might just leave the country altogether."

He shrugged. "Do as you please. I've got to get out of here before I throw up all over your desk."

After he left, I finished my beer and picked up the broken

deadlock from under the desk.

CHAPTER FORTY

It was 5.00 a.m. when the call came through. I was fast asleep, somewhere between Alice's wonderland and purgatory. Gérald was still asleep next to me like a newborn who needed his twenty-hour fix.

"Patricia Lunn?"

"Yes?"

"Detective Langford. Do you think you could come straight away to the Victoria Market?"

"Jeez, it's been a while. How have you been?"

"There's been a murder, and you're kind of implicated in it."

He told me the details.

After I hung up, I picked up my clothes from the floor and rushed to the bathroom. I pulled on a pair of jeans and a tee-shirt, and tied my hair back into a ponytail. Blood was rushing through my head, but I wasn't sure if it was because of the lack of sleep or what Langford had just told me.

I rinsed my face in cold water and wiped off the excess water with a clean hand towel.

Tyron was also asleep, but I woke him up by shaking his right leg.

He jumped up on the bed, rifle in hand. "What the—?"

"It's only me," I said. "Get dressed, we've got to go right now."

While he was putting on a pair of fatigue pants and a black shirt, I told him what Langford told me.

He said, "How did he die?"

"Langford didn't say."

"Christ, now the shit's really hit the fan!"

In less than five minutes, we were speeding up King Street, burning as many red lights as possible without causing permanent injuries to ourselves or anyone else.

When we arrived at the Victoria Market on Elizabeth Street, blue and red lights from emergency vehicles were beaming everywhere.

Tyron said, "How many cops do you need to contain one crime scene?"

There were tens of market stallholders trying to get a glimpse of what was going on.

We pulled in behind a marked car and made our way to the white-and-blue crime-scene tape. The whole place smelled of garbage and rotten vegetables. A uniform stopped us when we got there.

"Sorry, can't go in there," he said.

I stepped closer. "Detective Langford asked for me."

"And who might you be?"

I pulled my ID from my back pocket. "Patricia Lunn. He called me."

"Ah, right, that's you. Yeah, just go right through."

He lifted the tape and glanced at Tyron.

"He's with me," I said, and the uniform let him through too.

I saw Langford before he saw me. When I was in uniform, Langford had been my boss but at the time he had not made detective yet. We kind of lost track of one another over the years, so seeing him there with all his hair missing on top reminded me of how time was playing a dirty trick on all of us. We'd always been on friendly terms, and he had been more of a friend to me than a boss. He knew how difficult it was at times to be a woman in a world dominated by men, and he always made sure he was on my side when someone got out of line.

"Langford?" I said.

He was talking to a couple of men dressed in white overalls. He wore grey slacks, and the sleeves of his blue shirt were rolled halfway up his forearms.

Langford made a gesture with his hand to tell me to come forth and blinked nervously.

There was a body on the ground, face down. A pool of blood circled the head like an aureole. Hurst was still wearing the same burgundy shirt and black trousers he had on when he visited my office the previous day.

"How did he die?" I asked.

"Shot twice in the back of the head," Langford said. "He was one of our best men. I want to know why the hell your name and address was found in his pocket."

"Detective Hurst visited me yesterday. I had no idea his life was in danger. I was still trying to protect mine."

"What the fuck is going on here?"

"Might be a case I'm working on. Remember the State vs Bah Sheh Mohammed some ten years ago?"

He tossed me a look that implied I had rocks in my head.

"Hurst was working the case back then. I'm reviewing the details for Smith & Gordon."

"The law firm?"

"Yep."

"Shit, this is going to be a real mess." He scribbled something in his notebook. "You're not in a hurry, are you?"

"Nope, apart from needing another hour's sleep, I've got all the time in the world."

"Good, cause I'd like you to meet me at the St Kilda Road Police Complex in…say… one hour from now."

"Sure."

Tyron and I walked back to the car.

"You think they think you killed him?" Tyron asked.

"Not a chance."

"What makes you so sure?"

"I've never killed anyone in my life, and I've encountered people who deserved to die far more than Hurst did."

"Can't disagree with you on that point." He paused for a

few seconds. "Any idea who might have killed Hurst?"

"Right now, just about anyone he has ever come across."

"Well, that narrows it down then."

"And my guess is that we can draw up a list of the next potential victims. You can include yourself in that one."

"Thanks, your insight is reassuring."

"You're welcome."

CHAPTER FORTY-ONE

"He was our best lead," I said to Tyron.

"Maybe Morgan will open his mouth now that Hurst is gone. We can feed him all this shit about police protection."

At seven in the morning, outbound city traffic was relatively good. We were parked in front of the St Kilda Road Police Complex within ten minutes of leaving the crime scene. The realisation that Hurst had just been murdered was slowly sinking in, and the lack of sleep didn't help me feel rational.

I didn't comment. Tyron was right, if someone wanted to kill someone else, nothing could stop it.

"We're really going to have to watch our backs from here on," I said.

"Not like we haven't been doing so."

"True, but now we can't take anything for granted. I'm going to have to get Gérald to take his leave ASAP. I'll never be able to face another day if something happens to him."

"You know, it's time to step down from your moral pedestal and buy yourself a shining armour. I can get you a Smith & Wesson by tomorrow, 9mm, double-action trigger with a beautiful alloy frame and stainless-steel slide. I bought one for myself last Christmas. I can get you one for a fair price."

"I hear you, Tyron, and don't think it's not on my mind twenty-four hours a day." I reclined the seat on the driver's side and closed my eyes. "I'm going to rest for a little while. Wake me up when Langford gets here."

"Sure thing."

Half an hour later Langford entered the building and Tyron woke me up to let me know. I felt groggy to the point of wanting to throw up. We walked once around the block to get some fresh air before going inside the building. Tyron bought two apple pastries from a coffee shop nearby and ate them both.

"You're lucky you're not a diabetic," I said, "or you wouldn't have made it past the age of ten."

"Ah, come on, these things are full of fruit."

"The only fruit around here is you."

"Yeah, yeah, whatever...."

"You're right, my life ambition is to swallow a bucket of sugar."

"Patricia, why don't you save all the aggression for the bad guys.?"

"I'm sorry, I'm not thinking straight. I didn't particularly like Hurst, but that didn't mean I wanted him to die."

"None of us did."

We climbed up the steps of the building and passed the security checkpoint.

Once in the elevator, Tyron said, "You better keep your emotions under control when we get there. If you fall apart in front of everyone, they're going to pull you off the Donnelly case."

"I'm not falling apart, Tyron, it's just that murder is not something that goes too well first thing in the morning."

Langford was waiting for us with another detective, whom I had never seen before. He was about my age and wore rimless glasses. He seemed a little tired, but then so did the rest of us. His off-the-rack suit was a little too big for him.

We gathered in Langford's office, and Langford introduced us to the unknown detective.

"Detective Coyle will be working with me on this. He knew Hurst quite well, but obviously not well enough to know why he was killed."

The atmosphere in the room was buttery.

Langford turned to Coyle: "Patricia thinks that Hurst's death has something to do with a case she's working on."

"How's that?"

"Have you heard of Bah Sheh Mohammed?" I said.

Coyle shook his head.

I told him as much as I knew, whilst leaving my opinion out of it. That took a good part of ten minutes.

Tyron was standing next to me, his hands behind his back. He seemed somewhat impatient because he had lived through the story like I had, and listening to it all over again was somewhat irritating, a bit like listening to a politician making broken promises.

Coyle said, "So you said that he came by your office yesterday and threatened you?"

"He certainly did," I said. "He shoved his gun up my nose and told me to give him one good reason why he shouldn't kill me."

"Wouldn't that be a good enough reason for you to go and shoot him the next day? I mean, who knows, maybe he was going to come back and finish his job, and you got scared so you decided to jump him first."

I was going to let out some obscenity, but Langford got in first. "Patricia didn't kill Hurst, okay? I've known her longer than I've known you, and she would never do something like that, no matter how threatened she felt."

"All right," Coyle said, "just asking the obvious before we go any further."

You've got a theory on all this?" Langford asked me.

I looked at Tyron and then back at the two detectives. "I think Hurst was double-dealing some ten years ago. He was paid to frame Bah Sheh Mohammed, and he was also paid to get someone else off the hook."

"And who is that someone else?"

"I'm not sure, but at the time Donnelly was going out with a guy named Weinmann, a University of Highton student, and he certainly wasn't the cooperative type."

"And you think this guy killed Donnelly?" Doyle asked.

"Well, maybe he did, maybe he didn't. He comes from a family where money grows on trees, and if he did kill him and someone found out, then it would be the end of his life and his family's reputation. He used to tag along with two friends, who just happen by coincidence to have witnessed Donnelly's kidnapping and pointed the finger at Mohammed. The three of them attended The University of Highton, which is where Donnelly's body was found. It's most likely that Mohammed has never set foot at the university."

Doyle and Langford looked at each other for a few seconds.

"Shit, Patricia," Langford said, "so if what you're saying is true, then who the hell killed Hurst?"

"Maybe the same people who tried to kill me the other day, whoever wants this story buried ten kilometres underground. Hurst kept on saying that I didn't know who I was dealing with."

"Why don't you check Hurst's bankbook?" Tyron asked.

Everyone seemed surprised to hear Tyron's voice.

"Can we look into that?" Langford asked Coyle.

"Sure," Coyle said, "the man's dead, we can look into anything we want."

"You're going back some ten years here," I said. "His bank account might have changed since then. I certainly wouldn't have kept the same one."

We all stayed silent for the next thirty seconds.

"Well," Langford finally said, "we need to find out who these men in black are. If the person who tried to kill you on High Street is the one who killed Hurst, then hopefully the ballistics test should come up with something."

"And I'd be inclined to believe," I said, "that whoever killed Hurst is the same person who paid him a long time ago to frame Mohammed and to deal with Weinmann with caution."

Coyle shifted from around the desk. "I'm not all that convinced that Weinmann is involved in this. The only connection you have here is that he wasn't cooperative."

"Well, actually, the police file doesn't have his name in it. I mean do you find it normal that a bloke gets killed and the boyfriend is not interrogated? He wasn't even on the list of suspects. You know as well as I do that lovers and family members are always the first suspects."

"She's got a point," Langford said. "We're going to have to review the entire Donnelly file here." He turned to me: "I hope you're wrong because if Hurst is corrupt, this whole thing is going to look really bad for the department. You can imagine the joy the dailies are going to have splashing more police corruption headlines all over their front pages."

"It's a small price to pay for justice," Tyron said.

Coyle turned around to face him. "There's no such thing as a small price to pay—Hurst is dead."

CHAPTER FORTY-TWO

Peter Weinmann was at the National Theatre when I called in on him. I had no idea where he would be, but since he never gave me his home address, I thought it better to check out his workplace. He was in his office, going through some paperwork. His door was half-open, so I didn't bother knocking. The creaking of the hinges made him turn around.

"Jesus Christ," he said, "you scared the shit out of me. What the hell are you doing here? Didn't I make it clear that I have no desire to talk to you?"

I moved to the centre of the room. "Good morning to you, too."

"All right, I'm going to have to call security and have you removed."

"I just want to talk to you for five minutes."

"About what?"

"Donnelly."

"I've got nothing to say about Donnelly, I've already told you that. If it's information you want, why don't you go through the proper channels and talk to the detective who was in charge of the investigation."

"I've already done that."

"So why do you keep bothering me?"

"Well, I thought you might be interested to know that Hurst is dead."

"Who?'

"Detective Hurst, the man I'm supposed to be channelling with. But you already know that, don't you?"

"What the hell are you talking about?"

I moved one step forward. "Can I ask you a personal question?"

"Do I have a choice?"

"Steven Donnelly didn't have one when he got killed."

He shifted in his chair. "Why don't you get to the point. I've got a shit-load of paperwork to do here, and I'm not in the mood to indulge you with my time."

"How much did it cost to set up Mohammed?"

He stared at me blankly.

"Or maybe it wasn't you who paid for the deal, but someone who had an interest in protecting you and your clan. Getting warmer?"

"You're fishing deep and wide here, and you know it."

"Really? So, you don't think that whoever arranged to have Mohammed put behind bars has anything to do with Hurst getting bumped off yesterday?"

"This is bullshit," he said and stood from his chair. "You've got no right to come here and accuse me of all this stuff. I mean, who the hell do you think you are?"

"I'm not accusing you of anything, I just want your opinion."

He gathered some files from his desk. "I've got to be somewhere, so why don't you go back the same way you came. And if I see your face around here one more time, I'm going to get a restraining order."

"For what? For doing my job? I don't know if you are aware of it, but I'm licensed by the state to harass people like you."

"Don't you worry, I know which buttons to push."

"I've got no doubt about that, but you keep pushing enough buttons, and one day the only button you'll be pushing is the one attached to the toilet cistern in your cell."

He tossed his paperwork back on the desk and lunged forward.

Before he had time to sink his teeth into my neck, my right knee found its way into the soft pouch of his belly. He went down on all fours and breathed like a Pit Bull Terrier having an asthma attack.

"You fuckin' bitch," he managed to bark.

"Hey! Didn't your mother teach you to watch your language in front of a lady?" I kicked him in the ribs for good measure.

He rolled to the side, saliva trickling from the corner of his mouth.

"There's something that I don't get," I said. "Why would someone who has nothing to do with the death of another person try so hard to obstruct an investigation?"

His eyes met mine. There was a mixture of fear and anger in them.

I went on, "Okay, so maybe you didn't kill Donnelly, but I bet you know who did."

"You can't prove anything," he said. "And nobody is ever going to talk to you, so you're wasting your time anyway."

"I went to charm school, so in the end I always manage to use my charismatic personality to get what I want."

He massaged the spot where I kicked him. "Shit, I think you broke one of my ribs."

I went down and pushed his hand aside. "Let me see." I ran my fingers down his ribcage.

He pulled back. "Ouch!"

"There's nothing broken. You'll probably get some bruising, that's all."

"Where the hell did you learn to kick like that?"

"One of my hobbies. It helps me to relax."

"Jesus, yeah, well, maybe you should try netball. What are you on? Steroids?"

I helped him to get up from the floor. He held on to the corner of his desk.

"Can I get you something?" I asked.

"Yeah, the cupboard behind you, on the third shelf, behind those books, there's a small bottle of scotch. There's a glass in my top drawer."

I pulled the bottle from where he said it was and the glass from the drawer. I poured in a half measure and passed it to him. He drank it in one go and handed it back to me for a refill.

"Fuck, you know," he said, "why the hell did Murray hire you in the first place?"

"I never told you who hired me."

"Yeah, well, it's not the best kept secret." He sat back behind his desk. "I don't know what's with you, but I tell you one thing, you're not getting shit out of me, so why bother in the first place?"

He was right, if people don't want to talk, they won't talk, but in the past two weeks I had gotten pushed around and shot at, so I didn't mind tossing my weight around a bit.

"You don't have to tell me your secrets," I said, "and I can't really force you to. But I'll get to the bottom of this, one way or another, and if I find that you've had anything to do with Donnelly's death, you can bet your bottom dollar that there'll be hell to pay."

"I'm shaking. You come on to me like that one more time, and I'll see you in court on assault charges."

"That was self-defence. You threw yourself at me, remember?"

He didn't reply.

"Well," I said, "if you've got nothing else to add, then I guess I'd better be on my way."

He stared at me. "Messing around with people like that is not going to make you many friends."

"Thanks for the advice, Peter, but I've got enough friends as it is. If I feel the desire to acquire someone new in my life, I'll be sure to give you a call."

When I left his office, I heard the sound of my name, followed by a flood of profanity.

CHAPTER FORTY-THREE

Gérald was working late, so I had decided to take a stroll down the Esplanade. Tyron was asleep at our Port Melbourne retreat because he had been awake all night keeping guard diligently like a sentinel at a border check.

Though the air was warm, most people had gone home, and I was virtually alone enjoying the invigorating smell of the sea. I should have known better than walking around without company, but I refused to change my life so much that I wouldn't be able to go for a stroll whenever I wanted to. I thought that if someone wants to kill you, in the end he probably will. You can't hide in a shoebox forever.

I was getting close to Luna Park and thinking of committing a gastronomical sin, a quick bite at McDonald's. After having come on so strongly to Tyron about his eating habits, I felt a pinch at the back of my conscience. Maybe Tyron had finally succeeded in changing the way I saw food, grab whatever you can, while you can.

And that's when a bullet hit me just below the left ear. At first I thought a wasp bit me, but when I passed my hand to the side of my neck, there was way too much blood. The second bullet got me in the lower back and the third in the left calf. I went down like a sack of potatoes and smashed my right shoulder into the hardness of the concrete. The coppery taste of blood filled my mouth. So this is how you die, I thought, alone by the side of the road like the victim of a hit-and-run accident, bathing in the last amber rays of a stunning sunset.

I somehow managed to roll to my side and saw in the distance, towards the Esplanade Hotel, what looked like the man who shot at me outside Terry Bennett's in Prahran. In fact I was sure it was him, but my vision was getting blurrier by the second, and any certainty I had was slowly fading away.

My killer was coming towards me, his weapon in hand.

To my right, tram 96 was travelling city-bound.

The killer or the tram?

I gathered whatever strength I had left and crawled in front of the tram. The impact was merciless, like plunging head first into a lake of freezing water. I blacked out, but was still somehow conscious about what was happening around. Voices came and went, like distant roaring from far away traffic, and I felt myself floating in the air. It almost felt good, if somewhat a little unfamiliar. I thought of nothing in particular, like when going to sleep with a clear conscience.

And then there was a prick in my arm and long stretches of nothingness.

Sometimes I felt too hot, sometimes too cold.

My throat was dry, and I wanted a drink, but it was as if my whole body had vanished and only my consciousness remained.

More voices and the sound of metal.

The smell of industrial cleaner.

For a while, I didn't want to wake up and return to the harsh reality of life. This place, wherever it might have been, felt like the home I've missed after a long journey away.

And then a voice broke in: "She's waking up."

My eyes hurt from the brightness of the room. Everything was white, the sheets, the partition, the walls, the ceiling, the nurse's uniform.

"Where am I?" I said and felt a burn in my throat.

"At St Vincent's." My nurse was in her early thirties and had a welcoming smile, the type you would expect from an air-hostess or a hotel concierge.

"Can I have some water?"

"Sure."

She turned her back on me for a few seconds and reappeared with a glass of water. "There you go, and don't drink it too fast."

"Thank you."

She held the glass up and I drank from it. In spite of her warning, I gulped my water in five seconds.

"When can I leave this place?"

"Not for a while. You need to give yourself enough time to adjust back to the environment."

She vanished and let me soak in my own despair for almost three hours. I couldn't feel my arms or my legs. And then I remembered what had happened. The bullet that hit me in the lower back might have hit my spine and turned me into a person that would need the company of another twenty-four hours a day. I had never been one to rely on others' charity with ease, and my foreseeable lifestyle was not something I could easily come to grips with.

Tyron walked in the room unannounced.

The nurse was right behind him.

"They called me as soon as you woke up," he said, "but the traffic out there is metal-to-metal."

"How long have I been here?"

"Two weeks."

I let that sink in for half a minute.

"What about Gérald?"

"He's on his way from Clifton Springs."

"Clifton Springs?"

"He is staying as far away as practically possible from the action."

I nodded with approval. "Did they find him?"

"Who?"

"The weasel who shot me."

"Nope. No witnesses either, not even the tram driver who needed counselling after you dented his fender."

I felt a pain in my abdomen. "Don't make me laugh, it hurts like someone pulling teeth."

"Frankly, you're lucky to be alive."

"Is that so?"

"Yep, doctor says another quarter centimetre to the left, and the bullet would have hit a major nerve. If you'd played the lottery that night, you probably would have got a first division prize."

I tried to move, but nothing was responding.

I said, "I can't feel my hands or my arms."

"Doctor's still looking into that."

"How long is it going to take?"

"Dunno, but as soon as I'm told, you'll be the first to find out."

I closed my eyes, and the next time, Gérald was seated on a chair next to me.

He saw me open my eyes and took my hand in his, even though I couldn't feel a thing.

"How are you doing?" he said and pressed his lips against mine.

"Fine, given the circumstances."

"You're going to be okay. As soon as you're ready, we're leaving Melbourne."

There was no need to ask him why. My body wouldn't be able to tolerate another three bullets, let alone one. The killer would come back and finish me when he had learned that I had not been terminated.

"I'm really thirsty," I said. "Could you give me a glass of water?"

The nurse had left a jug and glass by the side table.

Gérald filled up the glass and brought it to my lips. The water was cool and soothed the dryness in my throat.

"Langford is coming to see you," Gérald said. "He should be here any minute."

I wasn't really in the mood for questioning, but if I had been out of it for a couple of weeks already, there was no point in making anyone wait any longer.

"What did he say?" I asked.

"He wasn't too happy. He blames himself for not having you pulled off the case immediately, especially straight after Hurst got shot."

I chewed on his comments and thought about all the wrongs we would be able to undo if time travel was as easy as backing a car from a driveway.

CHAPTER FORTY-FOUR

We stayed in silence for a few minutes. Noise from nurses and trolleys passing by my room were the only distinguishable things inside the hospital. Traffic in the distance reminded me that I was in the city, but I had no idea what the time was.

I was almost asleep when Langford came in with a man in a long white coat.

"How are you doing?" White Coat said.

I shifted my head to the right. "I've seen better days."

He grabbed a chart from the front end of my bed and flicked through the pages. "You're a very lucky woman."

"So everybody keeps telling me, jeez, why don't I suddenly feel overwhelmed by euphoria?"

White Coat smiled. "I'm Dr. Herbert, your best friend for the next few days. I'm sure we'll get on just fine. All you need is a little faith and strong will power."

"The willpower I've got, the faith, I think I left it under the tram a couple of weeks ago."

He shifted to one side of the bed, opposite Gérald.

Langford waited patiently for his turn to talk, like a good customer holding on to his ticket at the deli.

Dr. Herbert said, "Can I be honest with you?"

"Don't tell me you have to amputate anything, or you might as well go straight ahead with a lethal injection. You'll do everyone a favour that way, even the bastard who shot me."

"Well, now, Patricia, I don't want you to feel alarmed. In your state, it's always good to keep a positive mind, and that alone can make a whole world of difference."

I glanced towards Langford to see if he was buying any of this psycho-babble.

He smiled in return with that look Bozo the Clown is so good at doing.

Shit, now I was going to be the girl everyone feels sorry for!

"Okay, doctor," I said, "hit me with the truth."

"Every angle?"

"In plain English, if that's possible."

His chest heaved. "You might never walk or use your arms again, but we won't know for a couple of days."

"Well, that's good, at least I get to keep my head and both my eyes, right?"

Herbert stayed another ten minutes explaining all the medical and technical details of what had happened to the bullet that lodged near my spine, and the one that entered my neck, and the one that got me in the leg. He made me sound as if I were a vehicle that simply needed a tune-up, new parts and a good kick up the backside.

Halfway through the explanation Gérald decided to head back to Clifton Springs because of the two-hour drive. We never got a chance to say our goodbyes properly with everyone eyeing every move we made.

When Dr. Herbert realised I was losing concentration, he decided to leave me alone.

"Just get some rest," he said and he left the room. As if I were capable of doing anything else.

Langford asked if he could stay a few more minutes because he had some important questions to ask me.

"Did you get a look at the sonofabitch?" Langford asked. He was now sitting on the chair that Gérald had occupied for a good part of two hours.

"Enough to know that it was the same man who tried to do me on High Street the previous week."

"Well, I've got five detectives on the job as we speak. It'll only be a matter of time before we get the scum."

"Thanks, I feel totally reassured now. It's like, God, what could possibly go wrong?"

"I don't blame you, Patricia. In fact, I should have told you to pack it in when we found Hurst."

"It's all right, I'm not blaming you either. It's entirely my fault. I had been warned enough times, but I didn't listen. You know what I'm like."

He shifted closer to the bed. "We're working with the media on this one. No one knows you're here."

I tossed him a side-glance.

"You're dead, Patricia. Your funeral was held ten days ago."

I felt as if someone had knocked me on the head with an sledge hammer.

"What about my friends and relatives?"

"Everybody thinks you're dead, other than Gérald, Tyron and me. It's safer that way."

I could have argued with him, but I knew he was right. With my death came peace of mind for everyone involved in the Donnelly case. No one would go after Tyron or Gérald. I wondered how Bain felt since he was the one who gave me the job in the first place.

"Did you tell John Bain?" I asked Langford, just to make sure I had my facts straight.

"Can't do. If someone comes after him, and he snaps under pressure, they'll know you're still out there somewhere."

"You've covered every angle. I knew there was something efficient about you."

"Only doing my job, but my concern is that you don't get hurt anymore than you already have been."

"Thanks, I'm sure it's heartfelt."

He smiled and placed his right hand on top of mine, which might have been effective a month ago, but right now I couldn't feel a thing.

"I've really got to get going," he said, "the wife and the kids are waiting, and my working hours are already long as it is—"

"You go ahead, don't let me keep you. After all, how are you going to explain to your squeeze that you've been spending time with a dead woman?"

"You haven't changed, Patricia, even when I think you've come to the end of your rope, you keep pulling some more. That's a trait I've always admired in you. When this is all over, if you ever want to come back and work for us, I'll put in a good word. We sure could use someone like you around." He grabbed his jacket from the chair next to the bed.

"I'm flattered, but you know my uniform days are over."

"I was talking about making you detective."

The expression in his eyes told me he was serious.

"I'll give it some thought."

He was just about to go through the door when I said, "How's Tyron taking it?"

"Like a five-year-old who's lost his mother at the shopping mall."

CHAPTER FORTY-FIVE

Hospitals are a funny thing. No one likes being a patient, but once you're in, you don't really want to leave.

The good news came two days after Dr. Herbert announced that I might not be able to walk or use my hands again. It began with ants on my fingertips, and then I began to feel my toes. By the end of the week, I was on crutches, not without difficulties, but at least now I had real hope that I would eventually regain full control of my limbs.

When I left the hospital, the sun was high in the cloudless sky, and the brightness of the daylight hurt my eyes.

"Mission accomplished," Tyron said and helped me to sit comfortably on the passenger side of his 4WD. "Now it's a one way ticket to Clifton Springs until you're fully recovered."

"That could take months." I adjusted my seat belt.

"Nobody is in a rush here. Let them all think you're really dead, and then, just when they expect it the least, we'll take them by surprise."

He smiled when he said that.

"You're really looking forward to this, aren't you?" I said.

"Oh, yeah, I'm going to blow those motherfuckers to pieces." He caressed his sawn-off rifle as if it were a man's best friend.

"How's Garvy doing?"

"Feels like a fool that he let anything happen to you."

"But he was assigned to protect Gérald, not me."

"Still, he feels like an incompetent arsehole. That makes two of us."

"Where is he now?"

"With Gérald, like a flea on some pooch's back."

I nodded and realised how Gérald would be fed up having another man scrutinising his every move. Like me, Gérald was fiercely independent, other than wanting to get married ASAP, and his idea of freedom would not include a gun collector tagging along all day.

We passed the Western Ring Road junction and headed straight towards Geelong. I shifted on my seat, unable to straighten my legs to their full length.

"Whose pad is it that we're going to?" I asked.

"A friend of a friend of a friend's."

"Does this friend of a friend of a friend have a name?"

"Better if you don't know."

"Why? I'm not going to have it published in the classifieds."

He looked at me as if I had just drooled all over my tank-top.

"All right then," I said, "don't tell me, I don't care, you know what you're doing."

I lay back on the seat and closed my eyes and fell asleep for a good half hour.

When I woke up, Tyron had pulled into the McDonald's in Corio and was taking change from a teenage girl at the drive-through window.

The cabin smelled like cheeseburgers and French fries.

Tyron tossed a cheeseburger on my lap. "Eat something or I'm going to force-feed you."

I had lost fifteen kilos since I had been in hospital, and I was struggling to get my appetite back. The good thing was that I had no problems whatsoever fitting into my clothes. The downside is that I made Kate Moss look like a beached whale.

I washed down the cheeseburger with a Coke and tossed the empty container into the brown bag that came with our

181

food.

"You know what the odd thing is?" Tyron asked.

"What?"

"The bullets they retrieved from your body don't match those found at Hurt's autopsy."

I chewed on his comment for a few seconds. "So you don't think it's the same person?"

"I didn't say that, but it certainly wasn't the same weapon."

"There might be more than one person who's trying to keep the past buried."

"And that's only going to make matters more complicated."

"Can't argue with that."

He pulled out of the McDonald's car park and headed for the Geelong marina.

"God," I said, "I haven't been in this area for years. It has changed so much. When I was in my late teens, I used to live in Bell Post Hill, not far from here. It was the most depressing time of my life. I had no idea who I was or where I was heading. It's just so weird how life ends up taking care of itself."

Tyron looked at me for a few seconds, down at my legs, and then back at the road. "You not going all philosophical on me, are you?"

"Just thinking out loud, that's all."

"Well, you just hang in there, and we'll get to the bottom of all this."

We stayed quiet for the rest of the way, like a married couple waiting for the divorce papers to come through.

CHAPTER FORTY-SIX

The friend of a friend of a friend's house was hidden in a cul-de-sac, amongst tall trees and only a short walk from the ocean. It was a good hideout, although probably not as good as the Unibomber's one-room shack. The only way the 'bad guys' were going to get to us would be if someone had ingeniously managed to place a tracking device to Tyron's 4WD and had a satellite dish mounted to the rooftop of their own vehicle.

The three-bedroom timber home included an eight-person spa hidden amongst foliage in a separate hut built by the owner. From the back porch, you had an uninterrupted view of the hills and the blue sky. Wildlife had made the landscaped garden its habitat, and I particularly enjoyed spending my first hour awake sitting on a bench and listening to birds' morning choir in the midst of the rose bushes that surrounded the property. The earth smelled wet and flowery.

We spent the evenings in front of the television and watched videos that Tyron or Gérald had rented from the local Video Ezy. I had not seen some of those films for over a decade, and I have to admit that movies like *St Elmo's Fire* and *Basic Instinct* had dated rather badly, to the point of making the whole experience of watching them laughable.

During the day, I was forced to do some exercises to get my muscles and bones used to the bodily movements most people take for granted. Tyron helped with the workouts because he just enjoyed exercising by nature, and he gave me the psychological lift I needed when life seemed too much of a burden to bother with. And because we had been working out for years at Terry Bennett's, we had developed an effective routine that was as close to clockwork as humanly possible. We used a spare bungalow next to the spa room, which Gérald had furnished into a small gymnasium, complete with hand weights, a floor mat and a full-length mirror. The struggle I was enduring to regain the function of my legs and arms fuelled me with enough anger to realise that the day we returned to the city, my whole life would be devoted to finding the bastard who got me trapped in this purgatory.

Afternoon exercise consisted mainly of slow, long walks up and down the coastline and conversations filled with plans for days to come. As much as I was in turmoil with my body, I had not felt such peace in my life for a very long time. I had no bills to pay. Langford was taking care of all my financial needs through the Victims Special Fund, and I had income insurance, and no clients to see. It was as close to early retirement as I would ever get, and I could see clearly that it was a lifestyle I could get accustomed to.

On the Wednesday of the second week at our hideaway, we were walking the beach at St Leonards, Gérald on one side of me and Tyron on the other, like Madonna and two of her bodyguards. The world seemed so serene in this area that I really didn't feel the need to go back to the city with all its lunacy and mayhem.

Tyron said, "Someone could easily be behind one of those bushes," he pointed towards the main road, "and take the three of us in one go."

"With what?" I said. "Poisoned arrows?"

"I was thinking more in terms of a Holland & Holland fitted with a telescopic sight mount."

Gérald lifted his brows.

"A rifle fitted with a monocular lens," I explained. Then to Tyron: "Assuming they know where we are."

"Oh, it's probably just a matter of time. If they can buy the police, there's no telling how far they can go."

"Your confidence is reassuring, but I don't intend hanging around here long enough for our names to appear into the obituaries of the local rag."

I struggled to get to the last length of the beach that led to the pier. Often the mind was more than willing during those long walks, but the body lagged behind like of a cripple.

Within two months, my bodyweight was slowly creeping back to its former self, and I could even observe some roundness in my thighs. I worried somewhat at the prospect of never being able to undertake professional taekwondo again. The ability to defend oneself physically is far more reliable than private health cover.

Each day began to blend into the other, and soon we all lost track of what day of the week it was. At dinner, we talked too much, ate like monks at a monastery, and drank beer and wine in the same fashion. We were doing what retirees did around the area—nothing, and it was everything I had hoped it would be.

Early one morning, when my body seemed to function much better than it had since we'd moved to Clifton Springs, Tyron called me outside. I stood by the porch. He was holding his sawn-off rifle and polishing it with a yellow terry cloth.

"Want to learn target practice?" he said.

I thought he was kidding, but when I met his eyes, they weren't smiling.

"Sure," I said, "give me a minute, and I'll be down."

CHAPTER FORTY-SEVEN

I've never been particularly fond of firearms, but the moron who'd managed to put my life on hold most likely didn't reside on the same level of consciousness. Tyron had made that message loud and clear a few months back, but at the time I had not been ready to listen. Funny how a near-death experience forces you to accept yourself in ways you would never have thought possible.

"The neighbours are not going to complain?" I asked.

"No neighbours around here to complain about anything," Tyron said. Our closest neighbour was some two kilometres away.

Tyron and I were facing a line-up of empty beer bottles standing against the edge of the fence in the backyard.

"But a gunshot is not a radio turned on too loud," I insisted. "Someone might hear the shots and call the cops."

His eyes met mine. "Do you want to do this or not? If it's an excuse you're looking for, I can think of a million reasons not to bother with target practice."

I shrugged. "Let's do it then before I change my mind."

He removed the safety catch from the rifle, aimed at the line-up of beer bottles and shot twice. Two bottles exploded.

The loudness nearly burst my eardrums. The smell was acrid.

"Christ, Tyron, you're not scared of going deaf?"

He pulled a small, yellow plastic container from his right pocket and passed it to me. "One plug in each ear and all you'll hear is the sound of your blood pumping in your brain."

I did what he told me, but the ringing in my ear had already settled and would not stop bothering me for the next couple of days.

We spent the next hour killing empty beer bottles. I was waiting for two representatives from the community glass-recycling program to pounce on us and preach about the irresponsibility of our action. How dare we waste perfectly recyclable glass and not protect our beaches from further pollution and dilapidation?

I mentioned something to Tyron about our responsibilities as local citizens.

"For fuck's sake, Patricia, with everyone recycling glass these days, I doubt that shooting two dozen beer bottles is going to make a difference in the great scheme of things."

I pointed the barrel of the rifle to the ground. "Yeah, but if everyone thinks the way you do, there wouldn't be any recycling taking place."

"All right, since you're such a good samaritan, why don't you go and collect all the shells and bullets from the yard so that we don't bring lead and copper poisoning into the area."

"I might just do that."

I spent the next hour cleaning up our mess. This wasn't my turf and until I returned home, I felt the need to respect other people's property.

That same evening, we were sipping on light beer and watching re-runs of Law & Order on cable TV.

Tyron pulled a pistol from his backpack. "Heckler and Koch USP, double action, 9mm Para, 15 rounds, three-dot sights, windage adjustable, safety catch, de-cocking lever and automatic firing-pin safety, check it out."

He passed me the weapon. It had a black coated finish with a steel slide and frame-integrated grip. "Do you memorise all this information when you go to bed?"

"It's like buying a car," he said, "you have to know what's

under the bonnet before you commit."

"Where did you get it?"

"Special delivery. Picked it up from some underground dealer in Queenscliff while you were busy cleaning the backyard this afternoon."

The gun felt fairly heavy in my hand, but I knew it was because I was still weak from having been shot and hospitalised. "What do I owe you?'

"It's a gift to celebrate your rite of passage from martial artist to shooter extraordinaire."

I felt somewhat humbled knowing that buying an unregistered weapon on the black market cost three times the retail price of one over the counter. "You know, I would have got one eventually. You didn't have to go out of your way."

"Believe me, it wasn't a problem, and I got a discount for bulk purchase."

Gérald laughed. "What are you up to? Setting up your own militia?"

"The way the government is running this country," Tyron said, "it wouldn't be such a bad idea."

"Right," I said, "let's give everyone a weapon so that they can take the law into their own hands. Come on, Tyron, the average person hasn't got enough up there to be trusted with a weapon. Just look at what they've done to America."

Tyron shrugged. "I was only kidding, bloody hell, chill out, don't be so uptight."

Gérald and I looked at each other and chose not to reply.

Tyron said, "We can go and target-practice tomorrow, if you want."

I held the gun in my hand and aimed at the television set. As much as I wasn't keen on fire power, I had to admit it felt comfortable in my hand, like an expensive pair of gloves.

"Nice, euh?" Tyron asked.

I turned the H&K around. "Okay, it's nice, I admit."

"It's all in the way it makes you feel, Patricia. Two hundred years of handgun design is going to improve the product somewhat. These days you can get any colour, any size, engineered to accommodate your lifestyle."

"Comforting to know that weapon manufacturers have my lifestyle in mind when it comes to blowing someone's brain to

188

bits."

Gérald stood from the couch. "I'm hitting the sack before this conversations turns into a civil war."

"I'll join you in a minute," I said.

When Gérald left the room, we stayed silent for a little while.

"I really do appreciate the gun," I finally said.

Tyron shifted on his seat. "Don't mention it. I know you were not going to get one, so I thought I would take the initiative."

"You've probably done the right thing, even though it's going to take me a little while to get used to carrying this thing around."

"Ah, before you know it, you'll even be sleeping with your toy. When thunder hits, you'll be ready to strike back."

"To be honest with you, I hope I'll never have to use it."

With that, I left Tyron in front of the television and took the gun to bed with me.

After brushing and flossing, I joined Gérald between the sheets. He was reading a French paperback novel. I played with the safety catch of my H&K.

Gérald observed me from the corner of his eye. "You're not going to sleep with that, are you?"

"Does it bother you?"

"Well, yeah, it does. What if it goes off accidentally in the middle of the night?"

"Then one of us will have to be rushed to hospital."

He put his paperback down. "That's not funny, Patricia, not after what's happened to you."

I made sure the safety catch was on and placed the gun by the side-table. "Don't worry, I have no intention of leaving it under the pillow."

"*Bon Dieu*, why do I suddenly feel so reassured?"

"Come on, sweetie, don't be so dramatic."

His fingers touched my lips. "It's just that I am worried about you, I don't want you to get hurt again."

"Well, that's what the gun is for, protection."

"You've been listening to Tyron for too long. All this gun business is making me feel rather edgy."

I pulled him closer to me, the smell of his jasmine shampoo feeding my senses.

His finger brushed my right cheek. "Do you feel strong enough for a little love serenade?"

"You'll just have to be gentle with me."

We made love slowly, like soft summer waves crashing against the hot, white sand.

CHAPTER FORTY-EIGHT

Tyron and I woke up early to a breakfast of eggs, grilled tomatoes and wholemeal toast, and by nine o'clock we were shooting bottle targets in the yard. It took me a while to get used to the weight of the gun.

"You're holding eight-hundred grams with your arm stretched," Tyron said. "It's not that hard to remain steady."

"But the damn thing keeps on jumping every time I shoot."

"That's because you're not holding the gun properly. You need to be firm but relaxed at the same time. It's like holding a tennis racket, tight grip, but loosen your muscles in the upper and lower arm."

He made a V-curve at my right arm's joint.

"Now," he said, "instead of pressing the trigger, squeeze the whole gun. One shot, one squeeze. One shot, one squeeze."

I squeezed.

One green bottle on the fence exploded like a firecracker.

I aimed and squeezed again.

Another green bottle blown to bits.

Tyron re-loaded the gun for me. "Very good, you're a natural."

I smiled. This was actually more fun than I had imagined. Maybe I was turning into a trigger-happy moron.

"You think you'll be able to do it when it's a live target?" Tyron said.

"Don't worry, my compassion for bad guys has just about hit a wall. I'll blame it on self-defence if I have to."

"I don't need an excuse to blow the motherfuckers away I'll do it in the name of justice," he said.

Bang, bang, bang!

Tyron blew the rest of the bottles away with his sawn-off rifle.

I said, "Jesus, Tyron, where's all this anger coming from?"

"Some people drink, some people shoot up, some people visit whores. I like to blow up a few things now and then, it helps me to relax. You'll see, you're going to sleep like a baby tonight."

I collected the casings and bullets from the lawn, and Tyron placed the broken bottles into a recycling bin. When we came back inside the house, Gérald was making French pancakes with sauté mushroom in a Chardonnay sauce.

"Smells damn nice," Tyron said. To me: "You should get shot more often. At least we get to eat gourmet food twice a day."

We ate like school kids who'd been in class all morning without a break.

"We're going to have to work off all these calories this afternoon," Tyron said. "Gérald, want to come with us?"

"Don't think so. I'm going return the videos and get some food for tonight. I'll workout after you've finished yours. Room's too small for three people."

"Suit yourself."

Gérald took the car to town while Tyron and I did the dishes. I washed, he dried.

Half an hour later, we were in the bungalow-turned-gym. We did the obligatory stretches and headed straight for the bench press.

I went first. "We should have waited for digestion to finish before working out."

"Nah," Tyron said. "Old wives' tale. Better to work out straight after lunch. Saves you from the afternoon slump and you've got plenty of energy on reserve."

Tyron was spotting me doing a bench press with fifty pounds on each side. "Take it easy," he said. "Are you sure you're ready for this?"

"Time to get the show on the road. Okay, here we go."

I took a deep breath and lifted the barbell above my chest. Tyron kept his hands under the bar but without actually touching it.

"Just let me know when you can't anymore," he said.

I didn't reply but took a deep breath instead.

Down inhale.

Up exhale.

Down inhale.

Up exhale.

The muscles in my chest were tearing like paper.

"Come on," Tyron said, "you can do it."

Down inhale.

Up exhale.

Down inhale.

Up exhale.

You can do it, you can do it, you can do it.

Based on my mental calculation, I was only two away from ten reps.

The mind was willing, but my muscles were cramping up.

"Take it up," I said between two breaths.

Tyron obliged. He placed both hands on the bar and pulled it up to the rack.

"Damn it! I was so close. I'm going to make it, you know, it's not like I'm giving up or anything."

Tyron gently placed the bar on the rack above my head. "It's only you and me here, you don't have to prove anything."

I jumped from the bench and went straight for the punching bag.

One, two, three. I punched repetitively as if my whole life depended on it.

Tyron came up behind me. "Will you just take it easy?"

"I'm going to get through this even if it kills me."

"I know, I know, but destroying yourself is not going to help the healing."

He was right of course.
There was always tomorrow.

CHAPTER FORTY-NINE

There had been a summer storm overnight, the biggest one for the past one hundred years according to the morning paper. People were left stranded on flooded highways, and roofs were peeled from houses like lids from tin cans. Outside, in the yard where Tyron and I had been engaged in target practice, broken branches lay like cards scattered on a coffee table.

Beach sand had somehow managed to find itself in the middle of the road, but this was more likely due to sewerage flowing backwards from the ocean nearby than raging wind. Everywhere it smelled of seawater.

I walked with Tyron down the main streets of Clifton Springs to assess the damage. Rubbish lined the gutter, milk cartons, drinking cans, plastic shopping bags, leaves of all sorts, and rubbish bins left for collection had been knocked on their side, their contents displayed for everyone to see. Some pathways were gorged with rainwater, making it impossible to walk along them without getting soaked up to the knees.

Tyron said, "I haven't seen anything like this since I was a toddler."

I looked at the mess all around me. "Maybe the gods are trying to tell us something."

"Like what?"

"Like the world could end today, so whatever we have planned for the future, we might as well stop putting it off and begin working on it now."

We wanted to go for a jog down on the beach, but the storm had made everything soft and hazardous. Gérald was home cooking lunch. He was never into fighting the elements, so he refused to come with us.

The aftermath reminded me of the first day of the millennium when Gérald and I walked the city from the top of Swanson Street down to Flinders Street Station. People were strolling in a mist of tiredness, confusion and relief. The world had not ended the previous night, computer systems had not crashed, and the 1st of January was just another day. Mortgages still had to be paid, washing had to be hung on the line, and politicians still ruled the world, and doing a shockingly bad job at that.

We walked past a milk bar not far from a boat ramp. A sea breeze caressed everything it encountered, and all in all, it wasn't a bad sort of a day. The calm after the storm.

Tyron said, "Whenever you feel ready to go back home, just yell out."

"I need to work on my looks first. I think I'm going to go bimbo blonde."

"Sounds like you need therapy."

"You don't seriously think I can go back to Melbourne looking exactly the way I did two months ago? It's not like someone's not going to recognise me."

"You've lost a lot of weight, Patricia, so you don't look like your former self anyway."

"I can see that, but my face is still my own, and I don't intend to walk around town wearing a balaclava. I'm supposed to be dead, remember? It wouldn't take long for someone to figure out that I'm not."

"Okay, but bimbo blonde?"

"At least I get to find out if blondes do have more fun."

"Well, I guess you will bring in the element of surprise. Poor bastard who shot you won't even know what hit him."

I smiled.

After another one of Gérald's succulent lunches, baked potatoes with bacon cubes and fresh sour cream, Tyron and I headed back to the gym in the bungalow.

I still felt the pain from the previous day, but I knew I had to persist. I needed to gain back the full strength of my body in order to face the invisible enemy. All my senses had to be sharp and finely tuned, not like that last time when I was so busy with my own thoughts I didn't see death crawling down my back like a redback going for the kill.

We did our stretches and headed straight for the bench press.

"Same as yesterday?" Tyron asked.

"Fifty pounds per side," I said.

We lifted the barbell into position, and I lay on the bench.

Tyron stood at the top end of the bench. "And don't be a hero, you're not going to be any good to anyone if you end up in hospital again."

I closed my eyes, cleared my mind and placed both hands on the barbell. "Hit me."

Tyron lifted the weights from the rack, pushed the bar slightly forward and let go.

My arms took the whole weight to begin, but after I lowered the bar, my chest was doing most of the work.

Down inhale.

Up exhale.

Down inhale.

Up exhale.

Five down, five to go.

"Take it easy," Tyron said.

Down inhale.

Up exhale.

Down inhale.

Up exhale.

Two to go.

The tenth rep felt like needles piercing my lungs. The blood rushed through my temples, and I swore it was about to come out my nose.

"Okay, okay," Tyron said, "that's enough."

And then in my mind's eye, I saw the bastard who shot me in front of Luna Park. He was aiming his gun and firing point blank.

Bang, bang, bang!

One bullet below the left ear.

One in my lower back.

The last one in my left calf.

I pushed the weights up with all the rage I could muster. My arms had turned to steel. *Think machine, think machine, no pain, think machine.*

"Hey, hey, hey," Tyron said, "take it easy!"

Down inhale.

Up exhale.

Down inhale.

Up exhale.

I stopped at the sixteenth rep and felt the sweat trickle down the nape of my neck.

"Sonofabitch is going to pay for this," I said.

"Then just make sure you have enough energy left when you get to that point."

I looked up from the bench and matched his stare. "I'm much stronger than I look, Tyron."

"You don't have to convince me, I'm on your side."

We spent another hour and a half pumping iron like two athletes on steroids.

CHAPTER FIFTY

The week that followed was the one in which I made the best physical progress. The fifty pounds per side on the bench press had reached sixty by midweek, and I wasn't in more pain as a result. I did one workout in the morning and one in the afternoon. My diet was now supplemented with protein powder derived purely from egg white. My mind was in maximum gear and I felt better than I did before I got shot in front of Luna Park.

In the evening I went for a jog down by the ocean, but it took a while for my breathing to become adjusted. Every five minutes or so, I broke down to a walk, and when I caught my breath again, I accelerated, my feet splashing the edge of the saltwater, the smell of freedom feeding my brain like a junkie's last shot for the day.

In the distance, the skyline and the sea were almost one, and I found it hard to tell where one began and the other ended.

When I finished my run, I sat on the beach and tried to take it all in. Life wasn't as complicated as we made it out to be. It was simply a matter of choosing between A and B.

Tyron and I still practised our shooting skills every day, usually after lunch. I was getting much better with the H&K,

and one afternoon Tyron even suggested that I should join a gun club once I returned to Melbourne.

"You don't want all those skills to go to waste," he said as he re-loaded his sawn-off riffle.

"You're right, never know when the occasion might present itself when I will be forced to fill someone's head with lead."

He emptied his load into three stubbies lined-up at the back of the fence.

I said, "Don't know why you're practising. I haven't seen you miss a bottle yet."

"To keep you company, and it helps me sleep better at night."

I unloaded the contents of the H&K into the other three bottles and felt the adrenalin pump in my veins like acid.

CHAPTER FIFTY-ONE

Coming back home after a long break is never easy. St Kilda felt like a foreign country after having spent six months in Clifton Springs. Both were seaside suburbs, but it was like comparing a table with a chair.

My hair was bimbo blonde like I had intended, and my skin supple and coppery. My biceps were little lumps of steel. I pierced both my ears and choose gold sleepers as my weapon of choice. Aqua-coloured contact lenses added a finishing touch to my metamorphosis. Even I had trouble recognising myself in front of the mirror. It was like facing a twin who had suddenly re-appeared after going missing for twenty years.

Tyron had grown a long, shaggy beard that reminded me of Saddam Hussein when he got captured by US soldiers. Gérald was the only one who still looked like his former self. He resumed his work at the hospital so as to not raise any suspicion.

The inside of our apartment off Marine Parade was covered in dust, and it took us two good hours to get everything cleaned up. I opened all the windows to let the smell of seawater take over the place.

Tyron decided that he would stay with us for a little while, and he was more than welcome. We'd become so close to one another during our time in exile, I found it difficult to imagine him not being a part of my daily routine.

Wednesday morning, Tyron and I ate breakfast at Deveroli's, poached eggs, sausages, toasted bread, grilled tomatoes, capsicums and mixed salad. It had been months since I had been there, but my stomach wasn't complaining. It was good to be home, even if it felt a little strange, like moving back to the suburb you lived in as a kid.

Tyron sipped from his cappuccino and checked me out. "What do you think the odds are that someone's going to recognise you?"

"As likely as you becoming a supermodel."

He shook his head. "Stranger things have happened."

"You're probably right, but I think I'll place my bet on the obvious."

He resumed drinking his cappuccino.

"How are we holding up financially?" he said.

"I've got it covered."

"With what?"

"That's really none of your business."

He passed one hand over his bushy beard. "Wow, aren't we getting a little hostile here?"

I paused for a second. "Sorry. Must be the bacon in my breakfast. Not used to eating swine first thing in the morning." Then: "We had life insurance. When I got shot, I collected twenty thousand bucks for every bullet hole."

"Aren't you supposed to be dead?"

"Thought about that, but if Gérald collects the two-hundred thousand as a result of my death, we will have had to pay it back on resurrection day, not to mention being charged with fraud."

"Good point. What's the big plan?"

"I'll just lay low and spend my time painting my toenails fluorescent pink. Who knows, someone might just snap me up for the cover of Vogue."

"Shit, Patricia, at least you haven't lost your sense of stupidity."

"It's the company I keep."

"You are turning into a bitch, though."

We both laughed quietly and watched passers-by enjoying the summer sun.

That same afternoon my friends at the St Kilda Road Police Complex issued me with a full set of fake IDs, including a driver's license, passport, and two credit cards. My name was Tanja Barrett, and I was Gérald's new squeeze. Bastard got over my former self really quickly, especially at night when we were making love with the window open and the sound of the ocean drifting in like a caress against our bare skin.

"That blonde hair really suits you," he said as we lay in bed like a couple of seals stranded on the shore.

I turned to face him. "I thought you liked brunettes?"

"I do, but blondes do have a certain *je-ne-sais-quoi*."

"Such as?"

"I don't know, this look of freedom and carelessness, you know what I'm talking about."

"No idea, I've always considered myself free and exotic."

"Well, that hasn't changed."

"Yeah, try to smooth things over, why don't you?"

He caressed my bottle-blonde hair. "I don't have to do that, I'd love you even if you were bald and chinless."

"That's reassuring, but I'm keeping my chin, and I've got no intention of joining a skinhead militant group."

"Ah, ah, but you own a gun now."

"That's only to help someone with full facial reconstruction."

"Well, as long as it's not me."

He pressed my naked body against his.

"Don't push your luck," I said and kissed him.

CHAPTER FIFTY-TWO

Tyron and I were into some heavy cooking duties, and for the first time in my life, I had to admit that I was actually enjoying the whole process. We began with simple dishes, like pasta carbonara, and moved on to more elaborate things, Thai chicken curry, garlic king prawn kebabs, rice ribbon noodles with beef in oyster sauce, herbed leg of lamb.

I was slicing up carrots for a ratatouille, and Tyron was dicing beef into strips.

Tyron said to me, "What are we doing next week?"

"Get the bastard before he figures out that I'm still running around."

"The bastard is the guy who shot you, right?"

"You're very perceptive."

"Comes with the culinary skills."

I tossed the first sliced carrot into a bowl and began with a second one. "As long as he thinks I'm dead, he's not going to come running after me. If we give him too much time, he will figure out that I'm still alive and kicking, and then we're back to square one."

"That's it, that's the big plan?"

"Yeah, well, basically, he's the type of person who goes

around looking for prey, he'll never expect what's coming."

"The predator becomes the prey, and the prey the predator."

"Now I know why you're on such a good salary."

He giggled. "That's funny, Patricia, but on the subject of salary, you haven't paid me for three months, so—"

"I know, and I'm sorry. It's completely slipped my mind. You'll have the money in your account this afternoon."

He grabbed another chunk of beef and began dicing. "And what happens after you get him?"

"I'll find out who killed Donnelly."

"That easy, euh?"

I transferred the chopped carrots to a cooking dish. "No, Tyron, it probably won't be easy. But with you around, I guess the case is as good as closed."

"Can't argue with that."

After lunch, I deposited $10,000 into Tyron's account via Internet banking. That night, while Gérald was sound asleep after a twelve-hour shift at the hospital, I closed my eyes and dreamt about the hitman.

But this time I was doing the shooting.

CHAPTER FIFTY-THREE

From the look of the office, it was impossible to tell that Patrick Reilly was tied to the agency responsible for the majority of 'legal' assassinations in this country. There were no signs on the door of the room he occupied above a take-away pizza shop on Brunswick Street. There were no pictures or anything at all attached to the walls. Next to his desk stood a grey filing cabinet that was rusting at the corners. The room smelled like mothballs. He worked from a silver laptop, the type that could set you back five grand, fully equipped with wireless internet access, bluetooth technology and regular maintenance. He wore a standard, yellow business shirt and a purple tie. He was a bulky man with a full set of hair, which was kind of unusual for someone in his mid-forties.

"Patricia Lunn?" he asked.

I closed the door behind. "In the flesh."

"Jesus Christ!" He stood from his chair. "I didn't recognise you immediately with the new hairdo. What are you doing? Working Grey Street part-time these days?"

I closed the door of his office. "I'm in hiding."

His eyes lit up like two bulbs in darkness. "Shit, yeah, aren't you supposed to be dead?"

"Didn't like it much, too quiet for me."

"Well, I'll be fucked." He sat back behind his desk. "Take a seat."

When I sat, the leather of the chair squealed like a kitten.

Reilly leaned forward. "You look great, you really do. Blonde hair suits you, you know? You should have done that a long time ago."

"Yeah, it seems to have a strange effect on men, they start sucking their thumbs and buying me presents."

Reilly smiled awkwardly. "I see that your attitude hasn't changed."

"Comes with the territory."

"Still working for Langford?"

"Not for the past ten years."

"So it's true."

"What?"

"You being a private eyeball and all."

"Best job in the world, apart from the bit where you get used for target practice."

He played with his fat fingers. "Yeah, I heard that one." He shifted some paperwork on his desk. "What can I do you for?"

"I'm looking for the guy who forced me to change my hair colour."

"Uh-huh."

"Langford pointed me in your direction."

"Why? He's got his head so far up his arse he can't do the legwork for you?"

"Let's just say that you've come highly commended, and I don't have time to deal with red tape."

Reilly shifted towards the window and his eyes followed a tram travelling north on Brunswick Street. He made a good impression of looking like someone who was contemplating his options, but I knew he had already made up his mind the moment I stepped into his office.

He turned his attention back to me. "I've got no real reason to help you here."

"Do you want me to give you one?" I flicked my blonde fringe and began to undo my yellow blouse.

He blinked quickly. "You don't have to do this, Patricia. I don't work that way. But…if…"

I ignored him and tossed the blouse on the seat next to me.

I turned around, and with the index finger of my right hand, I pointed to the bullet wound in my lower back. "Is that a good enough reason?" I pulled off my stockings and showed him the bullet wound on my left calf. "There's another reason for you." I grabbed my blouse back. "What else do you want me to do? Suck your dick?"

If he had been a traffic light, he would have caused a major pileup.

"All right, Patricia, I get the point." He passed one hand over his round face. "You can get dressed now."

I buttoned my blouse, pulled up my stockings and sat back on the chair. "Good, at least now we can talk man-to-man."

His brain rattled like a half-empty box of cereal.

"Did you have a good look at him?" he asked.

"Enough to give you a description."

"I'm listening."

I told him the way I remembered it.

"Sounds like a professional, a loose cannon."

"A loose cannon?"

"Means we trained him, used him, and eventually he decided he didn't need us anymore. Happens all the time. Many end up leaving the country and working as mercenaries or get recruited by an overseas intelligence agency, mostly the CIA. Good shooters and professional killers are hard to find. Trained ones are a gold mine. Sounds like the bloke you're talking about is getting enough work in Australia to not bother going anywhere else."

I digested his words for half a minute. "Any chance of figuring out who he is?"

"Hard to tell. I'll have to run a check on who's deserted the agency lately and not relocated overseas. With fake IDs and dodgy bank accounts, it doesn't mean I'll get a name."

"If you could get cracking, I would be more than grateful."

He smiled. "Well, as you can see I'm flat out here, but for you Patricia, I'll see what I can do." He wrote something on a notepad. "You're still hanging around with what's-his-name-Maori-bloke?"

"Tyron."

"Yep, Tyron, the one who's built like a mountain."

"We're still together. He needs me as much as I need him."

"Good to hear."

I stood from my chair. "Well, thanks for your time. I got some leads to chase up."

"Uh-huh." He shook my hand. "You better watch your arse. If we trained this bloke, you've got little chance of catching him alive. If you do, he'll kill you before you get a chance to find him."

"Thanks for the warning."

"You're welcome."

I tossed my business card on his desk and aimed for the door.

I could feel his stare on my butt like a fishing hook.

CHAPTER FIFTY-FOUR

Two hours had gone since I had seen Reilly in his office. I was in my home office budgeting the next three month's rent and bill payments. The window was wide open, and the smell of seawater drifted in. I had just swallowed a cup of black coffee and was about to make myself another when my mobile phone rang.

"I got a name for you," Reilly said. He sounded distant, as if he were talking through a speaker-phone.

"Shoot."

"J. J. Logan."

"What does the J.J. stand for?"

"First one is Joseph, second one I wouldn't have a clue."

"What about background information?"

He hesitated. "You're on a safe line?"

"It's a new pre-paid account under a fake name. Keep talking."

"Okay, okay, just making sure." He paused for a few seconds. "He's ex-agency, I was right. Voluntary discharge. Got carried away in his assignments and ended up with a higher body count than what was required. According to inside information, Logan is a fruitcake. He actually enjoys killing more than target shooting."

I played with the telephone cord. "There's a difference?"

"Well, yeah, professional killers disassociate themselves from the victims otherwise they wouldn't be able to do the job. This bloke, however, gets off on the actual killings rather than the marksman skills. And it makes him an exceptionally dangerous man. Trying to find him might not be in your best interest."

"I think you already made your point clear when we met at your office this morning. Anything else you can tell me?"

"Works mainly in Sydney and Melbourne, but if the pay is good, he'll go just about everywhere. Takes half up front, half on completion, plus expenses. If he doesn't do the job properly, you get a full refund, no questions asked. To date, he's got a 100% success rate, not including you, of course, but he doesn't know since he thinks you're dead."

"How do I find this shit-for-brains?"

"Well, it's where I drew a blank. He's well protected in all the wrong milieus, so tracking him down is like Chinese water torture. He's pretty much an underworld figure, as one would expect."

"Mmmm…so what do you suggest?"

"I don't know, get in touch with people who live on the seedy side, you'll have a better chance than by asking the cops."

"I'll give it a shot."

"Good. If there's anything else you want, don't bother calling me."

"I won't. Thanks anyway."

"My pleasure."

I pressed the end button and finished my accounting work.

CHAPTER FIFTY-FIVE

Tyron and I were shooting beer bottles at Woodlands Historic Park, a twenty-minute drive north-west of Melbourne. The place was deserted, and it was just as well, because what we were doing was not totally legal, although there was no one around to tell us so. High dry grass and eucalyptus trees managed to survive on the dry, red earth left untouched for thousands of years. The entire area smelled of heat and dust. We drove to the location in Tyron's 4WD because the roadster would have had difficulties manoeuvring along the dirt road.

"I've spoken to Bud," Tyron said, "and he's arranging a little meeting with someone who might have used Logan in the past." He wore drill pants and a black tee that hugged his frame like a second skin.

I knocked three bottles out with my H&K. My grip was firm and my arm repositioned itself as if it were made of rubber.

Tyron smiled. "You're getting good at this shit. Maybe you'll be able to shoot Mr. Logan before he shoots you in the next round."

"Let's hope it doesn't get there." I changed my clip and added, "I thought Bud was small time. How would he know anything about Logan?"

"Small-time crooks know medium-sized crooks who in turn know big-time crooks. Not much different from your average multi-national corporation. If you want to get to the big fish, you have to bait the small fish first."

"Good to know you're reading *The Business Review Weekly* on a regular basis."

"I'm thinking of doing an MBA. Can I put you down as a referee?"

"When this thing is over, you'll get my full endorsement."

We emptied another two boxes of bullets before calling it a day.

CHAPTER FIFTY-SIX

Tyron and I were sitting with Bud at Zimmer on Acland Street. Normally, the place would be pumping with music via a live band, but it was early afternoon and not many people were around. Only recently Zimmer had been fined by the council for playing loud music. The penalty was much to the chagrin of the locals who preferred live entertainment to studio recordings blasted through twin 1000-watt speakers.

Outside, the sky was bright blue and the air filled with the smell of fried fish and saltwater. Inside, it was alcohol and cigarettes. Summer was upon us, and tourists would flock again on the weekend to invade every corner of every street. The beach-side suburb was arguably the grooviest place in Melbourne, and if you didn't live there, you ended up wishing you did.

We took a seat on green and blue, retro-style couches separated by a coffee table, and I ordered Tasmanian light beer all round. We were at the entrance and had a nice view of the frantic world outside.

Bud was not what I had expected. All my knowledge of Bud so far had come from Tyron's mouth, and for some reason, with such a name, I expected Bud to be some bony little man with a drinking problem. But Bud was sculptured at the gym, like myself and Tyron, and impeccably dressed, black designer suit and styled hair, and spoke with authority and calmness all at once.

"You've never met Logan?" I asked Bud.

"Nope."

My eyes crossed to the couch where Tyron was sitting. He told me with a gesture of his hand to be patient, but my patience was as thin as a sheet of ice on a windscreen in winter.

Bud went on, "Which doesn't mean I haven't heard about him. He's also referred to in inner circles as the ghost shooter, one dead person, no witnesses." To me: "Did anyone see this guy when you got shot?"

"Other than me?" I said.

"Other than you."

"No."

"Then it might be Logan after all."

"So where do I find this Logan?"

Bud played with the gold ring on his finger. "I don't think you want to find him. I don't think you *need* to find him."

I placed my beer bottle on the table. "Wow, hold on." To Tyron: "Did we agree to meet here so I could get the whereabouts of Logan? Is this going to be another morality lesson on how I should butt out of the Donnelly case?"

"Don't look at me." Tyron shifted uncomfortably on his seat. "Bud said he was willing to talk to you, so it's between you and him."

Back to Bud. "If we're going to sit here and argue, I'm going."

"Patricia, I'm just letting you know what you're getting yourself into."

"You're aware he shot me three times and I nearly died?"

"Yes."

"Then I think I know what I'm getting myself into."

"All right, all right, we're all friends here, there's no need to get chesty with one another."

I took a deep breath and sipped from my beer. "I'm sorry. It's just that I've been on a merry-go-round for a few months now, and I just want to get to the bottom of this."

"It's perfectly understandable, and I don't blame you for reacting this way. Tyron has told me a lot about you, and I respect you, which is why I'm here today. I would hate to be burdened with guilt if something ever happened to you resulting from whatever I'm going to tell you today."

I stayed silent for half a minute. "I'm a grown woman. Thanks for the concern, but I'm capable of weighing up the risks here."

"Message received loud and clear." He poured the rest of his beer into a glass and gulped a mouthful. "First thing you need to know is I can't give you an address or phone number for Logan."

"I'm listening..."

"It's kind of complicated. If you could contact him directly, it would be very easy for the police to go undercover and entrap him. No, Logan is far too clever to be entrapped so easily."

"So if I want someone killed, how do I work this out?"

"Through a solicitor."

I opened my mouth like a fish going for the bait. "I beg your pardon?"

"Logan takes his contract killings through a solicitor, this way if the police get involved, he can hide under the barricade of confidentiality red-tape. It's a clever tactic, and so far, he's gotten away with it."

"What's the name of the solicitor?"

"Don't know, but he works for Smith & Gordon. You know the firm?"

I nodded and felt a rush of blood. *What the fuck is going on here?*

He continued, "I've never met his solicitor because I haven't had the need to, and frankly if I did try to find out, it would come back to Logan one way or the other, and the next thing you know, my last supper would be served execution style."

I looked across the coffee table.

Tyron seemed as surprised as I was.

Bud caught my eye. "I take it you know someone who works for Smith & Gordon?"

"Well, yes, a solicitor by the name of Bain. He's the one

who got me on the case in the first place."

Bud shook his head and took another sip from his glass. "The world is a small fuckin' place after all. Just when you think you've got it half figured out, you get shit thrown all over your face." He saw the expression on my face and added, "No offence intended."

"None taken." My surprise was not his choice of words but what he had just told me.

Bud looked towards the street for a few seconds then turned back to me. "Can I ask you a question?"

"Fire away."

"Why are you doing all this?

"To find out who killed Steven Donnelly."

"To get Mohammed out of jail?"

"If he didn't do the crime, he shouldn't be rotting in jail."

He pointed a finger at my face. "I disagree with you. Mohammed is a danger to society, and he's better off where he is right now."

"I'm not saying Mohammed is an angel, but it doesn't mean he should do time for someone else's crime. It weakens our judicial system if we let innocent people go to jail because of their criminal history."

Bud digested my words. "I see your point, but it doesn't mean I agree with you. If it were up to me, the fucker would be dead by now. Rapists have no place in this world."

I agreed with his last statement but wasn't going to give him the satisfaction of acknowledging it. "It's a shame you're not running for police minister. It's easier to control the law from the inside than from the outside."

He smiled, but I wasn't sure if it was because he thought I was a complete idiot or because he agreed with me.

I emptied my beer bottle. "Look, I'm really enjoying your company, but do you know how I can get in touch with Logan's solicitor?"

"Go and see your friend Bain. I'm sure he will be more than happy to help you, unless he's the one who framed you in the first place."

"Yeah, well, it wouldn't be the first time I walked around with a knife stuck in my back."

He laughed. "It's the business you're in Patricia, eventually we all get fucked up by friends or family."

He left before we did, so I ordered two more beers. Tyron cracked the top of his bottle with his teeth. I sipped from my bottle and let the cold liquid cut through my oesophagus.

"Do you think Bain is in on this?" Tyron asked.

"Hard to tell. When I saw Bain in his office, he convinced me how in spite of the high perks and executive lifestyle he was still a decent man who believed in justice above anything."

"Yeah, well, sometimes it's the people you respect who are the ones you need to watch out for."

We drank our beers silently and watched passer-bys on their way to the Esplanade in search of an endless summer experience.

If Bain had set me up, there would be hell to pay.

CHAPTER FIFTY-SEVEN

Gérald and I were sitting on the balcony of our apartment, my bottle-blonde hair tied at the back of my head with an elastic band, and my yellow tank-top showing more cleavage I would normally allow. Gérald was wearing beige cargo pants and a loose, white shirt. He looked good, and if he had not been my other half, I most likely would have asked him out. The day was coming to an end, and the sky was painted in layers of amber over the apartments facing us. The smell of seawater whisked through the bay area.

"You know," Gérald said, "I really think this whole deal has gone too far. I mean I could understand your reluctance to get the cops fully involved until you knew exactly what was going on, but now Smith & Gordon are most likely tied to this mess, why not get Langford on the case?"

"Because all we have is circumstantial evidence," I said.

Gérald tried too hard to get involved, but I didn't have the heart to tell him where to go. "But if Langford can obtain a search warrant, surely we'll have a bit more to work with than just rumours."

"You're probably right, but nothing is conclusive. Think about it. All we know is Weinmann is reluctant to talk, Hurst got killed because he knew too much, and someone tried to end my life when they thought I was getting too close to the truth. What exactly do you want me to tell Langford?"

Gérald passed one hand through his hair, his eyes heavy from twelve-hour shifts. "Okay, but surely we can show how the sequence of events links all these people together. I mean, isn't it a bit of coincidence someone shot you pretty much after you started asking questions? You're not going to tell me it's not substantial evidence?"

"Actually it isn't if I'm going to argue the point, Mohammed got framed. How does it prove someone set up the whole thing some ten years ago? How does it prove someone doesn't want me dead for another reason?"

"Because we know it's not."

"Exactly my point. It's all based on instinct and hunches. You're a doctor, sweetie, you know the legal system is a science. Everything needs to be backed-up by solid evidence or by the time we go to court it's all going to smell like someone's garbage can."

He stayed silent for half a minute.

"Shit," he finally said, "I hate it when you're right, but your life still remains in danger."

I took his hand in mine. "Don't think I enjoy being in the current situation. But if we're going to win this game, we need to keep one step ahead of everyone. And giving up everything just to let the cops mess it up isn't my idea of justice."

Someone outside ordered his dog not to cross the road, and then we heard the screeching of tyres.

Gérald said, "So what are you going to do until you get your hands on Logan?"

"Apply pressure on everyone whom I think is hiding something."

"Everyone? You're supposed to be dead. How the hell are you going to proceed?"

"With violence and torture," I joked.

"Why don't you get Tyron to mess things up instead?"

I let go of his hand. "Don't want to put his life at risk."

"So you're going to play the lone ranger?"

"It might be the best thing to do for the time being. Nobody knows who the blonde chick living with you is, but everyone knows who Tyron is. I'm just some harmless slut who's taken over your household."

Gérald smiled. "I love it when you talk dirty."

"I always talk dirty."

"Yes, but it sounds so different with the blonde hair."

"How?"

"You sound like you mean it."

We kissed passionately and Tyron walked in on us.

CHAPTER FIFTY-EIGHT

"**D**o you want me to come back in half an hour?" Tyron asked.

I turned to face him. "No, not at all. Come in and join us."

"Well, jeez, I haven't even brushed yet."

Tyron did this rude thing with his tongue, and we both laughed.

"All right, people," Gérald said, "this is just a little too close for comfort."

Tyron sat on a spare chair that looked like it needed to be sat on. "Hey, chill out. The French are so fuckin' dramatic."

"Really?" Gérald said, "Then, how's this for dramatic: Patricia wants you out of the Donnelly case."

The announcement stopped Tyron like a bullet in the frontal lobe.

Tyron turned to me. "Is this true?"

"I don't want you to get hurt."

He held his hands together and flexed his biceps. "Do I look like I need protection? I'm not the one who got shot here. In fact, if I had been there, the chances are you'd still be in one piece."

I chose not to reply.

Tyron passed one hand over his face and grabbed Gérald's beer bottle from the floor. "Don't mind if I have a sip, do you?"

"Be my guest."

Tyron emptied what was left of the bottle. "All this light beer must be getting to your head, Patricia. I'm your partner, and with me around, you've got a better chance of survival."

"Maybe you're right," I said. "I was just thinking out loud before. Don't take it so personally."

"I won't then." Then: "So, whose head are we going to crack first?"

"She's going to go after Logan," Gérald said.

Tyron turned to me. "And when you come face-to-face with him, are you going to kill him or just knock him on the knuckles and tell him what a bad little boy he's been?"

I stood from my chair and walked the length of the balcony. "I'll do what I have to do when it happens. I believe in the art of improvisation."

"I think Logan might have graduated from the same course you have. It's all going to end up in a bloodbath." He cracked the joints of his fingers. "Know what I would do?"

Our eyes met. "What?"

"Pop the bastard before he pops you."

CHAPTER FIFTY-NINE

Bah Sheh Mohammed didn't look much different from when I had seen him last. It had been almost nine months, but he had maintained his composure, and other than his lack of verbal aggression, he pretty much looked as friendly as I remembered him. The orange overalls were a little tighter around his frame, so either the material shrunk in the wash, or he had been doing some extra-curricular activities at the prison gym.

We were sitting in the same visitors' room we had before I got perforated. Tyron was waiting in the 4WD in the prison's car park.

"What brings you back here?" he asked.

"I'm working really hard on your case," I said. "I think there's going to be a breakthrough soon."

"No shit. And what's with the blonde hair? You're modelling part-time now?"

I told him everything about me getting shot and how I was supposed to be dead. I showed him a clipping from the *Herald-Sun* reporting my murder in a gangland shooting.

He read the cutting with interest. "Can't say I didn't warn you. Bet you the next time the fucker is not going to miss."

"It's Bud's impression too."

"You've seen Bud?"

"Yesterday."

"How's he?"

"Doing real well. Doesn't think much of you, though."

"Well, fuck him, he's just a weasel in a Hugo Boss suit. He was my friend in prison, and now he's talking behind my back. Don't trust him for shit. What did he tell you about me?"

I leaned forward. "Listen to me, Mohammed: I don't care about your past. It's not why I'm here."

"So why are you here?"

"I know you didn't kill Donnelly."

He came forth, his nose almost touching mine. I could smell the foulness of his breath. "I'm touched, but your faith is not going to get me out of here."

I relaxed back into my chair. "Give me a little time, and you'll spend the next summer at the beach."

He stretched back on his chair and nodded. "Okay, but why you're telling me all this? What do you want me to do?"

"Just stay out of trouble."

He giggled. "What the fuck do you think I've been doing here? Causing a one-man riot?"

"Just don't get yourself in the shit. We might get a chance at an appeal and it wouldn't make a good impression if you turned up to court black-and-blue."

"Yeah, okay, whatever, I'll just be the little, white fuckin' mouse in the cage." He stood from his chair. "You know, it's not so bad here anyway. Kind of getting used to it."

I stood from my chair. "I'll keep you informed."

"Yeah, thanks. Appreciated."

We shook hands firmly.

A correctional officer escorted him out of the visitor's room.

Just another day in paradise.

CHAPTER SIXTY

Dusk was settling at the Queen Victoria Market, and traders were packing for the day. The smell of vegetables, fresh fish and exhaust fumes filled my lungs. It had been my idea to meet with Bain at a place other than his office. If Logan's solicitor was in fact working for Smith & Gordon, then my indiscretion might end up costing more than just one life.

"I haven't any fuckin idea about what you're talking about," Bain said. He was still shocked by the news I was alive.

"Can you look into it for me?" I said.

"How exactly do you propose I do this? Set up a meeting with all the partners? Excuse me, but do any of you by chance happen to have a client who works as a contract killer? Come on, Patricia, this Bud friend of yours obviously doesn't know what he's talking about. If the firm was somehow linked to a contract killer, don't you think I would know?"

I shrugged. "You didn't realise Mohammed might have been framed until Murray came to you."

Bain danced from one foot to the other. He wore an expensive suit with gold cuff-links and a matching tie pin. "True, but I do spend a great deal of time with the partners, and surely I would have heard if one of them had an account with a contract killer."

"I doubt you would find anything in the books. You know damn well contract killing is illegal, so it's not like the bookkeeping is going to be kept immaculate in case the ATO or the Law Institute decides to drop by for a coffee and an audit."

Bain was looking at an Asian store holder packing his cheap electronics into a white van. He was frowning, and I knew he was seriously worried about where this whole investigation was going.

"You know what?" he finally said, "why don't we just forget about the whole thing? You nearly got killed, and maybe it's just not so important any more. Fuck Murray and fuck Mohammed. It's their problem."

My jaw went slack.

"Ah, come on, Patricia," he went on. "You don't have to take on the world's hopeless cases just to prove a point. Even if you're wrong about Logan and his connection with Smith & Gordon, if word gets out the firm is dealing with homicidal corruption, we'll go down like the Titanic. We deal with white-collar criminals, for Christ's sake, not with pay-as-you-go murderers. The firm doesn't want blood on its hands. We have shareholders to think about, we need to focus on what's good for the majority, not for some Arab rapist who happens to be in jail because somebody wants him there. Fuck him. Don't know why I bothered in the first place."

I moved two steps forward. "John, you're a real jerk. What was the point of giving me all this pep talk about believing in the truth if you're going to break at the seams because you're worried about your shareholders? You're a broker now? Justice, remember? Doesn't it mean anything to you?"

Bain made a half turn and straightened his tie. "God, you make everything sound so simple. I'm a solicitor, true, but I'm also a businessman. I have financial responsibilities to the firm, my clients and the shareholders of this company."

"You asked me to dig up the truth, and it's what I'm doing."

"Yes, and now it's one huge fuckin' mess."

"Hardly my fault."

He checked his watch. "All right, I'm going to see what I can do, but I can't promise anything. There are a couple of people I trust with my life in this company, and I'll run it past them first. If they've heard something, we'll dig further. If they haven't, I'll have to let it go, and it'll be the end of it."

"That's all I'm asking, just a little co-operation."

He checked his watch again. "Look, I've really got to go, dinner with a client at six-thirty in Chinatown. I'll talk to you soon." He was just about to take off but turned around instead. "Oh, and I like what you've done to your hair."

He made his way between the market stalls, a tall figure in a designer suit, eyes to the ground like a sinner on his way to confession.

I stood on the exact spot where Hurst's body had been found.

SIXTY-ONE

Murray and I were at Big Mouth working on a café latte, a light beer and two five-dollar pastas. He was red from the neck up from being exposed to the sun and not bothering with sunscreen. His five o'clock shadow looked good on him and was more in tune with his personality than his off-the-rack suit. He had taken the 2.04 p.m. from Sydney and two hours later he was having dinner with me in St Kilda.

"What did you want to see me about?" he asked.

"You know I got shot?" I said.

"Yeah, well, it was all over the newspapers, you'd have to be blind to miss it."

"I think it might be important for you to lay low during the next few days. I'm going to be switching to high gear and pissing off a few people suffering from antisocial personality disorder, and not the supermarket checkout kind."

He nodded and sipped from his coffee. "God, you nearly gave me a heart attack when you left a message on the answering machine. No one told me you were still alive."

"It was better to say nothing, but now I've been reassessing the situation, and it's important for you to know."

"Why?"

"Because if the wrong person finds out I'm alive, you could be next on the list."

He rubbed the bridge of his nose with his thumb and forefinger. "Shit, I had a feeling it was going to come up eventually. The way Mohammed was warning me about those-bastards-who-will-stop-at-nothing, I knew we were dealing with some really dangerous people."

Two young men walked into the café. One was a blond with a red body-glove pair of pants, the other bald with a tight shirt and jeans. Murray checked them out from head to toes. They ignored him and headed for the upstairs lounge.

He turned his attention back to me. "I like what you've done with your hair."

"Yeah, seems to be the general consensus if you got a dick dangling between your legs. Don't know if blondes actually have more fun, but they certainly get more attention."

He smiled. "Well, I'm not that kind of man."

"Sorry, I forgot."

He pushed his empty cup to the side. "So who framed Mohammed?"

I gave him a non-biased run-down of what I knew.

"Shit," he said, "and Logan doesn't know you're running around looking for him?"

"Nope. But he will soon."

"And when he does?"

"Bang, bang, we're all dead."

"Fuck."

I finished my light beer. "You've got a place to stay?"

"I can hide with my folks in Moe for a little while."

"If I were you, I would travel as far as Tasmania and stay with your great-grand parents."

He shrugged. "What about you?"

"I'm coming out of the closet, so to speak."

I ordered another light beer for myself. Murray said no to a second coffee. He looked highly-strung enough as it was, so I didn't insist.

I took one sip straight from the bottle. "You've got any connections who get can get in touch with someone like Logan?"

Murray was lost in thought for what seemed like eternity.

"I might," he finally said.

"There might be a link with Smith & Gordon."

"No shit?"

"I've got Bain looking into it, but he seems a little reluctant. He's more worried about his financial position with the company than finding out what really happened to Steven Donnelly."

"Fuckin' lawyers."

I didn't comment. He was half the reason why we were all in this mess in the first place.

He went on, "Why don't I get back to you on this Logan fucker?"

"Sure." I handed him a new business card.

"Tanja Barrett? Nice."

"There's a new mobile number as well. Don't bother with the old one. Patricia Lunn's long gone by now, so she won't answer it anyway."

He placed the card in his wallet and ten dollars on the table.

"Well, it was good to see you again. I'm sorry about the shooting. If I knew anyone was going to get shot at, I wouldn't have got you involved in the first place."

"I'm kind of having fun here, so don't worry about it."

He walked to the front door, his jacket over his arm.

I finished the rest of my beer by myself and wondered how many more days I had left to live.

CHAPTER SIXTY-TWO

Surprisingly enough, Murray did get back to me the day after our meeting in St Kilda. My mobile phone had gone off just when I had stepped out of the shower after a two-hour workout at the St Kilda Sea Baths. My muscles had regained the firmness they'd had before I ended up with three bullets in various parts of my anatomy.

I told Murray to wait a sec while I wrapped myself in a towel I pulled from my gym bag. I also fetched a pen and paper I kept in the side pocket of the bag.

"What have you got?" I said.

"Not Logan's address and phone number, but someone who can provide you with the information."

"How did you get this?"

"Someone who knows someone who knows someone."

"Networking is the best way to get your information."

"You're free tomorrow?"

"I'm free any time."

He gave me a name and a place for my contact. I wrote it down in my address book.

"You know these people well?" I asked.

"Not as much as I would like to."

"I'm not going to get gunned down in the middle of a public place again?"

"Don't think so. Your contact doesn't even know you're Patricia Lunn. As far as he's concerned you're just a messenger who's collecting info for someone else."

"Good job."

"It's the least I can do."

I pressed the end button and walked all the way back to my apartment. The sun was high in the sky, and it looked as if it would remain so for the rest of the day. Traffic was relatively smooth on the Esplanade, but I knew in less than an hour rush-hour would take over.

When I got home, Gérald had dinner ready—sauté chicken in apricot sauce with sliced cucumbers and green salad tossed in balsamic vinegar.

"How's Wonder Woman going?" he asked as he set the plates on the kitchen table.

"Best workout I've had in ages." I told him about my little rendezvous for the following day.

"You better bring Tyron with you."

"I will, but he will be standing in the distance. This way he will have a bird's eye view of what's going on around me."

I threw the gym bag in the bedroom, and we sat at the table to enjoy our succulent meal.

"If anything should happen to me," I said, "I've left my banking details in the top drawer of my desk. You can transfer all the money from my account into yours via Internet banking. I've got no secret debts, so you don't need to worry about. And make sure you collect a cheque from Bain, no matter what happens."

Gérald dropped his fork. "Shit, Patricia, you're really scaring me here."

"I'm just being logical."

"And that's what worries me. The last time you were being logical, you got shot."

I shrugged. "You and Tyron just run as far as you can. You're still a legal French citizen, so it shouldn't be too hard to find a hideaway on the Riviera."

"I might just spend the rest of my life tracking down this sonofabitch."

"Please don't. This is way out of your league."

"And it's not out of yours?"

"Maybe it was six months ago, but now I'm ready."

We ate the rest of our dinner in silence.

CHAPTER SIXTY-THREE

Tyron and I were practising target shooting at the Flemington gun club. I was getting so good at handling the H&K, I didn't even need to fully concentrate in order to hit my paper target. The whole place smelled of metal and gunpowder.

"We're all set for tomorrow?" I said.

"As ready as a dog with a bone," he said.

"Good. Just leave your bone behind and bring your sawn-off shotgun."

"It's like asking a fisherman not to forget his rod."

I blew off the head of the paper target.

"Not bad," Tyron said. "Maybe if this all goes down well, you could apply for a job as an assassin. I heard Logan is not going to be around much longer."

"Funny how rumours circulate so quickly."

We left the gun club with two hundred dollars worth of ammunition.

In the car, I told Tyron what the big plan was.

He pulled on his seatbelt "Well, I'm not sure if the police are going to like the way you operate. I know Langford is on your side, but I doubt he would give you the green light to go ahead with your little plan."

I shifted the sequential gears of the MR2 and pulled into the main road. "If I'd waited for someone like Langford to give me the green light every time I want to get things moving, I'd still be in uniform spending the bulk of my day directing traffic."

"True enough."

CHAPTER SIXTY-FOUR

Murray's contact resided at the Parliament end of Collins Street, just above a takeaway joint serving the best chicken kebabs in town. The office was small but well furnished. It was registered as an outfit under the name of Corporate Business Consultants International, according to the gold lettering on the smoked glass panel leading to the reception. A secretary with my hair colour asked me if I had an appointment.

"Tanja Barrett, he's expecting me."

"I'll let him know."

She made me wait a couple of minutes on a green leather couch, the kind you'd buy if money is not an issue. I felt the H&K pressing against the small of my back when I shifted to the side. I had no idea who Frank McFadden was, but according to Murray he was the man who would be able to tell me how to get in touch with Logan. I knew by now Logan's real contact was a solicitor at Smith & Gordon, but since Bain was not willing to get involved beyond telling me to drop the case, I had to keep abreast of the situation. The gun was just in case someone decided to knock me out for a second time. I was prepared and not feeling the slightest guilt about pulling the trigger if the occasion happened to present itself.

I was ushered into a room consisting of a solid oak

conference table with matching chairs, a water cooler and photographic views of Melbourne framed and displayed on the three walls. The fourth wall was adorned with a floor-to-ceiling view of the blue-grey building on the other side of the street. The smell of floor polish reminded me of the State Library. Traffic noise outside was blocked by double-glazed window panes, which also kept the cool of the air conditioning on the inside.

"Tanja Barrett, please take a seat," McFadden ordered from the corner of the room. He crossed to the other side and closed the door behind me. "Don't worry about privacy. This room is checked for bugs on a regular basis."

"You conduct all your dubious activities in here?"

He didn't reply.

McFadden was in his mid-fifties with a surprisingly full head of hair and a body that could have benefited from a few hours a week at a gym. He wore a designer shirt under a two-piece, top-of-the-range black suit. He took a seat opposite me and scribbled something on a piece of paper.

I was wearing a short, black skirt and matching jacket.

"You don't know me, I don't know you," he said. "I've never seen you before, and I would prefer to never see you again. The kind of people you're asking me to get you in touch with are highly volatile, and if anything goes wrong, I'm going to end up with a bullet in my brain."

"I don't mean to place you in any danger, Mr. McFadden, so you can rest assured of my discretion."

He looked up and his eyes met mine for the first time. "Let's not start sucking each other's dick here. I'm not interested in your objectives or reasons."

Each other's dick?

"Fine," I said.

"The person you want to get in touch with at Smith & Gordon is Jamie Wagner. He specialises in corporate takeovers, and no one in the firm knows of his other speciality —contract killing. I believe your contact John Bain told you the truth when he said he didn't believe someone within Smith & Gordon was involved in a shooting."

"You seem to know a lot for someone who doesn't want to get involved."

"No more than I have to. Murray is not my favourite person on the planet, but he insisted how for you it was a matter of life and death, so here it is. I ask questions, I get answers, and if I'm satisfied, I oblige."

He pushed the paper he had scribbled on across the desk.

It had my contact's name, a room number and a telephone number.

"How much do I owe you?"

He told me, then: "I'll have my secretary type you an invoice on the way out."

"Kind of an expensive service you're offering here."

He smiled for the first time. "You don't expect people to put themselves in the front-line without being adequately compensated for it, do you?"

"Not at all. But for the price of your referral, I could get someone down town to do the job."

"True. But it would depend on whether you want to spend the next twenty years of your life in jail."

"So, you're saying if I'm rich and I've got the right contacts, then I'm more likely to get away with murder?"

He stood from his seat. "When you've been in the business for as long as I have, you know how to keep your mouth shut. I think I have serviced your needs, so now would be a good time to farewell one another."

I stood and we shook hands.

"Nice doing business with you," I said.

"You're welcome. I wish you all the best in your endeavours."

"I intend to make a killing."

"I wouldn't expect anything less."

I collected my invoice from McFadden's secretary, which detailed his services to Tanja Barrett as corporate business consulting. I knew the corporate world was a cut-throat industry, but I never anticipated that the smorgasboard of services made available to clients who treasured confidentiality at a high price included contract killing.

Maybe I should have been a murderer.

CHAPTER SIXTY-FIVE

Bain wasn't happy, and if I had been in his shoes, I wouldn't have been happy either. I had just told him the bastard who was protecting Logan was Jamie Wagner, a senior partner who used to be John's mentor when he first joined the firm.

We were sitting in his office, indulging in coffee and cream cookies. His dark hair was brushed back and his yellow tie undone to the first button of his white shirt. The door was locked, and the room smelled of cigarettes. Bain was up to his third cancer stick. He had a concentrated look on his face.

"Bastard," he said.

"It's a small world," I said, fully aware I was using the oldest cliché in the world, "but in one way it doesn't really surprise me."

He wasn't listening to me. There was anger in his eyes.

"I think it's better if I see him by myself," I said, knowing the state Bain was in might be more counter-productive than I would have liked it to be.

"I'd rather be there when it happens."

"I'd rather you wouldn't."

"It's my show, and since I got you into this mess in the first place, I think it would be better if I get to the bottom of it."

He stood from his desk, circled the room, and looked at the street below, but his mind miles away in the world of prospective retaliation.

I crossed my legs on the chair. "John, you need to trust me on this. If you really want to confront Jamie Wagner, you can always do so when this is all over. Just let me get to Logan first and then you can run Jamie over with your 4WD for all I care."

He let my comment sink in for a few seconds, then turned around. "Okay, okay, you go ahead and do what you have to do, but if he doesn't give you what you want, then come back here and I'm going to make him talk."

"You've got a deal."

Even with anger creeping all over his body, he still had incredible sexual magnetism. Part of me wanted to hug him and tell him everything was going to be all right, and part of me was afraid he was going to lose his temper and start breaking everything around him.

I added, "You weren't to know your firm was involved in this chaos."

"Yeah, but how long has it been going on?"

"How long has what been going on?"

"How many people got killed because of Logan's connection with Smith & Gordon? It's a heavy weight on my mind. Not something I want to sweep under the carpet."

"John, you can't hold yourself responsible for every wrong on the planet. The fact you took Murray seriously in the first place and contacted me shows the kind of person you are."

"Does it?"

"Well, yeah, you didn't exactly tell Murray to go and get lost. You said you believed in the truth, but now the truth has come out in the open, you don't know how to deal with it."

"I just never expected *that*."

"It's what makes life interesting and frustrating all at once."

"Doubt it's what you were thinking when you were lying in hospital with a bullet in your spine."

There was little to argue with here, but I didn't like to see him beating himself over the head for something clearly out of his control.

I got up. "You better tell me where Jamie Wagner's office is so I can get this over and done with."

He walked back to his desk and pulled a small digital voice recorder the size of a pen from the right top drawer. "Sure. Don't bother calling him or he'll have time to be prepared. And take this with you just in case we need to take the bastard to court in the near future." He handed me the digital voice recorder. "It's got fresh batteries, and you can record up to eighty minutes of conversation. If you don't record anything significant, I'll break every bone in his head instead."

I slid the recorder in the right pocket of my jacket.

CHAPTER SIXTY-SIX

Wagner was in his early sixties, an age when he should have been fishing with his grandchildren instead of arranging contract killings. He had an easy-on-the-eye face, reminding me a little of Robert Redford, except his nose was a little crooked and he carried more weight on the cheeks. His hair was speckled with grey. He wore a pinstriped red tie over a white shirt. His office was tidy, and he had a 19" desktop flat screen sitting on the right-hand corner of his desk. The place smelled of his citrus aftershave.

"What's your name?" Jamie Wagner asked.

"You don't need to know my name."

He nodded without arguing.

"What's your business here?" he asked.

"Logan."

The digital audio recorder in my jacket pocket began taping our conversation the moment I stepped into his office.

He smiled. "Who's Logan?"

"McFadden sent me."

"What do you need?"

"What do you offer?"

"You'll have to discuss the details with Logan. I'm only his lawyer. I don't provide or endorse his services. I'm just the channel to get to the man."

You arrogant sonofabitch, I thought. You're the channel which gets people killed, and at your age, you should know better.

"Fine," I said, "how do I get in touch with your client whose services you don't endorse?"

"You don't get in touch with him, he gets in touch with you."

"Do I need to send him a Christmas card or something?"

Wagner stared at me for a full thirty seconds.

I didn't blink or divert my counter-stare.

"Okay," he said, "hold on a sec."

He picked up the phone and dialled.

Fifteen seconds went by.

He said, "Got a client for you."

Somebody said something at the end of the line.

Wagner said, "Lady, mid-twenties, blonde hair, good looking, looks genuine."

He didn't need to know I was really mid-thirties.

Somebody said something else at the end of the line.

"Okay. I'll tell her."

He hung up, then to me: "Five thousand upfront, and you'll need to leave it with me."

"I thought you said you didn't endorse his services?"

"I don't. It's just a safety deposit so he knows you're serious."

"Oh, I'm serious, all right."

"I know you're serious, but *he* needs the re-assurance you are, and five grand usually gets the ball rolling on both sides."

"Do you take cash?"

He stared at me like people stare at monkeys behind cages at the zoo.

I added, "When do you need it by?"

"The sooner the better. Depends on when you want to get the job done."

"I'll have it by this afternoon."

"Good. I'll need you to leave me a phone number for Logan to contact you." He slid a pen and notepad across the desk.

I scribbled my Tanja Barrett mobile number.

He said, "You better pick it up when it rings because he doesn't leave messages or a return number."

"Fair enough." I slid the notepad back across the desk.

"Good. You'll get a call one hour after you've deposited the money with me." He smiled like someone who just told him he won the lottery.

I stood. "I'll see you first thing this afternoon."

We shook hands like regular business people who made an honest living.

"One word to the cops," he said, "I'll deny everything, and you'll get a free home visit from Logan."

"I don't think we'll need to be worried," I said.

I left his office.

The digital recorder in my right pocket had not captured anything significant. It looked as if Bain might get a chance at applying his knuckles against Wagner's crooked nose after all.

CHAPTER SIXTY-SEVEN

After I hand-delivered $5000 in $50 notes to the office of Smith & Gordon in a large brown envelope, Wagner arranged for Logan and Tanja Barrett to meet at the Bourke Street Mall, just at the entrance of the HMV store. Supposedly, I was only a contact who would provide some information to Logan about a job paying a generous $50,000 for one hit. Wagner told us Logan normally charged $10,000 a pop, so I thought we'd make him an offer he couldn't resist. Greed always gets the fish out of the water, and Logan was no exception.

Logan did call me on Tanja Barrett's mobile number exactly one hour after I handed over the $5000 to Wagner. These people were professionals. They did everything by the clock as if their life depended on it, which it ironically did. Tyron and I were sitting in the roadster near the corner of Spring and Collins Streets when the call came through. It was a beautiful sunny day.

"Tanja Barrett?"

"Speaking."

Logan's voice was deep and smooth, like the voice of a spokesperson on the radio who tells you why you should invest in an overpriced waterfront Dockland apartment if you want a life akin to the rich-and-famous.

"Three o'clock. Don't bring anyone with you. Wear a red cap, I don't care where you get it from."

"Okay."

"You're late, I'm gone, you lose the $5000."

"I'll be there, don't you worry."

"Good."

He hung up before I had time to slip in another word.

In less than an hour, we would meet face-to-face.

"What are the odds of us having a gunfight in the middle of the city?" Tyron asked.

"It wouldn't comply with the spirit of Christmas," I said, "but I've never believed in Santa Claus anyway."

"Want me to come with you?" Tyron asked.

"Yeah, but keep your distance. It's just a safety precaution. I want to take the bastard by surprise. He'll feel like a cat tossed into a lake."

"You gonna pop him?"

My eyes crossed his. "What would be the point? He was only doing his job. If I do him, how am I going to get to the source?"

Tyron shifted on his seat. "It's a valid observation." Then: "You know you've really got to get a bigger car. I'm getting piles sitting in this shoebox."

Tyron had a point given his size and the way his knees nearly ran into his chin when he was riding in the MR2.

"I'll think about it," I said. "Maybe after I'm done with the blonde bimbo look, I'll do the fashionable thing. Get a Toorak tractor and run everyone off the road like local housewives do."

CHAPTER SIXTY-EIGHT

Tyron was lodged near the 2 Dollar Shop, right opposite the HMV store, his sawn-off riffle inconspicuously concealed under a black, leather trench coat. He looked like Lawrence Fishburn's body double in The Matrix.

I wore tight, black leather pants with a matching vest ending just below my chest and exposed a lot more than a mid-riff. My blonde hair was tied up in a ponytail at the top of my head with the length running down both sides of my face and my neck. I looked like an undergraduate student looking for a sexual summer encounter.

I didn't bother with the red cap Logan instructed me to wear. This way he will be looking for a woman with a red cap, and when I'll be right under his nose, he'll get the shock of his life. As far as he was concerned, I was dead and gone. The papers said so, and he fattened up his bank account as a result.

The Christmas crowd was congested, which suited me to a tee. The more people, the less likely we were going to shoot our way through this one.

The 9mm H & K was tucked in my Astro Boy shoulder bag. Bain's digital voice recorder was running. I felt sexy, and with the gun, very powerful. It would have been a dream come true if I could have just pulled the weapon from my bag, shot him in the spine at the same spot he shot me, and then disappear into the crowd like another anonymous Christmas shopper. The difference between the sonofabitch and me was that I had a sense of morality. No matter how angry I was, I would never shoot anyone in cold blood the way he did for a living.

I was ten minutes early, which suited me fine because it gave me time to become familiar with my surroundings. I wasn't really sure what Logan looked like, but I trusted my instinct would nudge me at the back of the head when he would appear. I was standing by the window of a surf shop, which gave me a nice clear view of the east side of Bourke Street, even with crowds walking around and stocking up on presents. The sun was high in the sky and visibility was one hundred percent.

Tyron kept in the distance, and because Logan would be looking for a woman, he would most likely not even notice him standing like a sentinel at his post.

Ten minutes went by.

I knew it was him the moment I saw him.

He wore a Hawaiian shirt with palm-tree motives, and a red cap. His hair was greying on the sides, and he looked as if he adhered to a regular schedule at the gym and a tanning saloon. At least we had the gym in common. He never told me he would be wearing a red cap, but I knew now how he had expected me to recognise him. What were the odds of two people standing in front of the HMV store at the same time wearing red caps?

I walked with the crowd from the surf shop and looked towards the entrance of the HMV store. There was a man waving Hungry Jack's coupons in front of my face, so I grabbed one just to make it look like I was really a part of the shopping crowd. When Tyron saw me move, he came forth and stopped just before the tram track. Normally there would have been cops on patrol around the mall, but they must have been busy running errands in other parts of the city. It was just as well because we didn't need the complication of having street cops mixed up in our plan.

I walked past Logan once, but he didn't react. He was too busy trying to spot a lady in a red cap. His face was rectangular and free of expression. I guessed it was one of the job requirements when you worked as a contract killer, show no emotion, just get the job done. I wouldn't have been surprised if he was the type of bloke who tucked his kids to bed and hugged his dog goodnight. Killers have a soft side too, but unfortunately it's not what the victims end up experiencing.

Tyron had removed his mobile phone with his left hand and was ready to autodial. His right hand held the sawn-off gun through the hole he cut out in the right pocket of his trench coat.

I pulled the H & K from the Astro Boy bag and casually walked up to Logan. He had his back to me. The crowd was dense and kept the HMV security guard busy checking bags of potential shoplifters who exited the shop.

Without warning I pushed the cold steel muzzle against Logan's lower back.

CHAPTER SIXTY-NINE

"Walk away," I said, "and it will be your last step."

Logan didn't move, but I felt his muscles tense.

"Tanja Barrett?"

"Yes and no."

"Okay, I'm here. What do you want?"

"See the man in the long coat in front of you?"

A few seconds silence.

Tyron waved.

Logan said, "Yes."

"You know him, right?"

"Yes."

"Good, then you know if you do anything stupid he will shoot you from the distance."

"What do you want?"

I passed one hand around his waist and felt the hardness of his gun. I pulled it and in less than two seconds tossed it in my Astro Boy bag. No one had noticed. Maybe we looked like a regular couple in the middle of a public hugging session.

"You're carrying anything else?" I asked.

"Nope."

"How do I know?"

"You don't."

I pushed the H & K further into his back like someone pushes a thumb pin into a wall. This time he jerked slightly.

"What do you want?" he said. "Too many people around, you're never going to get away with this."

"It's probably the reason why I will get away with it." Then: "I want you to turn around slowly."

He did what I said. His eyes were grey. The surprise on his face was not something he learned at acting school. It seemed as genuine as the gun pointed at him.

"Recognise me?" I said.

He looked at my chest and then dug his eyes into mine. "Yes. What the fuck happened to your hair?"

"Thought I was dead, didn't you?"

"The thought crossed my mind."

"Your client is going to get really pissed off he paid you a lot money, and I'm still walking around like Jesus Christ after he got crucified."

"I always refund disgruntled customers."

"Not going to happen this time."

"I was told you were a really hard bitch to get rid of."

"Who told you?"

"People in high places."

"You were told right."

I made a hand signal to Tyron with my free hand while making sure the H & K was in close contact with Logan's belly. The security latch was undone, and I prayed silently he would give me an excuse to shoot him.

Tyron auto-dialled a number on his mobile and talked to our contact.

"We're going to be standing here all day?" Logan said.

"With all these people around? No. I've got some friends who would like to see you for a pre-Christmas drink."

An unmarked grey police car pulled into the mall from the corner of Swanston Street, its blue-and-red flashing lights like decorations on a Christmas tree. Two marked police cars pulled in right behind us.

Logan saw them from the corner of his eye.

I said, "Well, look who's come to join the party."

He gave me a hard stare.

"Don't even think about it," I said. "There are cops everywhere around."

Langford stepped out of the unmarked car and walked towards us. Four uniformed cops followed from the other two cars. People on the street stopped and froze as if my gun was pointed at them.

"Is this the man?" Langford asked me when he moved in on us.

"It's him." I removed the tape recorder from my bag with my free hand and passed it on to him. "There should be enough in there to keep him in a cell for a while."

"You better put the gun away. We'll take care of it from here."

The four uniformed cops surrounded us, guns in hand, making sure there was nowhere for Logan to run to.

Langford handcuffed Logan.

The crowd was watching with great curiosity.

The Christmas show had come to town.

Ho, Ho, Ho, who's having a jolly good time now?

CHAPTER SEVENTY

We were in an interrogation room on the thirteenth floor of the St Kilda Road Police Complex. It was just Logan and me in one room with a table and two chairs. Our conversation was videotaped, but I had been given enough rope from Langford to do pretty much as I pleased. If my little talk with Logan didn't go my way, the videotape would mysteriously record nothing but snow.

"You don't have enough evidence to mount a case," Logan said, sure of himself.

I said, "We have enough to start digging. After we've finished with the digging, the hole will be deep enough to toss your body in there."

He thought about what I said for a few seconds. "Should I be speaking to my lawyer?"

"You mean Jamie Wagner, the one who told me how to find you?"

It stopped him like a punch in the face. "What do you want?" he said.

"Are you really interested?"

"Well, I'm here for something, aren't I?"

I didn't say anything immediately. It was good to let him

simmer in his own juice for a little while, let him worry about what twenty years in prison would do to his lucrative career.

"Have you ever failed one of your assignments before?" I asked.

"No."

"Since this is a new experience for you, I assume you have no idea how to proceed?"

He threw me a look. "I improvise a lot in my field. It's why I'm good at what I do."

"I'm the evidence you're not fool-proof and your improvisation technique is getting a little rusty."

He chewed over my comment. "That's true."

"I'd like to help you, but I don't know how willing you are to cooperate."

He looked at the wall and then back at me. "What's in it for me?"

"I shut my mouth, you walk away."

He stayed silent for a few seconds. "What do you need?"

"The name of the person who hired you to kill me."

"What you're asking me to do is unprofessional. I'll never get another assignment, and someone will want to fill my head with lead."

"You're not going to get many assignments while you're rotting in jail. And we can place you into the witness protection program if it's what you're worried about."

"Yeah, right."

We stayed silent for half a minute.

He said, "How do I know you're going to let me go if I give you my client's name?"

"You've got my word."

"That's it?"

"Given the circumstances, this is as good a deal you're going to get."

He toyed with the fold on his neck. "If I tell you who he is, you're not going to rat on me, are you? If you do, you'll be fuckin' dead."

I smiled. "Do I look like the type of person who goes behind another person's back?"

"I guess not."

"Good, then just tell me who it is."

He told me.

"Why doesn't it surprise me?" I said.

"You knew all along."

"I guess I did."

"And now I've just confirmed it for you."

"I'll be sure to give you a good character reference when you go to trial."

His eyes did this strange thing, like the lights on a pinball machine. "You said I could walk free if I gave you a name. We had a deal."

"Sorry, I lied."

"You fuckin' bitch."

"Lying has always been a flaw in my personality."

"I should have shot you in the head when I had the chance."

I pulled my chair back and looked towards the hidden camera behind Logan's back. "Did you get everything?" I said to Langford who was watching us via a video monitor in the other room. "Now might be a good time to get him his lawyer."

"Fuck you," Logan said.

CHAPTER SEVENTY-ONE

It was time to kill off Tanja Barrett.

The blonde look had been fun for a while, but it just became too much of a sexual magnet for my liking. And the arseholes of this world tend to associate the colour of your hair with the number of your functional brain cells. I spent two hours at a designer hairdressing salon on Chapel Street getting my hair cut shoulder length and dyed chestnut. It was like peeling off an orange and revealing what was truly on the inside. When I stepped out of the saloon, for the first time in months, I felt like my old self again. Logan was behind bars awaiting his trial, so there was really no point in hiding behind the disguise which had kept me sheltered from my enemies.

When I got home, Gérald had just finished a shift at the hospital. I threw my handbag on the kitchen counter, and he stepped out of the bedroom, his blond hair wet from having had a shower. He came up behind me and hugged me, the soap-scented skin of his right cheek pressed against my left one.

"I didn't know if I was ever going to see you again," he said.

"Did you have doubts?"

"A bit."

"Tyron was with me. Nothing could have gone wrong."

"I honestly didn't know. You'd never been shot so badly before, so I didn't know what to expect."

I turned to face him. "I'm here and alive and back to my normal self."

He passed one hand through my newly dyed hair. "I can see that. Welcome back from the dead, Patricia Lunn."

"It's good to be back."

We kissed like two young lovers who have been separated for a whole month with nothing to connect us, not even a phone call.

"What happens now?" he asked.

"I need to tidy up a few loose ends."

"Like who killed Donnelly."

"And who paid Logan to kill me."

We kissed again.

I added, "The cops are on our side now, so life is much safer than when this whole mess began."

"I should hope so. I don't want to have this feeling I'm going to lose you again. It's not something I think I would be able to live with. I've never been good with emotions."

"Your emotions seem fine to me."

"I mean negative emotions, this engulfing sense of despair when you know you're walking down a dark tunnel and there's no way back."

"I think you're stronger than you think, my darling. Most of us are but we don't always get a chance to show it."

"I'll skip on the opportunity if it's all the same to you."

I pulled myself away from him. "I'm going to have a shower. Why don't you go to bed and take your clothes off? There's something physically challenging I'd like to try out on you."

"Is it dangerous?"

"It could be if you're not prepared."

"How does one get prepared?"

"A regular workout and a lot of imagination."

"I think I'm prepared."

"Good, I'll see you in ten."

I vanished into the bathroom and ran myself a cool shower.

The temperature outside was in the mid-thirties, but the inside of the apartment was relatively pleasant. I thought about how distasteful my next move was going to be, but probably not as distasteful as to those on the receiving end.

When I returned to the bedroom, Gérald had obliged my demand, his clothes thrown on the floor, his naked body stretched out in its full splendour. I dropped my towel and climbed on the bed.

We made intensive love.

"Do you fantasise about Tanja Barrett when you make love to me?" I asked.

"Why should I? You're better than her."

"You just don't like competition, all these men checking her out."

"I've never met anyone who likes competition when it comes to women."

"That's why you want to get married?"

"Maybe it is."

"I might just take you up on the offer."

He turned to face me. "You're serious?"

"Never been more serious in my life."

CHAPTER SEVENTY-TWO

Doug Carlton and I were sitting in the lounge room of his home in Malvern. Crystal was out Christmas shopping like half the world's population, maxing credit cards that would take the rest of the year and an incredible amount of discipline to pay back. Doug wore knee-length, bone-coloured shorts with a yellow polo shirt. I wore a red mini-skirt and a white tank-top.

The air conditioning was humming in the background, and the smell of toasted bread filled the lounge room.

"I don't know why he got Logan to kill me," I said, "but I know it's got something to do with you."

"I have no idea what the fuck you're talking about," Doug said.

"I bet you do."

"Fuck you."

I chose to stay silent for a little while. He was coming undone at the seams and soon something was going to give. He was a big guy, but it didn't necessarily mean he knew how to defend himself. Tyron was waiting for me outside just in case things got a little out of control. The H & K was tucked in my Astro Boy bag.

"We can make a deal," I said, "but you need to cooperate on this."

"You don't scare me."

His eyes stared at an empty spot in space. I had seen that look before on people who knew they were trapped and there was no way out. His whole life was falling apart, and he didn't have much time to think. He'll probably lose the house, the luxury cars, the high-paid executive job, the gold membership at the golf club, the circle of influential friends, the holiday house on the peninsula, everything in his life he had fought so hard to protect. His cookie was about to crumble.

I said, "I'm not trying to scare you, Doug. I'm telling it to you the way it is."

"Go on."

"Joseph Donnelly arranged for Logan to kill me. It was most likely Logan who killed Hurst. I was getting too close to the truth and too close to Hurst, so Donnelly panicked. His son got killed, and he's tried to cover it up. Which doesn't make a whole lot of sense...unless..."

"Unless what?"

"Unless Steven did something so unimaginable, his whole family was going to go down for it."

"You're fishing."

"Yeah? Well, you know what else I think?"

"I couldn't care less."

"I think you and Crystal killed Steven Donnelly because of something he did or said. I think he was a threat to your lifestyle, and a threat to Joseph Donnelly's lifestyle. And then you got Hurst to frame Mohammed because he was a sure thing, and the suspicion wouldn't fall back on you."

Doug stood from his chair and walked to the bar standing at the corner of the room. "I think you better leave now. I've got nothing to say to you, and you'll never be able to prove your fucked-up, little theory to anyone."

"Don't bet on it. Logan is in jail and he squealed. And Joseph Donnelly is going to squeak too because he doesn't want to spend the rest of his life in jail. Which means the only loose end is you."

Doug reached for something under the bar.

Before he got to it, I pulled the H & K from my small bag and aimed in his direction. "Whatever you're thinking of doing, think it over carefully. Mine's fully loaded, and I've had plenty of practice."

He pulled a bottle of Jack Daniel's from behind the bar. "I was just going to pour myself a drink. You're going to shoot me for drinking?"

"Step away from the bar."

He left the bottle of Jack Daniel on the bar and lurched forward. "Hey, fuck you! You're in my house, so you can shove your gun right up your arse."

"Or what? You're going to do it for me?"

"I'm done with your shit. If you want to shoot, shoot."

He walked past me, grabbed his jacket and his car keys.

I followed him to the front door, my gun still in hand.

He walked across to his car.

Tyron stepped out of the roadster and blocked his way.

"Let him go," I yelled across to Tyron.

Tyron moved sideways.

Doug got in his Mercedes Benz, burned some rubber and vanished down the street.

I let the gun fall to my side.

"Why did you let him go?" Tyron said as he came closer to me.

"He needs time alone to face his own demons."

CHAPTER SEVENTY-THREE

Gérald and I were sitting on the balcony overlooking the traffic on Marine Parade. The sun was high in the sky and the temperature somewhere in the mid-twenties. I had yet to get used to my non-blonde locks and city-slicker lifestyle.

"You're going get your head blown up, and this time I'm not going to be around to pick up the pieces." Gérald was not impressed with my gun-trotting adventure.

I said, "What? So you're going to give up on me so easily? I thought you wanted to get married?"

"I don't mean it that way. You know, like do we really want to go through what we've been through already? You in hospital for another year? I don't know how much more of this shit I can take."

"It's all going to be over soon."

"I hope so. I'm trying really hard to think positive, but it's just not happening."

I took his hand in mine. "Trust me, it's going to be all over soon. And then we can take our nice little vacation in Broome, and when we come back, we can get married, just like a fairytale."

He pulled his hand back. "I don't know. I've been doing a lot of thinking, and I'm not sure it's what I want anymore."

"What? You don't want to go on holiday?"

"No, no, the marriage thing. Maybe you're right. Maybe it just doesn't change anything other than turning two people into one item."

I was genuinely surprised. He had harassed me for the past twelve months about getting married, and suddenly he had a change of heart. "Wow! Where's all this coming from?"

"This world, your job, everything that's been happening lately."

I tried to catch his eye. "You think I'm in a high-risk category and therefore not worthy of marriage?"

"Well, yes...but no, not the way you put it. I think you're right about keeping things the way they are. If something was to happen to you, I don't want to become a widower. And marriage is just an institution devised by the church and the government to keep tags on people."

"You think that's all there is to it?"

He turned to face me. "I'm not sure anymore if it's going to make any difference at all. A gold ring on your finger doesn't create a chemical change. You're still the same person."

I took in a deep breath from the ocean. "I'm glad you're being honest."

"So you're okay with this?"

"I was okay with our lives all along. I thought you wanted the marriage."

"Well, I did, but now it just doesn't seem right."

I stood. "Good, at least we've got this little problem resolved." I walked to the lounge room. "I'm going to get a coffee. Want something?"

He followed me. "I'm surprised you're taking it so lightly. You only told me yesterday you wanted to get married."

"I was trying to give you what you want."

He placed one hand on my shoulder and turned me around. "You were going to marry me only because I wanted to get married?"

"Yes, Gérald, I was going to marry you because you asked."

"But why?"

"Because I love you, and if it meant marrying you to keep you happy, then it was something I was willing to do."

He smiled and held my head in his hands. "You're amazing, you know?"

"I know."

"And a little too sure of yourself."

"Which is why you can't get enough of me."

He kissed me on the lips.

If marriage was an institution, then love was the Holy Grail.

CHAPTER SEVENTY-FOUR

"You just shut the fuck up!" Joseph Donnelly said, the barrel of his .38 pressed against my left temple.

Twenty four hours ago I was sipping fine home-made cappuccino with Gérald, and now I was sharing a garage in Toorak with Joseph Donnelly, his wife, and Doug and Crystal Carlton. We were all sitting in a circle, like witches at a séance.

I said, "Shooting me is not going to get you anywhere. I've already left a report with Detective Langford, and it's only a matter of time before he gathers enough material to lock you up."

"It's not going to happen," Joseph said. "I always fix things, and this is no different to all the other times."

Doug and Crystal were sitting sheepishly, like two innocent passers-by who'd happened to drop in to see what the commotion was all about. But the sheep were really wolves in disguise. It was Doug who had arranged our little meeting. He had rang me half an hour ago and told me he wanted to make a deal. He said Joseph Donnelly would be there too and they would explain everything. Of course, I should have known better than to turn up without Tyron, but he was running an errand for his nephew who got caught shoplifting again. I felt pretty safe with my H & K tucked in my bag, but the bag was now feeling quite lonely by itself, next to the garage door.

I said, "Logan has already spoken to the police. He's given your name. You haven't killed anyone, so don't make this worse than it is."

"Fuck, fuck, fuck," Joseph said. He was losing it, and the situation was now very dangerous. He was capable of shooting everyone in the room in the state he was in.

"I told you we should have told the truth," Doug said. "It was an accident. It's not like Steven got killed on purpose."

I swallowed. "So there, it was an accident. Steven didn't get murdered. Can I go now?"

Joseph pushed the gun against my temple. "Shut the fuck up, I said."

"She's right," Doug said, "killing her is not going to solve anything. We've got to come clean with this."

"Fuck you, Doug. Do you think I want the family's name dragged through fifteen miles of shit? The only reason you're not in jail is because I helped you."

"You were only looking after yourself," Doug said. "I'm not ashamed of who I am."

"Can someone explain to me what's going on?" I asked.

"No." Joseph said.

"Steven liked it rough," Doug said.

"Shut up," Joseph said. He turned the gun on Doug.

"Oh, so, you're going to shoot me now?"

"Just shut up."

"Not anymore, I'm not." Doug turned to me. "I'm bisexual, and I was having an affair with Steven. Crystal joined in now and then and we had a ménage à trois."

Crystal's face picked up colour.

Doug went on, "We played rough sometimes because it heightened the stakes. Steven liked it with a rope around his neck, you know doggy style."

Mrs Donnelly began to sob.

Joseph said, "Doug, if you say one more word, I'm going to shoot you."

Doug ignored the threat. "I killed Steven by accident. Crystal was there, she can tell you how it happened. It was truly an accident, but we were young and we didn't know what to do. I couldn't tell my father, so I turned to Joseph. He had no idea his son was gay, so it shook the hell out of him. He didn't want the world to know the truth about Steven. He had connections with Detective Hurst from way back when they were in their twenties. Hurst saw it was a way to make a quick buck, and he set up Mohammed as a scapegoat."

I said, "And you let another man take the rap?"

"Mohammed was an arsehole. We were doing everyone a favour."

I couldn't disagree with Doug, but we all knew it was a lame excuse to cover the truth.

"I'm not going to jail for this," Joseph said.

He inserted the barrel of his gun inside his mouth and squeezed the trigger.

CHAPTER SEVENTY-FIVE

"Just make sure you keep your nose clean," Tyron said.

Mohammed was sitting in my office, cleanly shaved and dressed in a oversized white shirt and jeans I had bought him when I picked him up from jail. He looked good without his five-o'clock shadow, almost like a honest-to-goodness citizen.

"I've just spent ten years in jail for a murder I didn't commit," Mohammed said, "so I think I can appreciate the freedom I've now got."

"I don't know if I'm happy to see you back on the streets," I said, "because we all know you did some nasty shit in your time."

"I'm a changed man."

"Yeah, everyone who spends a decade in jail says the same thing. Don't disappoint me and find yourself back in jail in six months."

He smiled. "I was never caught, Ms. Lunn, I got framed, big difference."

He was right, but it didn't make him a saint. He knew it as much as I knew it. People like him had little chance of rehabilitation. By sending him back into the streets, innocent people's lives were at risk. If his face ever came up again in the papers for a crime he committed, I wouldn't be able to live

269

with myself.

I said, "Get yourself a job, maybe go back and learn a trade or something, and you'll learn how life is not as complicated as we make it."

He stood from his chair. "Thanks for the advice. If it's all the same, I'd like to skip the lesson on morality. Thanks for the help."

"Don't take it for granted," Tyron said. "Most people don't get a second chance."

He saluted us with his right hand and left the office.

I said, "Do you think we've done the right thing?"

"Which part?" Tyron said.

"Everything."

"Donnelly's dead. Hurst's dead. Logan's in jail. Wagner's in jail. Doug and Crystal got a suspended sentence and are doing four hundred hours of community service. Murray can't stop smiling. Bain's been promoted. Mohammed looks like a born-again-Christian. I don't know, maybe it's all going to be okay."

"Maybe."

All we knew for a fact was the reason Joseph Donnelly shot himself was because he couldn't take what was going to happen in the coming days. He would have spent the rest of his life in jail for arranging two murders, for concealing the death of his son, for perjury, for unlawful imprisonment and attempted murder. In a way, it was just as well he ended up taking his own life because the trial would have been long, tedious and painful for all parties involved.

"And all this mess because he couldn't accept his son was gay," I said.

"Yeah," Tyron said. "Isn't the world a fucked up place?"

"The world is a fine place. It's people who make a mess of their lives."

"Can't argue here." He touched his lips with his fingers. "Got anything to drink?"

I pulled two light beers from the bar fridge. He cracked the top with his teeth. "Has Bain paid you yet?"

"Got to pick up the cheque this afternoon."

"Good. Now might be a good time to give me a pay rise."

"The thought has crossed my mind."

"I'll be your best friend for another year."

We raised our bottles and drank half the contents in one go.

Tomorrow I would be on my way to Broome with Gérald for a well-earned holiday. Nothing but sun baking on the hot sand and lovemaking in the moonlight.

If Bain called me again to solve one of his past mysteries, I would turn him down flat.

Life was too short to clean up somebody else's shit.

www.ingramcontent.com/pod-product-compliance
Lightning Source LLC
Chambersburg PA
CBHW022003010726
47494CB00003B/869